THE CHILDREN FROM GIN BARREL LANE

LINDSEY HUTCHINSON

Boldwood

First published in Great Britain in 2020 by Boldwood Books Ltd.

A CIP catalogue record for this book is available from the British Library.

Paperback ISBN 978-1-83889-387-3

Ebook ISBN 978-1-83889-385-9

Kindle ISBN 978-1-83889-386-6

Audio CD ISBN 978-1-83889-388-0

MP3 CD ISBN 978-1-83889-693-5

Digital audio download ISBN 978-1-83889-384-2

Boldwood Books Ltd
23 Bowerdean Street
London SW6 3TN
www.boldwoodbooks.com

1

'Jack Larkin, get yer arse in here NOW!'

'I 'eard you, I ain't deaf!' Ten year old Jack yelled in response to his mother's call.

'Don't you back-chat me my lad or you'll find yerself out on the street with nowt but the clothes on yer back!' Nellie Larkin shouted, her hands on her ample hips. A single nod set a grimy mob cap wobbling on prematurely greying hair which could not be contained by its pins. Nellie wore a full apron which, although once white, was now stained and a similar colour to her hair. The dress beneath had also seen better days and the hem at her boots was ragged and worn.

Jack gave her the once over and shook his head. In contrast to his mother he was tall for his age and slat thin which belied his strength. His dark hair was thick and his brown eyes held a constant mischievous twinkle. His old trousers fell short of his boots and the collar and cuffs of his shirt were almost transparent. His jacket was threadbare at the elbows and his muffler was old and dirty. His flat cap, however, was brand spanking new having recently been liberated from a market stall, and Jack wore it with pride.

'Get on t'other end of that bar and get serving,' Nellie swung out her fat arm and Jack ducked just in time to avoid it colliding with his head.

Walking to the end of the long wooden counter, Jack surveyed the room. It was packed full of men and women drinking gin – as much as they could pour down their throats. The noise was deafening as some folk argued and others sang loudly. Women screeched with laughter as people came and went through doors which seemed never to be still. There were no chairs or tables, just a mass of bodies lit by the gas light chandeliers hanging from the ceiling. The etched plate glass window was obscured from Jack's view as men pushed forward to be served their half pint of mother's ruin.

Jack filled a glass from a bottle on the counter and picked up the coins. A row of huge casks stood behind him which were backed by large mirrors reflecting the light back into the room.

Serving another drink, Jack took the money and threw it into the massive black till with the handle on the side.

Feeling Nellie's eyes on him, he ignored her and continued to fill glasses and take coins. He knew his mother didn't trust him – she didn't trust anyone where money was concerned – but he would never steal from her. Thieving outside of family was necessary on occasion, and Jack had no qualms about helping himself to something he needed – like his new cap. After all, Nellie gave him nothing except his food and somewhere to sleep and a bawling out now and then. But all in all, Jack didn't think it a bad life; there were others in far worse circumstances than his. Some were forced into the workhouse; more were living on the street, so residing in his mother's gin palace was what could be considered a fairly good existence.

Jack reflected on this as he watched a man, who had been leaning against the wall, slowly slide to the floor without spilling a drop of his precious drink.

Gin – the opium of the masses. With a smile, Jack's attention was caught by a small hand tapping a coin on the counter. Standing on the sturdy wooden box that ran the full length of the bar, Jack leaned forward.

'Hello Ginny – usual is it?' he asked with a grin.

'Yes please, Jack,' the little girl said, passing over her money and a jug.

Filling the jug, he handed it to his small customer. 'You want me to see you home?' he asked amid the noise of the bar.

'No, s'all right, I can manage,' Ginny answered.

Jack nodded and watched her thread her way through the crowd being careful with her important cargo. He knew if she dropped it she would be given the hiding of her life.

'Stop lollygagging and get serving!' Nellie's voice soared over the hubbub of the bar.

Jack took a deep breath and closed his eyes tight for a few seconds, trying to hold on to his temper. As he went back to his work, he recalled the last time he had stood up to his mother. They had argued about Jack needing new boots. Nellie was loath to part with her money, even when Jack had showed her the soles he had fashioned from waste cardboard and tied on with string to cover the holes. With the profit she was making, Jack could not understand why he couldn't have a couple of pennies to buy second-hand footwear from the market. He had protested loudly at her refusal to provide the necessary funds which had subsequently earned him a sound beating. To add insult to injury, Nellie had battered him with the very boots they had disagreed about. With a few bruises and no money for arnica to ease them, Jack had fumed in silence for days. The question he kept returning to was – did his mother love him? Because, if he was honest, much of the time he felt unloved and only wanted for the work he could undertake.

Just then his attention was drawn to two burly men in the corner, their raised voices heralding an imminent fight. Jack glanced at Nellie who jerked her head towards the crapulous men and he sighed. Climbing over the counter he jumped down and pushed through the throng of unwashed bodies, all the while thinking, *'I shouldn't be doing this – I'm only a kid!'*

Walking over to the men, he shoved himself between them. Looking up at the first one and then looking to the other Jack yelled, 'Nellie sez to take it outside or shut the hell up!'

Simultaneously, the men glanced over at the large woman behind the bar and were immediately cowed by her frown. Jack nodded and returned to his post behind the bar wincing at Nellie's look which he was certain could sour milk. He heaved a sigh of relief when he saw those same men laughing and clapping each other on the back. He hated being sent to break up fights or disagreements; he could be hurt badly if one of those big blokes turned on him. So far he'd been fortunate, but how long would his luck hold out? One of these days he'd find himself thrown out onto the streets with his brains mushed from a pounding.

When a toothless old woman called Aggie picked up her skirts and began to sing and dance, Jack knew it was going to be a long night.

* * *

Early the following morning, Jack sprinkled sawdust on the bar-room floor to soak up the spillages, then began to sweep it out of the door and onto the street. The chill of early spring caused him to shiver as he looked around. The Crown Saloon where he lived with his mother, and which depended largely on passing trade, stood on the intersection between the tramway and Bailey Street and had been affectionately nicknamed Gin Barrel Lane by the locals.

Nodding to passers-by, Jack leaned on the besom and contemplated his surroundings and his life. Dirty cobbled roads, grimy buildings, their windows so filthy they shut out the light. Detritus of all sorts in the streets which threw off foul odours on hot days. Tramps and beggars loitered further towards the centre of town hoping for a hand-out from a kind stranger. There were out of work men standing on street corners grumbling about the poverty, some even having to accept the ticket to the workhouse for themselves and their families.

This was the heart of the industrial Black Country in the centre of England. It certainly lived up to its sobriquet, for everything was constantly covered with a layer of coal dust. Birmingham, a town growing rapidly which boasted a market hall housing six hundred stalls built at a staggering cost of twenty thousand pounds. Also built at an enormous cost to the town was New Street Railway Station which had opened three years previously.

Jack was unable to comprehend such a figure, seeing as he was more used to working with pennies. He did, however, like a stroll around the market on the rare occasion he was let out of The Crown Saloon.

The bar's name triggered thoughts of Victoria, the English monarch, then on hearing the lilt of an Irish voice, his mind shifted to the great potato famine in Ireland five years ago. This had prompted a mass migration to the mainland as many came seeking work.

The screech of Nellie's voice broke his train of thought and with a last sweep of his broom Jack re-entered the barroom.

'Oh, there you are! Stop clarting about and get some bloody work done!' Nellie yelled.

'What do you want doing now?' Jack asked, feeling exasperated.

'That new cask of Ladies Delight needs bottling and diluting – you know what to do, I shouldn't have to keep reminding you,' Nellie said as she pushed Jack towards the cellar steps.

'Are the bottles washed then?' Jack called over his shoulder.

'Yes, Poppy did 'em yesterday; gave 'em a good scalding she did.'

In the cellar, Jack began his task of half filling bottles from the cask, and his thoughts lingered on Poppy Charlton, the barmaid.

The Charltons had been forced to accept the ticket into the workhouse when Poppy was a child, and there she had been torn away from her parents to be put in the girls' dormitory. At fifteen years old she had signed herself out, preferring to take her chances on the street rather than live another minute in that dreadful place. She had ended up on their doorstep all skin and bone, begging for work. Nellie had taken her on as a scullion; cleaning and washing, and before long she had been promoted. Now, at eighteen, she had attained the position of barmaid and was popular with the customers. Tragically, when she had revisited the workhouse in search of her family, she had learned they had passed away.

Jack saw Poppy in his mind's eye, her blonde curls bouncing and her blue eyes sparkling. She was a beautiful young woman and admired by many who would have willingly taken her as a wife. She could be a force to be reckoned with too, for on many occasions she had saved him from a beating. Knowing Nellie could not manage without her now, more than once Poppy had threatened to walk out, taking Jack with her. She had made herself indispensable and Nellie was fully aware of it. Her bright disposition and sunny nature drew the crowds in, but to Jack she had been his protector and he loved her for it.

The thought made him smile as he topped up the bottles with water and stoppered them with corks; then stacking them in a crate he carried them up into the bar. Placing them in their rightful place in the space beneath the counter, Jack returned to the cellar to repeat the process.

This particular batch of alcohol was the roughest produced and therefore by dint was the cheapest to buy in quantity by Nellie. Sold as Ladies Delight – a much smoother gin – the price was the same. It was throat-searing stuff but if folk were daft enough to drink it, who was he to argue?

It was not against the law to sell or drink this foul beverage, and it was up to the individual as to how they spent their hard-earned coin. Besides, this was Nellie's business, and she didn't care as long as they spent their money in her saloon.

By lunchtime, all the shelves beneath the bar were fully stocked once more. Nellie had opened up after breakfast and rubbed her hands with glee as people poured in through the door. She had tended the bar throughout the morning whilst Poppy had scalded more bottles and their lunch was prepared by Nancy Sampson, the cook, and Nellie's long-time friend.

Jack shot into the kitchen for his plate of grey peas and

bacon with fresh crusty bread. He was looking forward to the afternoon – he and Poppy would be working the bar together whilst Nellie took a nap.

It was fun to work alongside Poppy; her quick rejoinders to smutty remarks made by drunken customers always made him laugh.

Finishing his food, Jack stepped into the bar and immediately found his name being called by folk waiting to be served.

He smiled. The afternoon shift had begun.

2

As afternoon faded into evening Jack propped open the doors, front and back, with cast iron doorstops shaped like barrels. Slowly, the smoke from clay pipes smoked by both men and women drifted lazily outside, and much needed fresher air took its place.

The sound of a trumpet heralded the rag and bone man's passing and Jack heard the screech of the tram wheels as it drew to a halt. In a matter of moments people scrambled from the tram and pushed their way through the open door.

Standing three deep at the bar, folk yelled to be served, desperate for their tot of gin as though afraid the place might suddenly run dry. The noise was deafening as Jack hurried to attend to waiting customers and he had only a second to glance at Poppy. Laughing as always, the girl was working flat out but was still having a hard time keeping up with demand.

As he moved along the line of waiting men Jack knew it was time to approach his mother about hiring some more help. He sighed, knowing she would balk at having to pay a wage but the three of them couldn't cope any longer. They were all exhausted; the long hours and very little sleep had begun to take its toll on them.

Nellie arrived in the bar to be greeted by a cheer from the crowd and she gave them a wide smile and a wave as if she was the queen.

Lowering the chandelier by way of a rope attached to the wall, Nellie lit the gas lights before hauling it back towards the ceiling and tying it off securely. Lighting the wall lights too, she passed a word or two with her regular customers before taking her place behind the bar. Hooking a thumb to Jack, she dismissed him from his work there; his job in the cellar, however, began yet again.

Sitting on a three-legged stool and filling bottles with diluted gin, Jack longed for the day he would be old enough to leave this place. He yearned to be out in the sunshine, on a farm maybe. Here he felt trapped, suffocated – rarely seeing the seasons change or the goings-on in the outside world.

Once finished, he went out into the back yard for a breath of evening air. Standing on the doorstep, he leaned against its jamb and watched the light give way to darkness which gradually surrounded him.

It was as he turned to go back indoors that he heard a sound which, if he was not mistaken, sounded like a sob. Leaning casually against the frame once more, he waited. Sure enough, a moment later Jack heard the sound again. It was definitely a sob – someone was in the yard and they were crying.

Tentatively, Jack stepped forward to search between the empty casks awaiting collection. Following the sounds, he eventually came upon a young girl hiding between two massive barrels.

Seeing Jack, she tried to push herself further back into

the shadows but was caught against the wall which surrounded the yard.

Frightened eyes looked up at him and Jack's heart melted. 'It's all right, I ain't going to hurt you.' Whispering so as not to scare the girl any more than she was already, Jack hunkered down beside her. 'My name's Jack and I live here. What's your name?'

The child began to shake but whether with fear or cold Jack wasn't sure.

'Are you cold? You can borrow my jacket if you like,' he said as he made to take off the garment.

The girl tried to scramble away from him and her sobs rang loud in the darkness.

'Hey, it's all right, gel, I promise I won't hurt you. Just tell me yer name then at least we'll be introduced. Once that's sorted out maybe we can become friends.' Speaking quietly Jack sat on the cold cobblestones and leaned his back against the wall.

Jack winced as Nellie Larkin screamed out his name.

'That's me mother. Blimey, she's got a voice like a glede under a door!' In the dim light from the saloon doorway he saw a smile creep across the girl's face and he went on in a mimicking tone. 'Jack, fill the bottles! Jack, roll them barrels! Jack, do this – do that!' He heard the girl chuckle quietly and swiftly moved on. 'This place belongs to her – my mother – the one with a gob the size of England.' Another giggle and Jack felt he was making headway. 'So, are you going to tell me yer name?'

'Dolly – everybody calls me Dolly Daydream,' came the timid reply.

'Oh, ain't that nice? I like it – how do you feel about it?' Jack asked.

'I don't mind it.'

'What's yer other name?' Jack probed.

'Perkins.'

'Well, Dolly Perkins, what brings you here to The Crown Saloon?' Hoping he was not pushing too hard, Jack kept his eyes on the doorway.

'I... my...' Unable to find the words, Dolly burst into tears.

'Oh crikey, now look what I've gone and done. I d'aint mean to upset you. It don't matter – just dry your eyes.' Jack passed over a handkerchief which was none too clean.

'There, that's better. Now then, what I need to know is – will anybody be missing you? Cos if not, you'd best come inside with me and have a bite of supper.'

Dolly shook her head. 'I have no family any more.'

Hearing another sob, Jack decided not to probe further despite wanting to know more about the girl. He wondered what had happened to her family, and why she was hiding here in their yard. Risking a quick glance, he noticed she was very thin; how long had it been since she had last eaten? Rather than pry too deeply at this juncture, Jack said quietly, 'I'm sorry to hear it, Dolly. In that case maybe you should come in and meet everybody. Firstly, there's me – Jack Larkin – and Nellie, my mother. Then there's Poppy Charlton the barmaid – oh and Nancy Sampson our cook.'

'What about your mum? What will she say about me coming in?' Dolly asked tentatively.

'Well, she'll probably say – "Jack, what're you bloody thinking bringing me another sodding mouth to feed? Don't I pay out enough already? What can she do to earn her keep?"'

Dolly giggled, then said, 'She'd be right though, Jack.'

'So, what's the alternative – leave you out here to starve? I don't think so. It ain't my way, Dolly, to ignore somebody in need if I can help. That being said, get yer bottom off that cold floor and come inside with me,' Jack grinned as he got to his feet and stuck out his hand.

Dolly grasped the lifeline held out to her and smoothed down her dirty dress. Grasping a walking stick she looked at Jack for his reaction to her being a cripple.

A single nod and a smile from the boy who had rescued her told Dolly all she needed to know. Having a crippled leg would make no difference to Jack.

In the warm kitchen, Jack introduced Dolly to their cook. Mrs Sampson was a big lady with a mouth like a navvy. Her arms had defined muscles from years of lifting huge heavy pans. Grey hair stuck out in all directions from beneath a mob cap and pale blue eyes gave the girl the once-over.

What she saw was a stick-thin child of no more than thirteen years old leaning on a walking cane. A simple cotton dress, dirty and tattered, hung on her tiny frame, its hem at knee length showing her withered left leg. Her boots were almost useless, the uppers and soles held together by string wrapped around the whole foot. The girl's dark hair was matted and would no doubt be alive with lice but her brown eyes were glistening like molten chocolate. Dolly also had the most infectious grin showing surprisingly clean teeth.

'Right, put yer skinny arse on that chair and get this down yer neck!' Nancy Sampson said as she placed a steaming bowl of mutton stew on the table.

'Thank you, Mrs Sampson, but I don't have any money,' Dolly said as she stood quite still.

Nancy harrumphed then the tirade began. 'Money! Did I ask for payment? No, I bloody didn't! Talk about ungrateful...' The cook ambled away still muttering and came back with a bowl of stew for Jack. 'Sit, the pair o' you before I take that sodding cane to yer backs! And I want to see them bowls empty!' Slicing fresh bread, she slapped a chunk next to each bowl before wandering away to make tea.

Dolly and Jack grinned at each other before tucking into their delicious meals. They chuckled as every now and then another expletive would escape the lips of the cook.

'Jack!' Nellie's voice came again.

'He's having his bloody tea, Nellie! Fer God's sake give the lad a break – poor little bugger is worn to a frazzle!' Nancy Sampson yelled back and then continued her mumbling as she pottered about the huge kitchen.

The two youngsters giggled, then Jack whispered, 'It's always like this. Nancy and me mother shouting and swearing but they'm great friends really.'

Dolly nodded and laid her spoon in her empty dish. 'Thank you, Mrs Sampson, that was lovely.'

'Good. Glad you liked it cos there's a bloody great pan full there and you've got to 'ave some more!'

Dolly nodded, her pursed lips holding back a laugh. Finally, their hunger sated, the children sat with a cup of tea and listened to the shouting match between Nellie and Nancy as the former called for help and the latter told her friend to go jump in the canal.

Suddenly Nellie was in the doorway, her hands on her hips. 'Jack – come on!' Then her eyes locked on young Dolly. 'What the…? Who's this?'

'Mum, her name is Dolly and I found her in the back yard,' Jack explained.

'Found her, did you? Well you can damn well un-find her! I can't take in every waif off the street!' Nellie yelled.

Jack glanced at the young girl saying, 'I told you.'

'What? What did you tell her?' Nellie enquired, directing her gaze back to her son.

'Look, Mum, Dolly ain't got any family and she was starving—' Jack proceeded to explain.

'Jack, it doesn't matter. I'll be on my way.' Dolly turned to the cook. 'Mrs Sampson, thank you for the delicious supper, I'm very grateful.' Again, to Jack, she went on, 'Maybe we'll meet again, Jack Larkin, I thank you for your kindness.' Grabbing her cane, Dolly limped towards the back door.

'Mum! You can't turn her out!' Jack protested as he jumped from his seat.

With an explosive sigh, Nellie relented as she heard the calls from the bar. Poppy was run off her feet and desperately needing help. 'All right! Dolly, if I take you in – and I ain't saying I will – but if I do, you would have to share a room with Poppy. As for work, you could fill the bottles and Jack would fetch them up from the cellar. I wouldn't be paying you a wage, but bed and board would be in.'

'Oh, thank you, Mrs Larkin!' Dolly said on a grateful breath.

'Don't be getting your hopes up yet, young lady, I'll want to know much more about you before you get to live in this house.'

'Nellie!' Poppy's voice filtered through to the kitchen.

'I'm coming!' Nellie yelled back as she grabbed Jack's arm, 'and so are you, young man. Dolly, you can help Nancy in the kitchen for now.'

Dolly exchanged a grin with Jack as he was hauled away to the bar, and she felt blessed to have met him.

After her mother's passing, her step-father had voiced the notion of Dolly taking her place both in the home and in his bed. It was the day of the funeral, following the interment, that Dolly had run away. That had been three months ago and she had scavenged to survive ever since.

Now her luck had turned and Dolly Perkins felt safe for

the first time in a long while. The family who might take her in off the street were a little rough around the edges but they appeared honest and hard-working. She felt sure she could fit in well once she came to terms with all the bad language. She smiled as she recalled her mother telling her it was a trait of Black Country women to cuss constantly. Dolly didn't care, for she would be eternally grateful to these warm-hearted people for saving her from the workhouse, should she be allowed to join their coterie, of course.

Leaning her cane against the sink, Dolly set to washing the dishes, humming a little tune as she did so.

Nancy Sampson watched and thought to herself, *'Poor little wench. She ain't got anything but a gammy leg and yet she's happy to wash dishes. God bless her!'*

'Thank you, Dolly, that's saved me a job I hate,' Nancy said, 'now come and sit down and tell me all about yerself.'

Plonking herself on a kitchen chair, Dolly related how she'd come to be in the yard of The Crown Saloon.

3

'So why are you called Dolly Daydream?' Nancy Sampson asked.

'My mum used to call me that on account of me daydreaming about the faraway places like in the books we read together,' Dolly answered.

'What sort of books?' Nancy was impressed the child could read and her interest perked up.

'I love atlases best, showing all the places in the world on the globe. They all seem so mystical and exotic,' Dolly said with a smile.

'Did you go to school, then?' Nancy asked, surprised at the girl's use of such fancy words.

'No, my mum taught me at home,' Dolly said sadly.

Seeing the distress that crossed the girl's face, Nancy decided it was best not to pursue the matter further for now.

'My mum told me my dad died of the consumption when I was about twelve months old and within a few months she married Arthur Micklewhite. He was horrible to us, Mrs Sampson; he used to hit my mum, and then he started to hit me too when Mum wasn't about cos I wouldn't...' Dolly's eyes filled with tears at the memories.

'You poor little thing. What did your mum say about that?' Nancy probed.

Dolly shook her head and lowered her eyes.

'You didn't tell her, did you?' Nancy was horrified that this little one had suffered her abuse in silence for fear of upsetting her mother.

'She lost a baby and I don't think she ever really got over it. Then a few months ago my mum died and after the funeral I ran away. I couldn't stay in that house with him, Mrs Sampson, I just couldn't!'

Nancy sighed loudly before an expletive left her lips; one casting doubt as to Arthur Micklewhite's parentage.

A giggle from Dolly caused Nancy to let out a loud belly laugh. 'I know I've got a bad mouth, but it ain't no wonder living here with Nellie Larkin. That woman fair rubs me up the wrong way at times I don't mind telling you!'

'Jack said you were friends,' Dolly said.

'Oh, we are, but that don't mean she don't get on my last nerve. She could make a saint swear could that one, but she's been good to me over the years.'

'Don't you have any children, Mrs Sampson?' Dolly asked innocently.

'No lass. I was pregnant once – a long time ago. My husband, Cecil, was robbed and murdered on his way back from work. They beat him badly and left him in an alley to die. It was all too much for me and I lost the babby. I ain't had anything to do with bloody men from that day to this.'

'I'm sorry to hear about your husband and baby, Mrs Sampson,' Dolly said, a feeling of guilt coming over her for asking the question in the first place.

'Ar well, as I say – it was a long time ago,' Nancy re-iterated, but Dolly saw the grief still evident in the pale blue eyes and her heart ached for the woman – and herself.

Dolly felt keenly the loss of her mother, but she couldn't imagine what it would be like to lose a child. It wasn't the natural order of things – surely it was supposed to be that older people passed first. This woman had lost her child even before it had been born; it had had no chance of a life. Mrs Sampson had been robbed of seeing her son or daughter grow, get married and have a child of their own, and Dolly felt the heartache as she looked at the woman inwardly mourning her baby. Was there anything Dolly could do to lessen the emptiness she could see Mrs Sampson was suffering? How could she make the woman feel a little better? Then an idea jumped into her mind, but how would Mrs Sampson view it? Would she think Dolly was feeling sorry for her? Would she see it as an act of charity? Dolly weighed up the questions in her mind before reaching her decision. Should she voice the notion now as she might not otherwise have the confidence to do so?

But before she could speak, the conversation swerved in another direction as Nancy told her all about the saloon and its patrons.

'You wouldn't believe the sort we get in 'ere,' she said, rolling her eyes. 'Their kids are running around in rags with bare feet but they still find the money for their gin. Some blokes have jobs but their wives spend their hard-earned coin in here.'

Dolly listened quietly, trying to understand why people would live like that.

'It's a mystery ain't it?' Nancy asked, as if reading Dolly's thoughts. 'They have a house and babbies to look after and what do they do? They come in this place and drink that shit which will eventually rot their guts. It's a strange old world, ain't it?'

'It is, Mrs Sampson,' Dolly concurred and nodded as Nancy held up the teapot. 'I always wonder why it is the good die young and those who care nothing for others appear to lead long and reasonably nice lives.'

'Well now, that's a deep thought for one so young,' Nancy commented as she poured boiling water over the tealeaves in the pot.

'My mum told me I should think things through from every angle before I make a decision or open my mouth to voice it,' Dolly said with a sad smile.

'Now that's a piece of advice Nellie could benefit from at times. That bloody gob of hers is gonna land her in trouble one day. I keep telling her – Nellie, I says – shut yer trap and give yer brain a chance. The problem is, I don't think her brain works at all half the time.' Nancy gave a little laugh as the fondness she held for her friend showed on her face.

'I think Mrs Larkin is very astute,' Dolly said.

'How come?' Nancy asked, her interest sparked.

'Well, she runs a business – a very good one by what I've heard. She works her staff hard but no more than she does herself.'

'You'm quite erstoot yerself gel, to have noticed all that in the few hours you've been here,' Nancy said, wiggling her silver-grey eyebrows.

Dolly smiled warmly. 'You all seem really very nice.'

'We am cocka! We'm bostin!' Nancy let out a howl of laughter which echoed around the kitchen.

Having met for the first time only hours ago, the two had bonded like it was meant to be. Nancy set the pots and kettle on the range to boil some water for the girl to have a bath. Clattering cups on saucers she marvelled at how the fates stepped in when the need was greatest. Before long Dolly was luxuriating in the warmth of the bath.

Nancy had been secretly dwelling on her lost child for some time and now Dolly had come into her life. A thirteen year old with a crippled leg might just be able to save her from going mad with grief despite the years gone by. Every now and then, the loss weighed desperately heavy, and Nancy Sampson had often contemplated joining her loved ones in heaven. It was only the love of her friends in The Crown Saloon that had prevented her throwing herself in the canal. Now she had someone to take care of, to love and be loved by, if God saw fit to grant it. Nancy had always adored Jack but had constantly wished for a child of her own. She doted on the boy and now there was another to share her affections. Her thoughts were interrupted a moment later when Poppy staggered into the room.

'Phew! It's insane out there!' Poppy Charlton said as she dropped onto a kitchen chair and began to rub her aching feet. 'Hello there, Dolly, I'm Poppy. Jack told me about you. Nice to meet you.'

Dolly smiled and returned the greeting shyly. 'Mrs Larkin said I was to share a room with you, if she takes me in that is. I hope it doesn't put you out.'

'Not at all, sweetheart, it will be nice to have some company,' Poppy said as she gratefully accepted the tea offered by Nancy.

'Thank you, but Mrs Larkin hasn't made up her mind yet – about whether I stay or go,' the girl answered with a little smile.

'I expect Nellie will be wanting a meeting after closing time – she'll want to know the ins and outs of Meg's arse!' Nancy said with a sigh.

Dolly burst out laughing at the turn of phrase which caused the others to join in.

It was gone midnight when Nellie closed the saloon, her podgy arms pushing the last customers out of the door before shooting the bolts top and bottom. Turning off the gas lamps, she and Jack wandered wearily into the kitchen for a much needed cup of tea.

After a long interrogation from Nellie Larkin, Dolly was told she would be allowed to stay provided she behaved herself.

'I ain't having you and Jack messing about,' Nellie said, 'you'll work same as we do. Now if I find out you've been lying to me about having no family and what happened to you before you came here, I'll throw you out meself. Do you understand me?'

'Yes, Mrs Larkin. I haven't lied to you, nor will I. You have been very kind to me and I wouldn't repay that kindness with lies or deceit.' Dolly spoke in a serious tone to ensure Nellie understood she was indeed telling the truth.

'Right, you girls get off upstairs. I want you up bright and early tomorrer.' Nellie said with a perfunctory nod.

Then with grateful thanks she and Poppy retired to bed.

'Come on, Dolly, I have a nightgown you can wear,' Poppy said as they left the kitchen.

Jack followed suit shortly afterwards leaving the two women to discuss what they had learned about the young girl found in their yard.

'Nell, I'm ever so glad you took young Dolly in,' Nancy said.

'I d'aint have much choice, did I? What with Jack's begging and you feeding her up, what was I gonna do? I couldn't chuck her back onto the streets, poor little bugger,' Nellie said with a shake of her head.

'What I was thinking...' Nancy paused, unsure how to say what was on her mind.

'Go on then let's have it,' Nellie said with a tired sigh.

'What if... well, I wondered...'

'Will you get to the point before Hell freezes over?!' Nellie's patience was fast running out.

'Dolly could be my little wench!' Nancy snapped back.

Staring at the woman who had been her friend for many years, Nellie couldn't believe what she was hearing. 'What?! Nance, you can't be serious!' Nellie said at last.

'I am so don't you be poking yer nose in my business!' Nancy retaliated.

'She could be lying through her back teeth about having no family! What will you do if somebody comes looking for her?' Nellie asked.

'Look, you've got Jack, but I ain't got nobody. Surely you can see the poor little mite needs somebody to take care of her.' Nancy said, taking umbrage.

'I suppose so. Well, if she's to stay she'll have to work the same as the rest of us, and that gammy leg won't do as an excuse!' Nellie said sternly.

'She's a game young thing, I can't see her shirking her work so don't you worry on that score,' Nancy said, already slipping into the role of protective mother hen. 'There's another thing an' all – when are you going to tell young Jack...?'

'Don't let's go through that again, Nance, I'll explain it all to him one day,' Nellie interrupted.

'You know, if you keep him in the dark much longer, he won't be happy when he finds out,' Nancy pushed her point forward.

'I know but I have to take that risk,' Nellie said with a yawn.

'I can understand that, but think about it, Nell. He needs to know and sooner would be better than later.'

Nancy could see how exhausted her friend was but continued nevertheless. 'What about the lies you told him when he asked about his father?'

'I know, Nance, but he doesn't ask any more,' Nellie replied, tired at having the same old conversation yet again.

'Nell, the boy needs to know you never had a husband and the bloke you said died of fever weren't his father. It ain't fair on the kid!'

Seeing Nellie yawn again prompted Nancy to continue with, 'And another thing, don't you think it's time to abide by the law and close this place at eleven o'clock?'

'Bugger that! The place was packed tonight. Besides, have you forgotten about the riots two years ago when Parliament had to lighten the Sale of Beer Act for Sunday hours? They said we now have to shut between three and five and close up at eleven. Can you imagine what would happen if I did that? I'd have the windows bosted and the gin pinched – there'd be murder done!' Nellie shook her head, dismissing the idea.

'The coppers will shut yer down, Nellie, the time will come – then what will you do?' Nancy tried again to persuade her friend to adhere to the law.

'It'll be all right; half the time the bobbies are in here anyway! Besides, I'm still paying back the distillery for financing my refurbishment in the first place.'

'I know that, but how long will that take? A lifetime, Nellie! I understand they paid to make this place nice in exchange for you only selling their gin, and that you have to repay them, but if you go on like this you'll kill yourself!' Nancy was pacing the kitchen like a caged tiger.

'It's all I know, Nance,' Nellie said with a huge sigh.

Hearing the tiredness in her friend's voice, Nancy

relented. 'Come on, let's get to bed – it's been a long and eventful day.'

The two friends tiptoed past Dolly's room in order not to disturb her sleep, but unbeknown to them she was still awake.

Snuggled up warm in the bed which she and Poppy had made up with linen from the landing cupboard, Dolly thought about the last months of living out on the streets. She had scavenged for food and slept in doorways. Her hand instinctively went to the necklace she'd worn since it had been willed to her by her mother. It was worth a great deal of money and she had a letter of authentication to prove its value. She could of course have sold it and used the money, but something always prevented her from doing so. The necklace had a higher purpose she was sure, but just what that was she had no idea. It would all become clear in the fullness of time she was certain.

Closing her eyes, she drifted into a deep dreamless sleep – the first she'd had in a long time.

4

The following morning over breakfast Jack asked, 'What happened to your leg, Dolly?'

'I was born with it like this,' she answered simply.

'Does it hurt?' Jack pursued.

'No, it's just not very strong, so I use a stick.'

'How ever did you manage after you ran away from home?' Nancy asked as she topped up Dolly's teacup.

'I begged mostly. I scavenged what I could from the market. I didn't ever steal because it's wrong and I couldn't exactly run from the police with this.' Dolly tapped her left leg and smiled.

'Where did you live?' Jack asked.

'I slept in doorways or in Park Street Gardens. It wasn't too bad, but it was hard to keep warm. A tramp told me to put old newspaper between my clothes which helped. Then someone stole my coat and bag while I wasn't looking so I was left with nothing.' Dolly answered with a sigh.

Nancy passed over more toast and muttered under her

breath which caused Dolly to giggle; the words having likened the thief to a bovine carry-all.

'Ain't you bitter about it all?' Jack was amazed at how Dolly had taken all that had happened to her in her stride.

'There's no point dwelling on what I can't change. It was bad luck, that's all.' Dolly shrugged her shoulders before she finished her food.

'Well, I think you're a brave little wench,' Nancy said as she stroked Dolly's hair. Clean and dry now, it shone like a raven's wing and Nancy longed to brush and plait it. The beaming smile she received back for her troubles melted her heart and Nancy was sure this was as close as she was ever going to feel to maternal love.

Nellie's voice was heard before she was seen. Boots stomping on the tiled floor, she swept into the kitchen yelling, 'Jack! Come on, lad, that bar needs a good clean!'

Jack rolled his eyes and banged his cup on the table. 'No rest for the wicked.' he mumbled as he slapped his flat cap on his head and got to his feet.

'You work that boy too hard,' Poppy said as she followed Nellie into the kitchen. 'He's only ten years old – he should be in school.'

Nellie rounded on the girl saying, 'It ain't none of your business, madam! I give you board and lodging to tend the bar, not to stick your nose into my affairs!'

'Yes, but you don't pay me a wage, do you? So, I think we should come to an arrangement about that else I'm off!' Poppy retaliated.

Nellie's mouth fell open at the girl's sudden change in demeanour. Usually a pusillanimous person, Poppy's outburst took them all by surprise.

'Just where do you think you'll find work in this God forsaken town then?' Nellie asked sarcastically.

'Somewhere – anywhere – I'll get a job doing something where I'll be appreciated and paid accordingly!' Poppy countered. Her blood was up and she was not about to relent.

'After all I've done for you! I took you in off the street when you were starving! Is this how you repay me?' Nellie was furious.

'I will always be grateful for that but there comes a time when gratitude is repaid in full. Now is that time, Nellie Larkin!' Poppy banged her hand on the table in emphasis setting her blonde curls bouncing.

Everyone stared at the young girl wondering what would happen next. Would Poppy make good on her threat and walk out? Would Nellie concede and pay her a wage for all her hard work?

Nancy debated whether to intervene and tell them both to quit arguing but she didn't think it was her place to speak out.

However, it was Jack who finally spoke up and broke the impasse. 'Mum, it's only fair. Poppy works hard and long hours in that bar, same as you and me.'

Nellie glanced at her son, angry that he had taken the side of the barmaid over that of his mother.

'A maid earns about six pounds a year and what do I get? Bed and board! And – I work a sight harder than a maid!' Poppy went on.

'Six pounds a year! You'm joking, ain't you?' Nellie snorted.

'What about Nancy? What do you pay her? About eleven pounds a year would be my guess,' continued Poppy.

'Don't you be dragging me into this, young lady,' Nancy said, all thoughts of trying to quell the argument now gone.

'Stop it! All of you!' Jack yelled, making Dolly jump out of her skin. 'This is getting us nowhere. Mum, Poppy deserves a wage of some sort so work it out with her. Me and Dolly will go and fill the bottles in the cellar, and by the time we've finished this should all be done as well!'

Jack stomped from the kitchen and Dolly limped along behind him.

Down in the cellar, Jack passed his new friend a bottle half filled with gin and Dolly topped it up with water. 'Do they argue like that often?' she asked.

'I ain't never seen it before,' Jack replied, shaking his head, 'but I believe Poppy was right to ask for wages.'

'Do you get paid, Jack?'

'No, bed and board, same as you,' he answered blithely.

'But you should,' Dolly pressed her point of view as she corked another bottle.

'I'm her son, Dolly, so she thinks I should work for nowt – being family and all that.'

'That's rather unfair though,' she said sadly.

'Ain't it just. But you saw what happened when Poppy broached the subject, God knows how Mum would react if I asked the same.' Jack stacked the bottles in a crate to be taken to the bar. 'I'll take these up if you can sawdust and sweep the floor.'

'All right, that sounds a fair deal to me,' Dolly said with a giggle.

Jack grinned. Dolly's positive outlook and happy nature was infectious.

Working quietly together in the bar they heard no more raised voices and a moment later Poppy came through sporting a huge smile.

'All sorted out?' Jack asked.

Poppy's blue eyes twinkled and she nodded. 'She's agreed to pay me six pounds a year and you two, three pounds a year.'

'Blimey!' Jack spluttered.

'So, don't either of you let me down after I fought your corner for you,' Poppy said in a whisper.

'We won't, we promise,' Dolly assured her; she considered herself very lucky for only a couple of days ago she was starving on the streets. Now she had a home, a job earning a wage, new found friends, and a surrogate mother as well if she could put her question to Nancy. Dolly determined she would work hard in exchange for Mrs Larkin's kindness.

Nellie bustled into the bar and nodded her approval at the work being undertaken.

'Thank you, Mrs Larkin,' Dolly said as she approached the woman, 'it's so very kind of you to think of me too. Not only have you taken me in when I had nowhere else to go, but now you've given me paid work, I'm very grateful.'

Nellie looked down at the girl with the eyes the colour of chocolate and felt her heart melt. She would have loved a daughter such as this but it was not meant to be. Suddenly all her bluster was gone and she held open her arms. Dolly stepped forward and Nellie hugged her tightly. Then in the next moment she let go of the little waif and stamped out of the bar, brushing away a tear as she went.

'Blimey!' Jack said again before he, along with Poppy and Dolly, burst out laughing.

Arthur Micklewhite picked up the newspaper to be greeted with a headline announcing that the Queen had given birth to a daughter, Princess Beatrice. He glanced at the date on the top of the paper, 14 April 1857, and worked the numbers in his head. Queen Victoria was thirty-eight years old and still bearing children.

He grunted as his mind took him to Dolly Daydream. Where was she now? Slamming the paper down on the kitchen table he was angry that his step-daughter had run away. That young'un would have kept his bed warm for a long time to come. She could have cooked, cleaned and maintained the house as her mother had previously.

Arthur looked around at the dirty dishes piled up in the old brownstone sink, the crumbs on the floor and the pile of washing by the back door. It was no use, either he undertook these tasks for himself or he had to find a woman to do it for him.

Wondering how he could find the money to pay a cleaner/washerwoman, Arthur ambled outside to the privy. On his return to the kitchen he searched the cupboard for something to eat. Nothing. It was empty, barring a few breadcrumbs and a fly. Batting away the pesky insect, Arthur dropped onto the chair feeling completely miserable.

He was hungry, but with no money, his cupboard would remain bare. It was time to go and find a few wealthy folk and relieve their pockets of their wallets. Maybe a trip to the market where unsuspecting housewives might leave their purses unattended in their baskets.

Pulling up his braces, Arthur then shoved his feet into his boots. Grabbing his jacket from the nail hammered into the back door he slung it over one shoulder and left the house. Number twenty-seven was at the end of Rea Terrace and quite a way from the market hall but it was a sunny day and Arthur walked with a spring in his step; the prospect of having a meal that day lightening his mood.

The Macassar oil on his centrally parted hair had kept it in place despite his having slept, so he had no need of a comb. Too lazy to sharpen his cut-throat razor on the leather strop, Arthur was out and about with a day's growth of whiskers. His shirt was none too clean but the waistcoat covered most of the grime. Worsted trousers would soon prove too warm in the clement weather as he strode forth towards the market.

Arthur Micklewhite had weasel-like features and eyes so dark they appeared to be black, giving him a sinister look. As he proceeded further into the town, he thought about the life he'd led when wed to Avril Perkins.

Scouring the newspaper columns of the deceased, he had spotted the notification announcing the funerary arrangements of a prominent manufacturer who lived in the wealthier area of Great Charles Street. Mrs Perkins, the widow, would be an excellent candidate to take care of him he had surmised, which had proven to be the case.

A smile lifted the corners of his mouth as he recalled attending the interment posing as one of her dead husband's business acquaintances. Over time he inveigled his way into her affections and, after a suitable period of mourning, had begun to court her. He had been especially kind to Avril's crippled daughter, Dolly, which had only added to his kudos as a prospective husband.

Eventually they had married. Before long, he'd sold on her late husband's business. Arthur never had any intention of working a day in that cardboard factory. It hadn't taken him long to spend the money from the sale and even before Avril's passing, he was on the lookout for another wealthy widow.

As for Dolly Daydream, she would have been no use to him other than as a housekeeper and occasional bed warmer. Her withered leg would have prevented her from working, and she would have just been another mouth to feed. So, all in all, he felt he was probably better off without her.

A frown replaced the smile as Arthur considered again how dire his circumstances were becoming. He had to find a woman with money – and soon. He could not afford to rely on the newspaper, he must now go in search of someone who would lift him from his impecunious state and restore him to being a sybarite. The question now was – how to go about it?

The lifestyle afforded him when he had acquired money had suited him admirably. The seemingly endless stream of parties, soirées and balls; the mixing with the higher echelon of society was dizzyingly addictive, and Arthur missed it now it was gone.

Folk were fickle; if you were monied, you were admired and welcomed. But once your wealth disappeared then so did your so-called friends. Now Arthur Micklewhite was alone and penniless, a situation he needed to remedy as soon as possible.

The market hall which had opened in 1835 and the wonderful big Town Hall were things Birmingham could brag about and frequently did. The town was now producing 50 per cent of the world's manufactured goods and would, in the future, be known as the city of a thousand trades. It boasted botanical gardens, gas street lighting and a wonderful new railway station. Five years ago, St Chad's had been raised to Cathedral status by Pope Pius IX, and in 1853, Birmingham Mint had been contracted to produce the first pound sterling coins. Although it was set in the heart of the Black Country, and constantly covered in a layer of smoky grime from chimneys and factories, the people were fiercely proud of their town.

Arthur passed the baker's horse with its bread panniers and the smell of warm fresh baked goods made his mouth water and his stomach rumble. A little further on, a blind beggar rattled a few coins in a pannikin, the clink of metal on metal ringing loudly. Stopping, Arthur dipped his fingers in the cup and took out a threepenny bit before moving swiftly on; the beggar's 'thankee guvnor' making him grin.

Wheelbarrows full of fruit and vegetables were being pushed between stalls, annoying crowds of women intent on finding a bargain. All around, vendors called out the prices of their wares, adding to the cacophony of noise. There was an excitement about the place as people pushed and shoved their way down the narrow aisles between the stalls. Here you could usually buy anything you needed, but if not, there was always a man who could get it for you.

Arthur slipped on his jacket and began to weave his way through the throng of people, his eyes finding an escape route in the event he was detected. It was very busy so he thought his best option would be to mingle in with the crowd. Should he be lucky enough to pick a wallet or purse, he would empty it quickly before dropping it on the floor.

Spotting a likely victim, Arthur stepped closer to the woman with a basket on her arm. Her purse was in full view and within reach but as he stretched to retrieve it the woman snatched it away. She gave Arthur a glare which could burn a man to a crisp. He muttered an apology as he leaned forward to examine a pair of second-hand boots on the stall. With a sniff, the woman paid for her item and pushed her way through the closely packed people. Arthur began to sweat – that was a close thing. Continuing on, he was determined to be more careful. He wanted to eat today – but not inside a gaol!

* * *

Micklewhite's jaunt into the market was successful and now back at home he congratulated himself on a job well done. He decided to steer clear of that particular place for a while as the bobbies would be out searching for the culprit once the thefts were reported.

Buying food on the way home, Arthur's larder was now fully stocked and sitting with a plate of bread and cheese and a hot cup of tea, he reflected on his life.

After running away from the orphanage at the age of twelve, he had lived on the streets and fallen in with a bad lot. They had taught him how to lie, cheat and steal and this had then become his trade.

Arthur had never worked a day in his life and with a smile he determined he would not start now. Early on he had learned how to target lonely women who were only too happy to buy him clothes and gifts in exchange for his companionship. He would escort them to balls and the theatre at their expense and he became accustomed to living the high life. Arthur gained a reputation as a perfect gentleman, and on odd occasions – an ardent lover.

He used to scan the newspapers every day and select wealthy women very recently in mourning. Attending the funerals, he would introduce himself as a colleague of the deceased. Thereafter he would go calling on the widow to assure himself of her wellbeing. The rest would fall into place with gifts and money following swiftly on.

Then he'd met Avril Perkins and had married her in order to get his greedy hands on her money. Avril was not so ready to part with her coin as the others he had courted and so a wedding appeared to be the only lucrative outcome.

Leaning back in his chair, Arthur rolled himself a cigarette and smiled. Avril was dead, Dolly had run off and the house and all its contents belonged to him. A little pelf every so often would keep him going whilst he sought out a future target or two.

An avaricious man, it was not Arthur's intention to remain low on funds for long. His acquisitive nature would ensure his rise to the upper middle class once more. He had been quite a rakehell in his time; he was proud of it and was determined to be one again very soon. For now, however, he was content to continue to relieve others of their hard-earned coffers.

6

Work at The Crown Saloon went on as spring melted into summer, and the blistering heat had everyone fractious. The sudorific air made for odiferous bodies which crowded into the bar, making for even worse working conditions than normal. Even with all the doors open there was not even a zephyr to ease the discomfort of the workers. Nellie seemed not to notice but Poppy complained bitterly.

'The smell in here is making me gag!' she called over the noise of the bar.

'What do you want me to do about it?' Nellie asked as she pushed a glass of gin into eagerly waiting hands.

Poppy shook her head, placed her scent laden handkerchief over her nose and breathed deeply.

'Exactly!' Nellie yelled.

'Come on, Nellie, I've been waiting half an hour for my gin!' called a man sporting a grin.

'No, you ain't, you lying cur, you've only just walked in! Hey, you lot – get a wash before you come in here again!' Nellie pinched her nose between her finger and thumb.

Boisterous laughter sounded and Nellie held out her hands as if in defeat.

Poppy sighed and went back to work. Evidently buying gin was more important to the punters than buying soap.

Jack and Dolly were filling bottles in the blessed cool of the cellar.

'Isn't this cheating? Topping up with water, I mean,' Dolly asked.

'Yes, but to get drunk they have to buy more. Money in the till always makes Mum happy,' Jack replied. 'At least we use water, some use turpentine spirit.'

'Oh my goodness!' Dolly was aghast at the revelation.

'There have been cases reported of folk going blind drinking this stuff,' Jack added.

'Why do they drink it then?' Dolly asked, hardly able to believe what she was hearing.

'People get drunk for lots of reasons, Dolly. For some it's so they don't feel the cold in the winter or the hunger gnawing at their bellies. For others it's because they're miserable with their lives or can't get long term work,' Jack explained as best he could.

'All the gins have nice names though,' Dolly noted.

'True, but all these are the same gin – the cheapest Mum can buy; she sells it on as the stronger one for which she charges more. It don't matter cos it's all diluted anyway.'

'Do you like gin, Jack?'

'Never tried it; don't think I ever will. It destroys lives, Dolly. I've heard things that would make your hair curl.'

'Like what?'

'Like a woman killing her child and selling his clothes to buy gin. Another bloke sold his daughter for his drink money. It's addictive and the time comes when they can't do without it, so they'll do anything to get the pennies for their choice of drug.' Jack shook his head sadly.

'You're very wise,' Dolly said shyly.

'I watch and listen and in turn, I learn. One day I'll get out of this place and live on a farm,' Jack said dreamily.

'Can I come?' Dolly asked, full of innocence.

'Don't see why not. You could feed the chickens while I milk the cows,' Jack said with a grin.

The two chatted on for a while, fantasising in a childish way about living together in a cottage in the country before Nellie's voice broke their reverie when she called for more bottles.

'It must be really busy up there tonight cos I filled all the shelves this afternoon,' Jack muttered as he hauled a crate up the cellar steps.

'It's very warm, Jack, people are thirsty from the heat,' Dolly said, following behind him.

Jack was surprised to see Poppy and his mum working flat out and people yelling to be served.

'Come on, help me put these under the counter then I'll show you how to serve. It looks like Mum needs the help tonight.'

Above each shelf was a name tag denoting the different gins on offer with their price alongside it so there could be no mistakes made.

'Make sure they keep the same glass – it saves on washing up later,' Jack called to Dolly over the noise.

Dolly nodded and climbed up onto the box step, leaning her cane against the bar.

'What can I get you?' she asked a woman waving a glass under her nose.

'Tot of White Satin,' the woman slurred.

Checking the labels and price, Dolly grabbed a bottle and

began to pour. Glancing at Jack she saw him nod and smile. Taking the woman's money, she grabbed her cane and went to the till into which she dropped the pennies.

A moment later Nellie rushed along the bar with a large cigar box which she placed under the counter. 'Here, use this for now to save you the walk to the till.'

Dolly thanked her and set to serving one person after another and by the time Nellie closed the doors on the last customer to be thrown out, she was so tired she could barely stand.

Hobbling to the kitchen for a bite of supper, Dolly excitedly began to tell Nancy about working the bar with Jack. 'I sold White Satin and some Cream of the Palace; somebody bought Out & Out and one man asked for a Kill Grief!' Dolly was very pleased at learning the names so quickly. 'Mrs Larkin gave me a box to put the money in so I didn't have to walk to the till. Wasn't that kind of her?' she asked as a plate of sausage and fried onions was placed before her.

'Yes, sweet'eart. Now eat your supper then off to bed else you'll be good for nowt come the morning,' Nancy coaxed.

The question she had wanted to ask Nancy when she first arrived came to mind again at hearing the endearment. Despite her exhaustion Dolly steeled herself and plunged in.

'Mrs Sampson, do you remember the day when I was taken in by Mrs Larkin?'

'Yes, lovey, why?' Nancy asked, wondering what the girl was about to say.

'Well, you told me about – losing – your family and I explained about my mum...' Dolly was struggling to find the adequate words.

'Yes, and I've been pondering,' Nancy cut in. 'How would you feel if I was to become a sort of – mum – to you?'

'That was my thinking too!' Dolly gushed, relieved she didn't now have to ask. 'Would you – please?'

'Oh, bab! You little love – o'course I would if that's what you'd like!' Nancy gathered the young girl in her arms as a lone joyful tear ran down her cheek. Dashing it away with the back of her hand, she let go of Dolly and fussed with cups and saucers, a wide grin on her face.

Jack and Poppy had sat silently witnessing the whole thing and they now exchanged an open-mouthed glance.

'Well, young lady!' Nellie boomed as she entered the kitchen holding the cigar box.

Dolly withered beneath the gaze of Jack's mum. Should she have stepped in to help without being asked? Was Mrs Larkin furious with her now? Did she think Dolly might have stolen some of the money?

Placing the box on the table, Nellie flipped open the lid. Then she looked at the young girl sat at the table, fork in hand. 'This is what Dolly took tonight – well done, gel!'

Applause sounded and Dolly blushed to the roots of her hair.

'I should have asked if I could help first, rather than just stepping up, but you were so busy...' Dolly began.

'We needed that help so you did the right thing,' Nellie assured her. 'I think we might need you again, especially in this hot weather.'

Dolly clapped her hands in delight at having been asked.

Nancy and Nellie sat in the quiet kitchen after the others had trod wearily to bed, the aroma of onions still hanging in the air.

'You know I ain't in agreement with those kiddies tending the bar,' Nancy said, eyeing her friend over her teacup.

'I know, but with the way business is at the moment, I'll be able to pay the distiller off quicker,' Nellie answered.

'You'm allus thinking of yourself, Nell! Besides, it will still take years.'

'Maybe, but I ain't got a choice, Nance.' Nellie said, ignoring the jibe.

'My little 'un was tired to the bone, Nell.'

'*Your* little 'un?' Nellie asked.

'Ar, Dolly and I had a chat and we've decided it's what we both want,' Nancy answered.

'I see, well I'm glad for yer both, Nance,' Nellie said and her smile was warm as they both nodded together.

'Still, an' all, Dolly was done in tonight, Nell,' Nancy reiterated.

'Ar, but she was happy. I tell you what, Nance, she worked bloody hard tonight. She laughed and joked with the customers but never missed a beat. It's like she was born to it. She'll be an asset here, you mark my words.' Nellie poured herself another cup of tea, a smile gracing her rounded face.

Nancy yawned. 'I'm away to my bed now, don't forget to put that money away,' she said, pointing to the cigar box.

Nellie nodded. As she counted out the coins from the box, her smile broadened.

Well done indeed, Dolly Perkins!

7

Early one morning, Nancy donned her straw hat and prepared herself for the long walk to the fish market down past the Bull Ring. Taking some money from the household funds kept in the drawer set into the table she called out, 'I'm off to fetch some fish, Nell; do you need anything?'

Nellie came through from the bar shaking her head. 'No, but you can take young Dolly with you if you like. She's been working hard and deserves a bit of a rest from this place.'

'Righto,' Nancy nodded and gave Dolly a shout.

A moment later the girl appeared and was excited at the thought of a jaunt to the market.

'It's a long way, can you manage with that leg?' Nancy asked.

'Oh yes, I'm just not very fast,' Dolly answered. 'Can – can Jack come too?'

'Jack's got work to do,' Nellie said sternly.

Dolly lowered her gaze, feeling sorry for her new friend at being cooped up in this place all day. She had asked knowing how badly the boy wanted to be outside in the sunshine. He had been so kind to her and she wanted to do something nice for him in return. However, it seemed Mrs Larkin was not about to let him out today.

It was then that he came through the open doorway. 'Shelves are full; empty casks are ready for collection; floor is swept and now Poppy's scalding bottles,' he said breathlessly. 'Oh, you two off out?'

'Yes, I'm going to the fish market with Nancy,' Dolly said, almost apologetically.

Dashing into the hallway Jack returned with a battered old parasol and handed it to Dolly. 'It's as hot as a desert out there today.'

'Thank you, Jack,' Dolly said with a shy smile at his thoughtful gesture.

'Right, what's next, Mum?' he asked, suddenly aware that everyone was looking at him.

'You take yerself off with Nancy an' all; you deserve a break as well, lad,' Nellie said, 'but mind you ain't out all day cos we'll be run off our feet here later.'

'Thanks, Mum,' the boy said with a grin like a Cheshire cat.

The three went out of the back door into the yard, through the gate into the alley and then onto the main thoroughfare.

Nancy smiled as she walked down Gin Barrel Lane behind the two chattering children sharing the shade of the parasol. They couldn't have been closer if they'd been siblings. Dolly Daydream had the makings of being a real beauty in the next few years, but Nancy couldn't see the time when the girl would marry – not with that bad leg of hers. She'd probably grow up and grow old within the confines of The Crown Saloon for it was doubtful any man would take on a cripple for a wife.

Hearing Dolly's laugh, Nancy felt love surge through her. Everything about the child was gentle; her giggle was like water trickling in a brook, her eyes sparkled like stars and her brain held a wealth of knowledge for one so young. The words and phrases she used came naturally to her which showed a good education, but were never said in such a way as to make others appear or feel stupid.

Thirteen years old and an orphan, Dolly had endured more than any child should. Left only with an abusive step-father, the poor kid could take no more. Surviving on the streets with a gammy leg was a wonder in itself, and Nancy gave an imperceptible shake of her head at the thought.

As they continued on their way, Nancy watched Dolly's strange gait beneath the little summer dress Nellie had purchased from the market for her and wondered what had caused the leg to be damaged. Maybe the umbilical cord had wrapped itself around that little leg whilst still in the womb and thus cut off the blood supply. Could that have happened? Would it have resulted in a withered limb? No-one would ever know now, but what *was* apparent was young Dolly refused to be cowed by it. She did not see herself as disabled; to her the leg was nothing more than an inconvenience.

The smell of the fish market hit them long before they arrived. Leaving Corporation Street they turned into the High Street and on towards the stalls in Bell Street.

The difference in temperature caused them to shiver as all around them fish of all sorts were displayed on ice to keep them fresh. The calls of the mongers rang out, enticing buyers to their stalls.

'Mussels – fresh this morning!'

'Skate, come and get your skate here!'

'Last of the roe, ladies, so be quick!'

Dolly stared around and giggled at Jack as he opened and closed his mouth and used his hands as flippers.

Nancy grinned at his antics and cuffed him gently on the back of his head. 'Stay close, you two, I don't want you getting lost.'

As they meandered between the stalls, Nancy named the different species laid out before them. Cod, Pollock, Hake – the list went on before Nancy stopped to make her purchases. Rollmops – pickled herrings – were a firm favourite, and Pouting, which was cheaper than cod, were wrapped and placed in her basket before they moved on.

Nancy wisely kept her purse in her hand after hearing stories of a pickpocket targeting unsuspecting women.

'I just need to pop into the market hall quickly before we go home,' Nancy said as she ushered her charges out into the street once more. Pushing them before her into the massive market hall, she stopped at a stall selling Teddy Gray's sweets. She bought two ounces of boiled sweets each for a delighted Dolly and Jack with the firm instruction the confectionary was to be made to last.

'Don't crack 'em, you'll bost yer teeth. They'm called suck for a reason,' Nancy said with a grin. Refusing the bag proffered by Dolly she added, 'No, thanks, pet, they'm no good for me figure!'

Jack snorted and received another cuff for his cheek.

The walk home was made in silence as the youngsters sucked on a sweet, savouring its flavour like it might be the last they ever had.

Unbeknown to them a pair of weasel-like eyes had followed their progress. They had not seen the man watching, but Arthur Micklewhite had seen them.

8

Emptying the purse he had just stolen before dropping it to the ground, Arthur pocketed the money and pushed on through the fish market. That's when he had spotted Dolly and her friends. Surprised, he had not thought to see her again; after all, Birmingham was a large town.

Staying a good distance behind, he followed them up Corporation Street; he wanted to know where they were headed. Sauntering along in the mid-day heat, Arthur kept a beady eye on Dolly.

Eventually he stopped at the end of the tramway and leaned against a house wall. He watched in astonishment as the three entered The Crown Saloon. This was something he had not expected and he rubbed his whiskers as his thoughts swirled. A gin palace. Dolly Daydream had landed on her feet and no mistake.

He rolled himself a cigarette and lit it with a Lucifer, waving the match in the air to douse its flame before flicking it into the gutter. Puffing on his smoke he stared at the saloon.

Large plate glass windows etched with huge crowns stood

either side of the door. He could see, even from where he was standing, that the massive room, which he suspected had once been two, was full to bursting. Ornate gas lamps hung on the wall on either side of the door which was perpetually opening and closing as more bodies shoved their way inside. The sign which displayed the name of the place would also be lit up when darkness fell, he noted. The doors and window frames were painted burgundy and the brickwork looked as if it was cleaned regularly.

Pushing away from the wall, Arthur dragged his dirty fingers through his well-oiled hair. Pulling the dog-end from his lips he flicked it high into the air and watched its trajectory before it landed with a bounce and then rolled close to the discarded match.

His mind was working overtime as he walked home to Rea Terrace. Arthur considered the options. He could march in there all bluster and accuse them of stealing his daughter before he dragged her away. She could then take care of him as she should and he could finally get his hands on that necklace her mother had left her, once she revealed its hiding place.

Or, he could tell them he would report them to the constabulary for child theft unless they paid him to keep his mouth shut.

Arthur wondered if business was good at the establishment, which would mean he had another choice – breaking and entering. The takings would be a good haul but thieving such as that could only be undertaken once. The bobbies would no doubt patrol there regularly afterwards. There was a deal to think on concerning this and now Arthur knew where that girl was, he was in no hurry. He didn't think she'd be moving on any time soon as it would appear that she'd landed squarely on her feet. He guessed she was being well cared for and would settle herself in nicely.

Once he was back in the house, Arthur emptied his pockets onto the kitchen table. Five pounds, six shillings and nine pence – not a bad morning's work but not nearly enough for him to re-join the higher ranks of society. It was time to make himself some serious money. On that thought he flipped open the newspaper he'd purchased from a boy standing outside the market. Scanning the columns, his eyes lit up. There were two possibilities; businessmen about to be laid to rest. Making a note of the details, Arthur went upstairs to brush down his best suit. He was going to a funeral the following day and so he had to look his best.

Taking the suit from the tallboy, Arthur chuckled. He felt the old thrill rush through him at the thought of returning to the life he'd missed. He had known Avril's first husband's money would not last and he had enjoyed the spending of it. Now he was going back to doing what he loved – cheating women out of their inheritances. Catching sight of himself in the old mirror on the wall, Arthur saw how he had let himself go.

'This won't do at all, Arthur m'lad,' he muttered, 'you need a bath and a shave.'

Laying the suit on the bed he ran downstairs to drag the tin bath into the kitchen from the back yard. Whilst pans of water heated on the small range, Arthur sharpened his razor on the leather strop.

He shaved carefully; he couldn't attend a funeral with bits of paper stuck on cuts and nicks. Then he poured the warm water into the bath and began to strip off his dirty clothes. As he washed away the grime and sweat accumulated over the past weeks, Arthur's excitement mounted. In the very near future he would be a man of means once more, and revel in the respect and deference shown to him.

Whistling a little tune, Arthur grinned and then remembered – he'd better clean his teeth too!

At two o'clock the following day Arthur Micklewhite followed the mourners to a graveside at St Bartholomew's Church and stood back to watch the interment. Mr Bradshaw's coffin was lowered into the ground with great reverence and it was all Arthur could do not to smile wickedly. He recalled the details he'd read in the paper about the man these people were saying goodbye to. The late Mr John Bradshaw ran a large nail making business which, according to the law, would now pass to his widow. Arthur glanced over at the woman dressed all in black, a small net veil covering her eyes. He guessed her to be in her sixties, she had a trim figure in her widow's weeds and what struck him most of all was – there was no mopping away of tears. Was she all cried out already or was she glad to see the back of the man she'd been married to? Either way, Arthur intended to find out and in short order.

The mourners began to drift away and Arthur realised it was time for introductions. He was the last in line to pay his respects and engage the bereaved woman in conversation. As the line moved along, he realised there did not appear to be any offspring attending Mrs Bradshaw. Excellent, no family to avoid!

'Mrs Bradshaw, I was so sorry to hear of your husband's passing, please accept my condolences,' Arthur said as he took her black lace gloved hand in his and kissed the back tenderly.

'Thank you, Mr...?'

'Short, Gabriel Short,' Arthur answered.

'Did you know John, Mr Short?' Mrs Bradshaw asked.

'Not in the social sense, Mrs Bradshaw – we were colleagues.'

'Ah, I see. I'm afraid I know nothing of business, Mr Short, and now it seems I own one. I'm sure I don't know what I shall do about it.'

'If there is anything I can help you with, you simply must let me know. In fact, if you would allow, I would dearly like to call on you next week – to assure myself of your wellbeing, you understand,' Arthur said, giving the lady a look which he considered may cause her to feel less afraid of this stranger.

'It's not necessary, Mr Short,' Mrs Bradshaw said as they walked together towards the church gate.

'I agree, madam, but it would please me immensely. I would very much like to know more about you – your husband, that is,' Arthur made sure she had picked up on his deliberate slip of the tongue.

She turned to him with a frown, 'Are you flirting with me Mr Short?'

'God forbid such a thing and at this sad time! Mrs Bradshaw, you cut me to the quick!' Arthur feigned effrontery and with a small bow went on. 'If I have offended you then I apologise most profoundly. Now I will leave you. Goodbye, Mrs Bradshaw.'

'Mr Short!' Mrs Bradshaw called as he turned away from her and Arthur stopped. 'I'm sorry, it's just that this is the first time we've met and I'm not used to having gentleman callers.'

'It was not meant to be anything untoward, madam, I am merely worried for you,' Arthur smiled showing clean teeth.

'Forgive my rudeness, Mr Short, but I'm sure you understand it has been a trying time for me. Please – feel free to call any day next week. Thank you for your concern.'

Kissing her hand again, Arthur helped her into the driving seat of her cabriolet and handed her the reins. They exchanged a brief smile then she snapped the leather straps together, telling the horse to walk on. Arthur gave a small wave before turning to walk away, a broad grin splitting his face.

Once home, Arthur hung his suit in the tallboy and returned to the kitchen wearing only his long johns. Putting the kettle to boil on the range, he prepared himself a sandwich of cheese and salad. He propped open the back door with a chair to allow the air to circulate then made a pot of tea. As he busied about, he congratulated himself on his performance at the churchyard. He should have been an actor, but having said that, acting was not a lucrative profession. If the next funeral went as well as it did today, he would be off to a flying start.

Pulling the slip of paper towards him, Arthur checked the details of the service arranged for the following day – St Phillip's Church on Temple Row at eleven o'clock. Mr Roderick Chilton, carriage maker, was leaving a wife and daughter.

Munching his food, Arthur hoped the daughter was not a youngster. With a little luck the girl would be grown and married.

Lifting his cup, he made a toast, 'Don't worry about yer wife, Roderick, I'll take care of her.'

Arthur propped his bare feet onto another kitchen chair and finished his food feeling all was well with his world.

9

Whilst eating his breakfast, Jack Larkin was trying hard to read the newspaper. His reading skills were deficient due to lack of schooling, but he persevered with help from Dolly.

'The mutiny of sepoys in Meerut, forty miles north east of Delhi in India, is still raging,' Dolly read aloud as she took over after Jack had pushed the paper away exasperatedly.

'Record attendances to see the Art of Treasures of Great Britain exhibition in Manchester in the month since its opening.' Dolly looked up dreamily. 'I'd love to see that.'

'Go on, cocka,' Nancy encouraged, amazed at how easily Dolly read the headlines.

'The British Museum Reading Room was opened in May and appears to be in full use,' Dolly continued.

'When you've all finished with discussing world affairs, there's work to be done!' Nellie Larkin stated firmly.

A banging on the doors of The Crown Saloon had Nellie sigh then leave the kitchen.

Poppy and Nancy were chatting quietly and Jack and Dolly were clearing away their empty plates when raised voices were heard. Silence descended in the kitchen as all ears strained to hear what the ruckus was about. A moment later Nellie was back muttering obscenities under her breath.

'What's going on, Mum?' Jack asked.

'Nowt, lad, can you and Dolly fill the shelves? Poppy sweep the bar floor before you scald the empty bottles, there's a love,' Nellie said.

With only Nancy and Nellie in the kitchen it was the former who asked, 'What's up, Nell?'

'Henchmen from the distillers; came round to tell me I have to up my payments!' Nellie dropped onto a chair with an explosive sigh.

'That shouldn't be a problem with the way business has been lately, should it?' Nancy asked.

'Hmmm,' Nellie wasn't listening, she was trying to work out a way of paying off what she owed in one go. Firstly, she needed to discover how much she still owed, then check her savings before deciding whether she could afford to dispose of this debt completely. Then she made her first decision – she would visit the man who had lent her the money to convert The Crown Saloon from a run-down pub into a glittering gin palace.

'What are you going to do, Nell?' Nancy asked.

Nellie said nothing and shook her head.

'You're going to see *him,* ain't yer?' Nancy pursued her line of questioning.

'Looks like I'll have to.'

'I bloody knew it! Oh, Nell, be careful! You know what that bugger is like – everybody does!'

'I know. Ezra Morton is a nasty piece of work if he gets riled, but I don't see any way around this. I can't pay any more than I am already,' Nellie said as she rubbed a cheek with her palm. 'While I still owe Ezra, this place is a tied house. That means I can't buy my gin from anyone but him – so I'm stuck on that point. I ain't got enough to pay him off completely, I don't think, so that's no good either. The only option to me is to talk to Ezra to explain my circumstances and hope he's amenable to finding a solution to suit us both.'

'We could do with a big burly bloke around here to deal with men like Ezra Morton!' Nancy snapped.

'I could take Jack with me...' Nellie began.

'Are you out of your stark staring mind?!' Nancy exploded. 'The lad's ten years old for God's sake! What do you think he could do if Ezra turns nasty?'

Nellie dragged her hands down her face then nodded her agreement. 'You're right. I'll go on my own.'

'You want me to come with you?' Nancy asked tentatively.

'No, Nance, you need to stay here with the kids and oversee the bar. Even if I'm out, we still need to open up else there'll be murder done,' Nellie answered. Getting to her feet with a groan she added, 'I'll go tomorrow morning.'

Nancy sat with a cup of tea and pondered on the person they had discussed. Ezra Morton, a man of wealth earned mostly from dishonest practices and bullyboy tactics, so the rumours said. He would lend money with extortionate interest rates, and when folk couldn't pay, he would send his team out to put the fear of God into them.

The stories were rife about men being beaten when late on a re-payment to Ezra while women were threatened with having their children stolen and taken into Ezra's employ until the debt was paid off.

With a sigh Nancy considered whether these tales were true or whether they were circulated by Morton's men as a warning to others not to default. Either way, Nellie would be putting herself in harm's way and Nancy was terribly worried for her.

An image of Ezra formed in her mind and she could not deny the man was handsome. He was tall with dark hair greying slightly at the temples. Hazel eyes that could twinkle with mischief or bore into your very soul. Well-dressed at all times, Ezra was shown deference by those around him. Always taken to the best tables in restaurants, the proprietors being careful not to upset the man who could see them out of business in the blink of an eye. Staying on the right side of the law, Morton was untouchable. Hiding behind a cloak of being an honest business-man, Ezra's suspected underhand dealings could never be proved.

Nancy couldn't understand why such a good looking man had never married; maybe he had just not met the right woman. Or, it might be his desperation to make money which ruled his life. Whatever the reason, he lived alone but was always surrounded by his men; was this for protection against anyone who would do him harm? Nancy doubted it was for companionship.

Having finished her tea, Nancy thought it time to begin preparing their lunch. Whatever she said, she knew Nellie would proceed with her visit to Ezra the following day. All she could do was pray it went well and her friend returned home safe and sound.

* * *

Dolly and Jack had been busy in the bar with Poppy. The place was packed to the gunnels as usual and folk were already inebriated to the point of falling down. Dolly smiled when Jack dug her in the ribs and pointed to a man trying to dance a hornpipe. They watched as his legs tangled and he landed hard on his rump. Dragging himself to his feet he looked at the ground for whatever had tripped him over, and the youngsters collapsed in a fit of giggles.

'Hey, take it outside, ladies!' Poppy yelled as two women began to argue. Ignoring the girl, the disagreement became heated so Poppy shouted again. 'Stop that or there'll be no more gin for either of you!' That immediately got their attention and with a harrumph the women moved away from each other – another crisis averted.

'Ah, Poppy, give ush a kish,' a drunken man slurred as he leaned forward across the counter.

'Not on yer life,' Poppy replied with a smile as she pushed him away, 'you ain't even got yer false teeth in!'

The drunk smacked his lips and gave her a toothless grin as he staggered backwards.

'Now if it was him who was asking...' Poppy grinned at the handsome young man leaning on the bar watching her.

The rest of the morning went on in the same vein; customers arguing, women singing, men tottering – all drinking as fast as they could get served.

Joining Poppy, Nellie shook her head. 'All enjoying their destructive love affair with gin I see.'

Poppy nodded and sighed. 'Have you seen old Aggie over there?'

Nellie's eyes roamed the crowd in search of the woman. 'Oh, blimey! What happened?'

'She pawned her frock to buy her drink!' Poppy answered as they both stared at the old girl dressed only in her drawers, chemise and long petticoats.

'Aggie! Get off home and get dressed!' Nellie called out.

'Can't do it, Nell, this is all I've got left!' Aggie shouted back.

'Shall I get—?' Poppy began.

'No. Don't give her one of your dresses cos she'll pawn

that as well,' Nellie interrupted. 'Don't worry we won't see her again after today until she's got some pennies in her hand.'

'Nell, this gin tastes like camel p—' a man started to complain about the dregs in his glass. Clearly, he was hoping for a free refill.

'Don't you bloody dare say it!' Nellie jumped in. 'You don't like it – don't drink it!'

Turning to Jack she said, 'You and Dolly go and get your dinner now.'

Nancy welcomed them into the kitchen with a plate of faggots in rich gravy, peas, fresh bread thick with butter and a cup of tea. She laughed loudly when told about Aggie drinking gin wearing only her underwear.

During the afternoon whilst everyone was busy in the bar, Nancy spent her time thinking while she baked. She was making a meat and potato pie which she knew was everyone's favourite. Rolling out pastry she wondered how Ezra Morton would react to Nellie's visit the following morning. Nowt to do now but wait and see.

10

It was in the early hours of the morning when Arthur Micklewhite stole silently into the yard of The Crown Saloon. The place was in darkness and he checked around, assuring himself he couldn't be seen in the light of the half moon. Trying the back door he was not surprised to find it locked. He tried the windows – firmly closed. Screwing up his mouth in frustration, he realised the only way in would be to smash the glass pane and that would alert the occupants. Standing back, he looked up, hoping a bedroom window may have been left open against the heat of the summer. He was disappointed, there was no way in. He knew he could charm anyone into giving him their money and he was a nifty pickpocket but breaking and entering was not his forte. He decided it might be prudent to give up this idea before he was caught by a patrolling constable.

Slipping back through the gate into the alley, Arthur made his way home, thoroughly disgruntled at being no richer for his efforts. What he didn't realise was that all the time he was scouting the yard, a pair of eyes was watching his every move.

Dolly, unable to sleep for the suffocating heat, had been about to open her window when she saw the figure furtively creeping about in the yard below. Staying in the shadows she waited and kept her gaze on the intruder until he had given up and left. All she could tell was that it was a man, his features indiscernible in the shadows of darkness.

Unwilling to open the window now, Dolly returned to sit on her bed feeling unnerved. Evidently the man had been trying to break in, but his efforts had been thwarted by the place being sealed tight.

Happy at being given her own room after a clear out of rubbish, she wished for a moment she was still in with Poppy. Unable to rest now, Dolly placed a chair by the window. She would keep a look out until the morning when she would tell Nellie about what she'd seen. Despite the cloying heat, Dolly shivered. Who was that man and what was he after? Had he intended to rob the Saloon of its takings? Or did he have a more sinister intention? Was he out to murder them in their beds?

Dolly shivered again as she willed the morning to come quicker.

It was very early and Dolly was downstairs first. She fed the range with coal and set the kettle to boil. Into a massive frying pan, she dropped the rashers of bacon taken from the cold slab in the scullery. It wouldn't be long before the aroma of cooking food would bring the others from their beds.

By the time tea was made, Nancy and Nellie were in the kitchen with astonished looks on their faces.

'I couldn't sleep,' Dolly said in reply to their surprise.

'Why, gel? Is it cos you've a room of your own now?' Nellie asked.

'No, it was lovely of you to let me have it.'

Dolly smiled, passing the cosy-covered teapot to Nancy. 'I was overheated in the night and I was about to open the window when I saw a man snooping around in the yard.'

'You what?!' Nellie almost gagged on her tea.

'I guess he was trying to find a way in,' Dolly added.

'Bloody thieving—' Nellie began. 'It's a good job all the doors were bolted. I wonder if whoever it was might try again. We'll have to make sure everything's locked up tight.'

'You don't think it could have been one of Ezra's—?' Nancy began.

'No!' Nellie cut her off mid-sentence, tilting her head to Dolly who was tending the bacon. 'I suspect it was an opportunistic effort that came to nowt.'

Nancy also glanced at Dolly and nodded. 'I expect you're right.'

Poppy and Jack filed into the kitchen sleepy-eyed.

Nancy sliced bread to go with the bacon now on everyone's plate and they all tucked in. Between bites of her breakfast, Dolly explained again what she'd seen the previous night.

'You d'aint see who it was?' Jack asked.

'No, but – there was something familiar about him. I can't put my finger on it, but I'm sure I've seen him somewhere before. It was dark, Jack,' Dolly said apologetically.

'What are we going to do, Mum?' Jack asked.

'Ain't nothing we can do, lad, other than to make sure the place is locked up as tight as a duck's arse,' Nellie replied.

Dolly choked on her tea at the phrase and Poppy patted her back gently.

'Anyway, I have to go out later so I'm relying on you lot to get the bar stocked and the doors open on time,' Nellie added.

'Where you going?' Jack asked, eyeing his mother suspiciously.

'I have to go and see Mr Morton about an extra delivery because we've been so busy these last weeks,' Nellie lied.

Jack nodded. 'Me and Poppy will...'

'Poppy and I will...' Dolly corrected him with a cheeky grin.

Jack sighed but with good humour. 'Poppy and I will fill the shelves and Dolly can sweep.'

Titters were stifled then Nellie said, 'Right, let's get to it then,' as she ushered them out of the kitchen. Turning back to Nancy she raised her hand and crossed her fingers. Nancy did the same with a nod of her head.

* * *

Nellie looked at the building in front of her – Ezra Morton's brewery. Just off Nova Scotia Street, it occupied a massive piece of land. Here the workers brewed beer and distilled gin and Ezra supplied many landlords and owners of pubs in the area.

The smell emanating from the works was pungent and Nellie felt her stomach roil. She was nervous but knew she had to keep it in check; she could not allow Ezra to detect her fear.

Taking a deep breath, Nellie marched through the open wrought iron gates and into the red brick building.

'Where would I find Mr Morton?' she asked a man wearing a filthy apron who was sweeping the floor.

'Through there, missus,' he said pointing to a door.

Nellie nodded her thanks and knocked on the door. Without waiting for an answer, she strode into the office, her head held high.

Ezra Morton was sat behind a huge wooden desk and he looked up from his writing as Nellie walked in.

'Well now, Mrs Larkin, how very nice to see you. Won't you sit down?' His eyebrows lifted in surprise at the unexpected visitor, and calling so early to boot.

'Ezra.' Nellie said as she took a chair facing him.

'To what do I owe the pleasure of your visit, Nellie?' Ezra's honeyed tones were quiet as he leaned back. With his elbows on the arms of the chair, he plaited his fingers over his flat stomach.

'Oh, I think you know as well as I do, Ezra Morton. You sent your bullies to scare me into paying you more money each week. Well, I'm here to tell you it ain't gonna happen. What I need to know is just how much is left on my debt,' Nellie said as she raised her eyebrows.

Ezra chuckled. 'Always the strong one, ain't you? I always admired you for that, Nellie. You're about the only one who's not afraid of me.'

You couldn't be more wrong! Nellie thought but gave a confident smile instead.

Pulling open a drawer he took out a large ledger and flipped it open. Running his eyes down a page with her name written on the top he said, 'Hmmm, it's a lot, Nellie, and it's my guess you don't have it. So, what we have to decide now is – where to go from here?'

Turning the ledger so Nellie could see the total owing, he then snapped it shut and returned it to the drawer.

With all credit to Nellie she never batted an eyelid, even after seeing she still owed two thousand pounds.

'Indeed Ezra, where do we go from here?' she asked, a little smile lifting the corners of her mouth.

'You've got a young lad, ain't you?' Ezra asked, matching her smile.

'I have, and he stays with me. Don't even think about drawing him into your web of dirty dealings.' Nellie kept her voice even despite her heart hammering out of her chest.

'I'm sure I don't know what you mean,' Ezra said, a grin spreading over his handsome face.

'Look, Ezra, let's not play games, eh? I owe you and I'm paying back each week. I've never missed a payment yet, not like others you deal with, and I only sell your muck – the stuff you have the nerve to call gin.' Nellie sniffed.

To her surprise Ezra let out a great belly laugh. 'I have to hand it to you, Nellie Larkin, you've got style. If you were a man, you'd have balls the size of mine.'

'And if bullshit was music, you'd have yer own orchestra!' Nellie countered.

Ezra's booming laughter sounded again. Then leaning forward he said, 'All right, how about this? You pay an extra sixpence a week and we'll leave it at that – for now.'

Nellie stood and proffered her hand to seal the deal. They shook and she turned and left his office.

For a long time, Ezra stared at the closed door shaking his head. That woman had some nerve.

Nellie walked from the building quickly, a feeling of relief flowing through her. Two things had been achieved. Firstly, she had discovered the sum owed, and secondly, she had struck a deal which she could live with. Furious that she had only been paying off the interest, which was not what was agreed, Nellie determined to pay off the debit in one go as soon as she could. She congratulated herself on her calm dealings with the man everyone feared. Now she had to find a way of gathering two thousand pounds together, then she could visit Ezra again. She would present him with the money, get a receipt and tell him to shove his gin where the sun don't shine. For Nellie Larkin, that day couldn't come fast enough.

Whilst Nellie was bandying words with Ezra, Arthur Micklewhite was readying himself for a funeral.

The widow, Sylvia Chilton, would not know him, of course, but would accept that Arthur was a colleague of her late husband. It was a ploy he'd used time after time and it had never failed him yet.

Walking to the appointed place, Arthur scanned the crowd in order to identify the grieving woman and her daughter. There, in the middle of a huddle of black-clad figures was the person his eyes sought, and to his delight so was the daughter – and the man he presumed was her husband.

Arthur really did feel his luck was changing for the better despite his failure to break into The Crown Saloon the night before.

Going through the motions was second nature to him now and everything went smoothly. Gabriel Short was invited for afternoon tea the following week. No doubt the scowling daughter would be there too, but all he had to do was hold his nerve and charm them both.

Arthur returned home a decidedly happier man.

11

Ezra Morton was contemplating his meeting with Nellie Larkin when one of his men walked into the office.

'I wish you would remember to knock!' Ezra spat.

'Sorry, boss,' the big man said looking suitably chastised.

'Now you're in, what do you want?'

'Erm... Mr Aldritch has just taken over The Comet Inn over at Cheapside, boss.'

'And?' Ezra asked with a sigh.

'And – do you want me to pay a visit?' The big man was shuffling uncomfortably from foot to foot.

'Yes, Frederick, please do that,' Ezra replied.

The man nodded and left his employer's office quicker than he entered.

Frederick Dell was a giant of a man and Ezra likened him to a big stupid dog, always at his master's heels, but he was handy to have around. People walked around him rather than tangle with him and Ezra had been glad of him more than once. Having been threatened with violence on occasion he had been happy to let Frederick step up and protect him.

Ezra liked this huge dim-witted fellow despite his having to explain every little thing over and over to ensure Frederick understood. Now he was off to visit a new landlord to explain the lie of the land – protection offered for a small fee each week and the offer of a refurbishment loan.

Rubbing his hands together, Ezra knew by the end of the day he would have another 'tied house'.

Donning his bowler hat and grabbing his silver topped walking cane, he decided it was time to see just how good business was for Nellie Larkin at The Crown Saloon.

Hailing a cab Ezra climbed aboard calling out the address. As they rolled along, he stared out of the window at the dirty streets with poverty-stricken people ambling about aimlessly. He shook his head at seeing beggars standing on the street corners – someone should do something about all this – but he knew it would not be him. Ezra Morton enjoyed his money too much to be spending it on improving the town; that's what the council was for. Despite the sun shining down, the dirty grey smoke emitted from factory chimneys hung low over the town, the pall giving the whole area a look of dirty degradation.

They passed The Gaiety Palace where Ezra had spent many happy hours. He was fond of attending the shows and socialising. The clip-clop of the horse's hooves on the cobble-stones echoed off the buildings lining either side of the road and the bouncing carriage rattled his bones. Shanks' Pony would have been kinder on his body, but it would not do to be seen walking – not a man of his status.

As the carriage drew to a halt, Ezra looked out onto the façade of The Crown Saloon whilst waiting for the jarvey to jump down and open the door.

Alighting, he slipped half a crown into the man's hand.

'Thankee, sir!' the coachman said, tipping his hat, his eyes as wide as saucers at the incredibly large tip.

Ezra stood a moment looking at the frontage of the building as the carriage rolled away. Nellie Larkin had done wonders in turning her old pub into such a showpiece. Plate glass windows, gas lamps, a new sign depicting a golden crown.

Stepping through the open doorway, Ezra couldn't believe his eyes. It was wall to wall with bodies. Revellers singing and dancing, some debating what they felt to be important topics, such as the strength of the gin. The odour of unwashed bodies caused him to wrinkle his nose as he parted a way through the crowd with his walking cane until he reached the counter. There he found himself staring as Poppy Charlton smiled at him.

So far nothing had been as he expected, but for a moment this beautiful young woman had taken his breath away.

'What can I get you, sir?' she asked.

'Nothing, thank you,' Ezra murmured.

'Sorry, mister, but if you ain't drinking then make way for them as is,' Poppy tempered her words with another dazzling smile.

'C'mon Poppy!' a customer called.

'All right, keep yer hat on,' she yelled back as she moved to serve the impatient man.

Poppy! What a delightful name!

Ezra felt his heartbeat increase a little hearing the girl's laugh, and again when she glanced back at him. He watched her laugh and joke with those on the other side of the counter.

'When you gonna marry me, Poppy?' an old man with a grizzled expression called out.

'Not until you're a millionaire, Mr Cartwright,' Poppy answered jovially.

'Oh, bugger!' the man replied as he was jostled in fun by those around him.

The girl certainly was a blonde haired beauty with eyes the colour of cornflowers. She had a sense of humour too. Ezra continued to stare, unaware that Nellie had spied him and was now glaring at this man who had the audacity to be checking out her business, as well as her bar staff, for that was surely why he was here.

'Mr Morton! To what do I owe the pleasure of your visit, Ezra?' Nellie used the words he had said to her earlier that day and she saw him smile.

'I was curious about what you'd done with this place. I haven't seen it since you renovated. Very nice, Nellie,' he said, glancing around but then his eyes lingered on Poppy.

Nellie's stomach turned over as she saw the look on his face. Oh no! Not Poppy! Somewhere deep inside she knew her plea would go unheard. If Ezra Morton set his sights on something – he usually got it. And if she was not mistaken, what he wanted now was Poppy Charlton.

'Was there anything else?' Nellie snapped, bringing his focus back to herself.

'No, only – who is that girl?

'She's my barmaid and I'll thank you to get yer beady eyes off her. She ain't for you, Ezra.' Nellie's voice sailed across the room and heads turned to listen in to the conversation.

Seeing the warning in Nellie's eyes, he smiled. 'We'll see,' he said as he tipped his bowler and shuffled out through the throng to hail a cab again.

Nellie sighed with a relief which she guessed would only be temporary for she was certain they would be seeing a lot more of Ezra in the near future.

Answering a shout with an expletive, Nellie returned to her work but her mind was on how to shield Poppy from Morton's attentions.

* * *

That night when everywhere was securely locked up, Nellie related her account of her meeting that morning.

'So now you know where I went and what for,' she said.

'Two thousand pounds! Blimey, Mum, that's a fortune!' Jack gasped.

'I know but the sooner we get it, the quicker I'll be out of Morton's clutches. So, I need some ideas as to how to raise that much money.' Nellie laid her hands on the kitchen table they were all now sitting around.

'I'll work for free, Nellie,' Dolly piped up. 'After all, you were good enough to take me in off the streets. You saved my life and it's the least I can do to repay you. Bed and board is enough.'

Nancy's eyes brimmed with tears at the girl's thoughtfulness.

'Me an' all, Mum,' Jack said, following suit.

'Me too, even though we've only just started to get paid,' Poppy added.

'I will as well,' Nancy said finally.

'Thank you, but I fear it won't be enough, so you all keep your money. I do thank you very much for the offer though. We have to find a way of getting all that cash together in one go so I can tell Morton to shove it up his—'

'What about a bake sale?' Nancy put in quickly.

'Ar, it would help,' Nellie agreed. 'What else?'

Heads shook as silence fell and tired brains worked hard but produced no answers.

'Right, let's sleep on it then,' Nellie said and with that everyone retired to their beds feeling thoroughly exhausted.

Despite being desperately tired, Dolly spent long hours thinking about the discussion around the kitchen table. Nellie was in great need of funds and there was a way Dolly could help. Staring at the moonlit ceiling she murmured, 'Nellie has been so very kind to me these last weeks, what would you do, Mum?'

As if in answer, a gentle wind took up outside and rattled the window. Dolly smiled into the shadows. She knew now what had to be done, and the sudden wind on such a balmy night – to her at least – was an omen. It was her mum's approval on the decision made.

12

Dolly was up early the following morning and was out before anyone else roused. She was on a mission. Limping down Corporation Street her eyes searched each building. The place she was looking for was on this major thoroughfare somewhere. Then she spotted it – the Abyssinian Gold Jewellery Co. Ltd. Stopping to stare into the window through the wrought iron shutters, she was mesmerised by the gold glinting in the sunshine. It was not open yet and Dolly waited patiently by the door for someone to arrive. Leaning on the doorframe to ease the burden of her weight on her good leg, she heard the church bell strike eight.

Just then a tall thin man walked up to her. 'Be off with you, you can't beg here!' he snapped as he unlocked the door.

'I'm not a beggar, I was waiting for you,' Dolly replied.

Casting an eye over her old clothes he shook his head. 'My dear girl, I'm certain there is nothing in this establishment you could possibly afford!'

'My dear man, I'm not here to buy!' Dolly said with her nose in the air.

'Oh,' he said as he pushed open the door.

'Indeed.' Dolly followed him inside and again waited while he opened the shutters.

'Right, what can I do for you?' the man asked in a tone that said this urchin was wasting his precious time.

'My mother bequeathed me a necklace and it has already been valued so I know its worth. What I wish to know is whether you are interested in purchasing the said piece.' Dolly stared the man straight in the eye, daring him to try and dupe her.

He nodded. 'May I see it please?' He had been surprised by her elocution and wondered if he had misjudged the girl.

Slipping the gold chain from around her neck, Dolly laid it on the counter. The pendant held a brilliant stone which sparkled like fire as the rays of the sun rested on it.

Lifting it, the man's eyebrows flicked up and Dolly, who was watching him carefully, caught the movement. He was impressed. Inspecting the diamond with his jeweller's magnifying glass he asked, 'How do I know this belongs to you? It could be stolen.'

Dolly reached into her chemise and pulled out an envelope which she laid on the counter.

The man picked it up and pulled the papers from the envelope with the tips of his fingers having seen where it had been kept. It was a letter of confirmation of the weight, carat, clarity and price of the diamond from a prominent London agent. There was also was a copy of her mother's will and Dolly's birth certificate.

'Well, you've certainly come prepared I must say!' the man gasped.

'It pays to. When you saw me outside you instantly took me for a beggar. Looks can be deceiving, sir, and it's important not to judge a book by its cover. If you read that book

first then you have entitlement to make your judgement.'
Dolly gave him a smile and flicked up her own eyebrows.

'Touché,' he said grudgingly. 'Now, you wish to sell this?'

'Yes, I have a dear friend in desperate need of the money
it will bring,' Dolly answered.

Again, the man was surprised. 'I must apologise for my
faux pas,' he said, waving a hand towards the door.

'That's all right, everyone makes mistakes at some time or
another.'

Another shock – she understood precisely what he had
said.

'If you are sure?' the man asked, dangling the chain over
his hand before placing it on the counter.

'I am,' Dolly confirmed.

'Very well, if you will give me a moment to retrieve the
money from the safe.' The man disappeared into a back room
and returned soon after with an envelope in his hand which
he passed to Dolly.

Taking out the money, Dolly counted it quickly.
Nodding, she replaced it in the envelope and pushed the
will and birth certificate in with it. The necklace and its
letter of authenticity she slid across the counter towards
the man.

'Thank you, Sir.'

'Thank you, *Miss Perkins*,' he said as he shot round to hold
the door open for her.

'Good day,' Dolly said.

'To you too,' the man said. Watching her limp away he
shook his head, hardly able to believe the whole transaction
had taken place.

* * *

Back at The Crown Saloon there was mayhem in the kitchen when Dolly walked in.

'Oh, there you are! We've all but had the bobbies out looking for you! Wherever have you been?' Nancy said tearfully as she rushed to fold Dolly in her arms.

'I had to go out. I'm sorry if I worried you all,' she replied.

'Well, you're back now so—' Nellie began.

'Nellie, I have something to say to you first if that's all right,' Dolly interrupted. With everyone sat around the kitchen table, it was evident Nellie had delayed opening the doors to the saloon in case they had to go searching for the girl they thought was missing.

'When my mum died, she left me a necklace that my stepfather wanted, but in the will it was bequeathed to me. I took the item and the will when I left. Now I have sold it, that's where I was this morning.' Reaching into her chemise she removed her birth certificate and the will and handed the envelope to Nellie. 'Take what you need to pay off Mr Morton, the rest I'll keep for a rainy day.'

Nellie pulled out the money and gasps sounded all round. 'I can't take this! My God, Dolly, I... It was left to you by your mum, you should keep it!' Nellie was aghast at the girl's generosity.

Nancy's hands had shot to her mouth as she stared at the notes on the table. She had never seen so much all in one place.

Dolly grabbed the money and counted out enough to repay Nellie's debt. The rest she shoved into the envelope and back into her chemise, birth certificate and all.

'Please take it, I want you to have it and I know my mum would want the same.' Dolly spoke quietly, and as she looked around at the faces watching her, she saw tears streaming from their eyes – even Jack's.

'Thank you,' Nellie sobbed, 'I'll repay you somehow – someday.'

'It's a gift Nellie – a thank you for saving me,' Dolly said as she sank into Nellie's outstretched arms.

They all hugged her – all except Jack that is, who was too shy to join in and instead patted her back in a 'well done' gesture.

'Tomorrow I'll be paying Ezra another visit – and it will be one I'll treasure for the rest of my life!' Nellie said, wiping away tears with her apron.

That night, Dolly sat in the chair by the window of her bedroom, gazing up at the stars. She wondered if Arthur Micklewhite had discovered the will was missing yet – or indeed the necklace. She had no doubt he would have searched for both.

She recalled their visit to the solicitor's office for the reading of her mother's will and Arthur's rantings when he was told the jewellery now belonged to Dolly even though the house and its contents were his to do with as he wished. The kindly solicitor had handed the necklace to Dolly who had slipped it over her head and beneath her dress before Arthur could see it clearly. He had also given her the envelope with the authentication letter and her certificate of birth which Dolly had made sure were kept safely hidden beneath a floorboard in her room.

Dolly smiled up at the moon casting its silvery beams down onto her face. 'Thanks, Mum. It was a wise decision not to let him have your jewellery. I hope you are pleased with my helping Nellie with the money. I think you always knew I wouldn't stay at home once you'd gone, didn't you?'

Just then, a star twinkled brightly and Dolly nodded. In her mind she felt her mum had heard her and approved.

With a yawn, Dolly crawled into bed with a feeling of warm satisfaction settling on her.

'I'm going to get off and see Ezra Morton early so I'll be back before it gets too busy,' Nellie said the next morning.

'May I make a suggestion?' Dolly asked tentatively.

'Yes, lovey, what is it?' Nellie asked as she grabbed her bag, checking the money was safe inside.

'If Mr Morton is, as you say, a liar and a cheat – might it be prudent to take someone with you to act as a witness to you paying off your loan?' Dolly asked.

'That's smart thinking, Nell, I would never 'ave thought of it,' Nancy said.

'It's a good idea, Dolly, but everybody needs to stay here and run the bar,' Nellie replied.

'You could ask my mum's solicitor, Mr Sharpe. I'm sure he would be happy to accompany you for a small fee,' Dolly responded. 'If you like I'll show you where his office is.'

Nellie exchanged a glance with Nancy who nodded her approval.

'Come on then, darlin', let's get Ezra bloody Morton paid off as soon as possible.' Nellie grinned, her excitement at the prospect of being free of the man evident as she headed for the back door.

Out on the street Dolly said, 'We have to get to Union Street, and the office is almost at the end of Corporation Street.'

Looking down at the girl's withered leg, Nellie nodded. 'It'll be quicker by cab.' Curling her forefinger and thumb to form a circle she stuck them in her mouth and gave a loud whistle.

Dolly winced at the sound but smiled as she saw the cabbie steering his horse towards them.

Nellie helped Dolly inside, then she climbed aboard giving the cabbie the address. 'Bottom end of Corporation Street please.'

What would have been a long walk was a short journey by cab and as Nellie alighted, she asked the driver to wait. Then she and Dolly entered the office of Sharpe & Derby, Solicitors. In but a moment, Mr Sharpe was greeting them warmly.

It was Dolly, at Nellie's prompting, who explained what they were there for Nellie dug into her bag and produced her little notebook with the amounts paid up to date.

Checking through the small ledger the solicitor nodded. 'I see,' Mr Sharpe said thoughtfully. 'Well, I agree it would make perfect sense. By having a witness, there can be no comeback on you, Mrs Larkin.' Seeing her puzzled expression, he explained further. 'You pay what is owed to Mr Morton who in turn provides you with a receipt. This is signed by him, yourself and me thus making the transaction legal. It would mean you are paid up in full and final settlement so Mr Morton could not then come back to you at a later date claiming he was still owed the sum.'

'So, I'll be free and clear?' Nellie asked.

'You will indeed, Mrs Larkin,' Mr Sharpe confirmed.

'Right then, I suggest we get this over and done with,' Nellie said as she got to her feet.

'Am I to take it you are engaging my services?' Mr Sharpe asked.

'You bet your arse I am! If you're free that is,' Nellie said with a laugh.

'For payment?'

Nellie nodded, 'Of course.'

'Then give me a moment to get my hat!' Mr Sharpe grinned as he stood.

On the journey, Mr Sharpe checked the small account book again and questioned Nellie about her repayments.

'I borrowed two grand but there was interest to go on top of that. Morton showed me how much I owed and it was still two thousand so I must have only been paying off the interest.' Nellie said a little sadly.

'How much interest?'

'I ain't sure,' Nellie said, feeling rather stupid now as it was said out loud.

'No matter. I think I have this worked out so don't worry,' Sharpe answered.

A short while later, Mr Sharpe, along with Nellie and Dolly, entered Ezra's office on the brewery site.

'Nellie! Another visit – and so soon after the last,' Ezra said, but his eyes remained on the official looking man.

'Mr Morton, my name is Sharpe and I'm a solicitor of law. My services have been retained by Mrs Larkin to witness a transaction between the two of you.'

'Which is?' Ezra asked, only now looking at Nellie.

'This – payment in full,' Nellie grinned as she slapped the money on his desk. 'I'd like a receipt.'

Ezra's eyes widened as he looked at the money. 'How...?

Where did you get this?' he asked.

'That ain't none of your business. Now if you don't mind, Mr Sharpe ain't got all day.' Nellie's voice held a touch of weariness at his prevaricating.

Ezra gave her a sickly smile and wrote out a receipt, passing it across to her.

'This ain't right,' she said, placing it into the solicitor's hands.

'Two thousand, five hundred, Nellie, that's what you borrowed,' Ezra said slyly.

'I borrowed two grand. It was you who added that extra five hundred as interest! That money there covers all of what you showed me was owed the other day – two thousand – check your ledger again!' Nellie fumed.

'You knew there would be interest to pay, Nellie,' Ezra said with a shrug of his shoulders.

'Ar, but five hundred! Bloody hell, Ezra! You're a blood-sucking parasite!' Nellie was beside herself with anger.

'However, there is the money already paid back to take into account if you recall,' Mr Sharpe interjected quickly.

'Therefore, Mrs Larkin is correct, Mr Morton.'

Nellie glanced up at the solicitor, as did Ezra.

'Two thousand borrowed plus five hundred interest added by yourself equals two-five if I'm not mistaken. Mrs Larkin has already paid off the interest as well as five hundred from the capital sum loaned which she appears to have forgotten about. Therefore, by my reckoning she is only in debt to you for fifteen hundred.' Picking up the money, he retrieved five hundred pounds which he passed back to Nellie.

'I assure you, Mr Sharpe, my books are in order,' Ezra scowled.

'And I assure you, Mr Morton, they are not. Mrs Larkin

provided me with her accounts and *my* adding up is precise.' The solicitor eyed Ezra, daring him to challenge or argue the point further.

'Now that we have that sorted out may I request a receipt for my client – this time for the correct amount. Also, if I may be so bold, I would suggest you abide by the law – at least on this one occasion.' Mr Sharpe pushed his spectacles further up on his nose.

'You don't know what was agreed between us, Mr Sharpe,' Ezra said.

'Mrs Larkin informed me on the way over here, and as I said previously, she provided her accounts, so if you continue to argue the point, I'm sure a Judge will be able to sort out the whole thing in court. Are you willing to go that far, Mr Morton?' Mr Sharpe smiled at the man sitting behind the huge desk.

'My mistake,' Ezra said with a scowl.

At last the deed was done and Nellie was satisfied. Tucking the receipt in her bag, she turned to Dolly. 'If you and Mr Sharpe will wait for me in the cab, I have something to say to Mr Morton. I'll be with you in a moment.'

Once Dolly and the solicitor had left the office, Nellie leaned her hands on Ezra's desk. 'That's you and me finished, Ezra, which means I won't be coming back here. It also means you ain't welcome at my place. So any designs you might have on my barmaid, you'd best forget. I told you before, she's not for you – she deserves better. Now, that money I've paid – you can stick it as far up yer backside as it'll go! Tarrar Ezra.' Nellie laughed as she heard him growl then, giving him a wave, she left him to stew in his own juices.

Ezra picked up the money and wondered how Nellie had managed to get this much together. Laying it back on the desk, he rubbed his forehead; it was a mystery, but somehow he would solve it. He was determined to know the truth.

She had told him that he was no longer welcome at The Crown Saloon. This was a blow for it meant he wouldn't be able to see Poppy. He guessed the girl was given very little time off from her job, so it was unlikely he would bump into her in the town.

Without realising he began to tap a finger on the money. Somehow, he had to find a way to introduce himself to Poppy. That young lady belonged on his arm and Ezra had every intention of making that happen. One way or another, Poppy would be his; the question was – how to go about it?

Opening a drawer, Ezra slid the money across the top of the desk. He smiled at the satisfying sound it made as it dropped inside, before his mind returned to Poppy. Grinning widely, Ezra left his office to inspect the works.

Back at Mr Sharpe's office Nellie paid the solicitor his fee saying, 'Mr Sharpe, I need to thank you so much for every-thing. It was damned lucky you were there otherwise that bast... bleeder would have taken all that money.'

'You are most welcome, Mrs Larkin, and thank you for this,' Mr Sharpe smiled as he waved a five pound note in the air – a welcome bonus for his efforts.

'You've earned it, sir. Ezra was trying to pull a fast one there, but you outsmarted him,' Nellie grinned.

'All's fair in love and – money!' Sharpe said with a laugh. 'Should you need my help in the future please feel free to call on me.'

'Judging by what's just happened it looks like I could do with someone to help me with my books,' Nellie said.

'I'd be more than happy to help should you wish to engage my services,' Sharpe answered.

'Consider yourself on the payroll, Mr Sharpe,' Nellie nodded as she shook hands with the man.

'Good day, ladies. It was nice to see you again, Dolly.' Mr Sharpe smiled as he bid them goodbye.

The waiting cabbie then took Nellie and Dolly home where they regaled Nancy with the tale.

'That Ezra is a thieving bugger!' Nancy said. 'I would never have believed he had the gull to try it on!'

'The word is gall, Nance,' Nellie said gently.

'I don't give a bugger what the word is, I'm just glad Mr Sharpe was there!' Nancy replied tartly.

'Sharpe by name, and sharp by nature,' Dolly said with a grin.

'It's all thanks to Dolly,' Nellie said at last, once the laughing and dancing around the kitchen had ceased.

Digging into her bag, Nellie produced the money the solicitor had given back to her. 'You should have this back, sweetheart.' She pushed the notes across the table to the girl watching her.

'No, Nellie, you hang on to it, you may need it in the future,' Dolly said with a warm smile.

'It's yours, lass. Put it somewhere safe with the bit you have left over from the sale of that necklace. You'll never know how grateful I am – all I can say is thank you.'

'If you're sure?'

Nellie nodded.

'Then I'll put it away with the rest, but if you should need it, please let me know.' Dolly answered.

'Mum, you're back! It's busy as hell out there!' Jack said as he popped his head round the kitchen door.

'All right, I'm coming,' Nellie replied.

Nellie turned to Dolly. 'I'll never be able to thank you enough, sweetheart.'

'No need, Nellie. I love being part of this family, and that's because of you.'

The two hugged then Nellie ran out of the room to lend a hand in the bar. Seeing a woman so drunk she was about to drop her baby, Nellie shot round the counter just in time to catch the screaming child. Herding the woman out of the door she pushed the infant back into its mother's arms and sent her packing. She watched as the woman staggered away up the street. *Bloody hell that was close!* she thought.

Going back indoors, Nellie set to work in earnest. It was after lock-up when Jack and Poppy were informed about the visit to Ezra Morton.

'So, what this means is, we can order our gin from anyone now without any reprisal from Ezra,' Nellie said with a smile which had not left her face all day.

'Well, it should be soon, Mum, because we're running low,' Jack said with a yawn.

'First thing tomorrow,' Nellie answered, 'you three get off to bed now.'

Left alone in the kitchen with her friend, it was Nancy who spoke first. 'That little 'un ain't half clever, Nell.'

'Surprising, ain't it?'

Nancy nodded. 'I hope you realise how lucky you are.'

'Oh, I do, Nance. How many folk would do what she has for us? She doesn't have a spiteful bone in her body. I know she's only been here but a month or so but I've come to love that young wench,' Nellie confided.

'Me an' all. I can't imagine life without her now,' Nancy replied. 'Anyway, I'm for my bed, I'm exhausted.'

Left alone, Nellie's mind went over yet again her visit to Ezra and she sighed with complete and utter satisfaction.

14

For Arthur, the next week was busy as he took afternoon tea with grieving widows. Outwardly, he was the perfect gentleman, while on the inside he was eager to get his hands on their money. It was going to be a long, slow process and his frustration mounted with each passing day. In between visits, Arthur had replenished his cash flow by way of picking pockets and stealing purses.

Hovering around the entrance to New Street station, Arthur had watched people coming and going. Checking out their attire he had targeted the wealthy; men with top hats and walking canes were the easiest to steal from. They were careless with their wallets, almost always carrying them in a jacket pocket, making them easily accessible. Once lifted, they were emptied and dropped, then Arthur strolled away from the scene of the crime. The crowded platforms also provided good pickings as he meandered through the crowds eagerly awaiting the steam train's arrival.

The station was noisy, with people talking loudly to be heard over the chug of the train pulling in and then the loud hiss of steam as it came to rest. Folk pushed and shoved their way to the doors then had to step back for passengers to alight.

Arthur wove his way between the bodies packed tightly together, his hands moving swiftly, before he turned and joined the throng now heading for the exit. Then he headed home to count his blessings and give thanks that he had not been caught pilfering from the rich.

One morning, Arthur decided to clear out Dolly's room and sell the furniture, and he suddenly remembered again the necklace the girl had inherited. When she had run away, he'd looked for it but had found nothing. Now would be a good time for a thorough search; if she didn't have it with her then it had to be hidden in this house somewhere.

Throwing open the door to Dolly's room, he glanced around. Where would she have hidden that jewel? His mind travelled back to the day of the reading of Avril's will. Dolly had been given the necklace and its letter of authenticity. She had slipped the chain over her head – would she still be wearing it? Where was the letter? Had she taken it with her as well?

Then there was the will and Arthur tried to recall where he'd put it. He'd find it later, for now he was going to be busy turning Dolly's room inside out. He needed to find that jewellery; once sold he would live like a king on the proceeds.

The hours passed as Arthur searched in every possible place. The tallboy and chest of drawers revealed nothing as he turfed out the girl's clothing; nor did the bed and mattress.

Then he checked the floorboards and on finding a loose one he ripped it up. Nothing.

Damn the girl! Where had she hidden it?

The whole day was spent looking in drawers and cupboards in the kitchen and living room to no avail. There was no sign of the piece or its letter – and the will was missing too.

Crafty madam!

Arthur knew he would have to find a way of getting hold of Dolly Daydream now, and when he did, he would rip that jewel from her throat before he wrung her neck.

You won't get the better of Arthur Micklewhite, you little varmint! You'll rue the day you took off with what should have been mine! Watch out, Dolly Daydream – I'm coming for you!

* * *

Whilst Arthur was ransacking his home, across in Nova Scotia Street, Ezra Morton was eyeing the big man standing in his office.

'Frederick, I'd like you to do me a favour.'

'Anything, boss.'

'I want you to find out everything you can about Nellie Larkin – on the quiet, you understand,' Ezra said touching the side of his nose.

'All right Guvnor,' Frederick said with a nod.

'Good man. I'll make sure you're recompensed.' Ezra smiled, then, seeing the look of confusion he qualified his statement with, 'You'll get a bonus in your pay packet.'

Frederick's frown turned to a grin.

'That will be all,' Ezra said, dismissing the man from his presence with a wave of his fingers.

Big and stupid – but very useful, he thought as he watched Frederick leave the office.

Ezra considered his request regarding Nellie. Everyone had a skeleton in a cupboard somewhere, and he was sure Nellie would prove no exception. If he could discover some-thing hidden in her past it would be an excellent bargaining tool. He would threaten to expose her to the town if she didn't sack Poppy. Once the girl was free of The Crown Saloon, he would swoop in and save her from a life on the streets – but it would be a ruse. On her last visit she had brought that damned solicitor with her who had caught him out trying to cheat more money out of Nellie. So, he would strike back by taking her barmaid.

You're a sly old fox, Ezra, and make no mistake! he thought as he clipped the end of his cigar. Lighting his Havana with a Lucifer, Ezra watched the plume of blue-grey smoke with satisfaction. On occasion it was not who you knew – but what you knew. He wondered whether there might even be something dire enough discovered in Nellie's past for her to relinquish the saloon to him.

Nellie Larkin had stood up to him – which he admired, but if word about it got out, he would lose all credibility. He could not afford to let that happen so he must strike first. He had to take Nellie down by blackening her name – and soon. He refused to be bested by a woman.

An image of Poppy formed unbidden in his mind. There was no denying he would like a dalliance with the girl; she was pretty and she definitely turned heads. She would warm his bed until he tired of her and then he would be rid of her.

His main intention in all of this was to endeavour to dupe Nellie out of her livelihood somehow. He'd made up his mind, The Crown Saloon was a little goldmine – and he wanted it.

Cigar held between his teeth, Morton smiled wickedly. Before too long he would have Poppy and he could well be the owner of the gin palace.

Sniff out what you can, my faithful bloodhound, he thought as his mind returned to Frederick Dell.

* * *

As he'd left his employer's office, Frederick had wondered where to start with the task he'd been given. Who would know anything about Nellie Larkin? He could quiz some of her customers he supposed. A drunken brain speaks a sober mind. How forthcoming they would be was anyone's guess, however. Either loyal to her or too inebriated to speak, Frederick knew he would have his work cut out. He didn't dare return to Ezra with nothing to report, for that could see him floating face down in the nearest canal.

Sweating now in the well-tailored suit Ezra insisted his employees wear, Frederick ran a finger around his stiffly starched collar. Lumbering down the street, he was off to The Crown Saloon where he might have to endure drinking that God-awful gin whilst chatting with the other customers. He prayed he didn't go blind from it in his endeavour to uncover some juicy gossip about the landlady.

* * *

In a dress she had acquired from somewhere, old Aggie sidled up to the bar and hooked a finger to Nellie.

Seeing the sign, Nellie nodded. 'Another, Aggie?'

'Ar, but I need a word. There's a big ape in a fancy suit outside asking questions about you,' Aggie said as she slapped her coins on the counter.

'About me? Nellie asked with a frown.

Nodding, Aggie gulped her drink. 'I know for a fact as he works for that Ezra Morton an' all.'

'Does he now? Thanks Aggie – here, have one on the house,' Nellie said as she topped up the woman's glass.

Pushing through the crowd Nellie made her way out into

the sunshine and squinted around. Finding the big man easily she walked up to him.

'My name is Nellie Larkin, and I believe you're asking questions about me,' she said as she looked up at the giant of a man.

Frederick visibly shrivelled under her gaze. Damn, he'd been found out already! Ezra would be furious with him.

'Erm...' He shuffled from foot to foot looking like a naughty schoolboy.

'Why? Who sent you?' Nellie asked.

'Erm...' Again, Frederick searched for answers.

'It's Ezra Morton ain't it?' Nellie pushed.

Frederick nodded and looked down at his huge feet.

'What's he after?'

'I don't know, Nellie, and that's the truth. He just told me to find out what I could about you,' Frederick said, feeling wretched.

'I see. Well Mr...?'

'Frederick Dell.'

'Mr Dell, be kind enough to go back to that – to Mr Morton and tell him this. If he wants to know about me, he should come and ask me himself.' Nellie's hands moved to her hips as she spoke.

'All right, Nellie, but he won't be happy. He'll be so mad with me, I'll probably get the sack.'

'If that should prove the case, then you come back here to me. I'll see if I can find you a job in The Crown.'

'Ta, Nellie!' Frederick beamed.

'Right, now you go and tell Ezra what I said.' Nellie shook her head as she watched him stride away. A child's mind in a man's body, she felt a little sorry for him.

Going back indoors, she went directly to the kitchen where she told Nancy what had transpired.

'What's it all about, Nell?' Nancy asked, perplexed.

'I don't know but I don't like it, Nance,' Nellie responded. 'I know Ezra's got his eye on our Poppy though.'

'Oh, blimey!' Nancy dropped into a chair.

'He can't get at her though, unless...' Nellie's hands shot to her mouth.

'What? Unless what?!'

'Nance, it's my guess he's going to try to get me to sack Poppy!'

'Why?' Nancy asked, aghast at the thought.

'So he can—' Nellie began.

'Steal her away!' Nancy finished. 'Oh, Nell! Whatever shall we do?'

'We have to tell Poppy – tonight! Everybody needs to be in the know so we can all look out for her.' Nellie said as she paced the floor.

'So why did he want to know about you?' Nancy asked.

'That would be to blackmail you,' Dolly said as she hobbled through the doorway. 'I'm sorry, Nellie, I wasn't eavesdropping, but I did hear what was said.'

'It's all right, sweetheart. You said blackmail...?'

'Yes, it sounds like it to me. He'll find out your secrets – if you have any – and use them against you,' Dolly explained.

'How, though?' Nellie asked.

'If he *is* after Poppy as you suspect, he'll threaten to disclose your secrets to everyone unless you sack her,' Dolly answered. 'At least that's my thinking anyway.'

'How come you're so clever?' Nellie asked with a smile.

'My mum ensured I had a good education, and I suppose I have a quick brain,' Dolly said shyly.

'Nell, what about Jack!' Nancy gasped.

'Oh, no!' Nellie closed her eyes. Then she said, 'I suppose the time has come to tell him before Ezra Morton does!'

15

Sitting in the parlour of the fine house in Ladywell Walk, Arthur gazed around him at the expensive paintings and porcelain figurines. His mind was adding up how much each item could be worth.

The house was large with six bedrooms, parlour, living room, dining room, kitchen and scullery, plus an indoor lavatory, so he'd been told. It was tastefully decorated and the furniture was comfortable and beautifully upholstered. French windows opened onto expansive lawns with neat flower borders, and Arthur could hear bees buzzing around the arbour. The carpet beneath his feet was of a rich Turkish design and it was as he placed his cup and saucer on a small mahogany table that Ann Bradshaw spoke.

'I have two tickets for the theatre, Gabriel, and I wondered if you would be kind enough to accompany me,' she said.

'Alas, I must decline, Ann. You see, my wardrobe is somewhat depleted due to a flood in my home. My clothes were all but completely ruined I'm afraid,' Arthur lied.

'You really should replace them,' Ann smiled sweetly.

'Of course, I would, but my capital is tied up in various ventures and not easily accessed. I apologise most profoundly as there is nothing I would have liked more.'

'Then there is only one option open to us. Come, Gabriel, we are going shopping – we must get you kitted out appropriately.' Ann reached out a hand for Arthur to help her to her feet. She was astonished when Arthur fell to his knees in front of her.

'Thank you, Ann, please be assured I will recompense you as soon as my funds are released!'

'Oh, my – Gabriel!' Ann said as he kissed her hands.

Dragging her to her feet Arthur wrapped his arms around her and gazed into her eyes. 'Ann, I can wait no longer to tell you of my feelings for you. In the short time we have known each other I have come to love you. Oh, Ann, I think of you night and day! I know you are still in mourning, but I can contain my feelings no longer!' Arthur gently pressed his lips to hers and felt her respond to his kiss.

Pulling away slightly, Ann stared at the man she'd only known for a matter of weeks. 'We should respect my period of mourning,' she said on a breath.

'In public certainly, but in private...' Arthur again kissed her gently and smiled inwardly as he felt her arms snake around his neck.

As they parted, he asked, 'Shopping now, my love?'

Ann nodded, suddenly feeling like a young girl again.

Later that day Arthur hung his tail coat and trousers in the tallboy and stood back to admire them. Despite being off the peg, they fitted him beautifully. New clothes in exchange for a false declaration of love and a couple of kisses – money for old rope! And a visit to the theatre into the bargain. Arthur chuckled; Ann Bradshaw was hooked. Now to cast his line in Sylvia Chilton's direction. Tomorrow would tell whether or not she would take his bait. Mentally slapping himself on the back, Arthur ran downstairs to contrive a plan to kidnap Dolly Daydream and retrieve that necklace!

* * *

Whilst Arthur was wooing Ann Bradshaw, Ezra sat in his office in the brewery staring at the man stood before him and his voice boomed out. 'For God's sake, Frederick! Can't you do anything without fouling it up?!'

'Sorry, Mr Morton, sir,' Frederick replied, feeling thoroughly ashamed of himself. 'Somebody must have told Nellie I was asking after her.'

'Obviously, how else would she have known?'

Frederick began to shuffle about, clearly uncomfortable beneath his employer's gaze.

'What *did* you find out then?' Ezra asked.

'Nothing, boss.'

Ezra sighed audibly. 'All right – get out!'

Frederick fled the office before Ezra really lost his temper.

Leaning back in his chair, Ezra realised he would have to put someone else on Nellie's case. He needed information and the sooner the better so he could get Poppy by his side and into his bed. Once that was accomplished, he could concentrate on the ruination of Nellie Larkin.

Frederick was relieved he was still breathing and although not very bright, he was intelligent enough to wonder if it was time to find a new job. It would, of course, mean telling Ezra he was going to leave his employ. He didn't know which would be worse, leaving or staying. He sat in the outer office and pondered. Nellie had told him she could find him work and shifting barrels would be a lot easier than having to scare people into parting with their money. His conscience would be clear too.

How would Ezra react if he said he was quitting? Would he be angry? Or would he bid Frederick a fond farewell? Shaking his head, he feared it wouldn't be the latter.

Hearing his name being called, Frederick gulped. If he was going to do this, now would be the perfect time.

Going to Ezra's office once more he tapped the door and walked in. Standing by the desk he waited, his hands clasped in front of him.

'Find me somebody to do what you couldn't!' Ezra said, without looking up from the papers on his desk.

Frederick didn't move and remained silent.

'Did you hear me?' Ezra said, glancing up.

Frederick nodded.

Ezra sighed, 'What now?'

'I'm leaving, Mr Morton,' Frederick said quickly.

'Leaving?'

'Yes, sir, I'm quitting,' Frederick said.

'Oh, I see.' Ezra's eyebrows shot up. This was something he hadn't expected. 'Where will you go and what will you do for work?'

'I ain't sure as yet, but I've had enough, Mr Morton. I can't do this any more. It ain't right taking money from folk who don't have much anyway.'

'Frederick, these people borrowed the money in the first place, so they have to pay it back. Surely you understand that?' Ezra explained as if speaking to a five year old.

'I do, but frightening them into it is wrong and I ain't doing it any more,' Frederick's hands clenched as he spoke.

'After all I've done for you!' Ezra boomed out. Seeing the big man wince, he went on. 'All right, fair enough. But know this, Frederick, you say one word about me or my business and you'll wake up dead one day.' Ezra's voice was quiet now and tinged with menace.

'I won't say a word, Mr Morton, I promise.' Frederick was familiar with the old Black Country saying – it was a thinly veiled threat to his life.

'Good. Now get out.' Ezra's eyes returned to the papers he had been reading through.

Frederick left, rather pleased with himself. It had gone better than he could have hoped, and he felt free for the first time in a long while.

Now what he had to decide was whether or not to go cap in hand to Nellie Larkin. He was sure she would make good on her offer to employ him, but how would Ezra react when he found out, as he surely would? Then again, it was no longer Ezra's business what Frederick did. Once he realised this, he felt much better about approaching Nellie, and there was no time like the present.

Walking with his head held high, Frederick's spirits lifted at the thought of good honest work, and by the time he arrived at The Crown Saloon, he sported a wide grin. Stepping inside he elbowed his way to the bar.

Nellie spotted him standing there – it was hard not to, the size of him – and guessed what had happened. Tilting her head, she called him to the end of the bar.

'Come on through,' she said as she lifted the end of the counter and swung open the little gate.

In the kitchen he was introduced to Nancy and Dolly.

'I don't work for Ezra no more, I jacked it in,' Frederick said, his eyes lingering on Nancy.

'Well, there's a job here shifting barrels and kegs if'n you've a mind to do it,' Nellie replied. 'Small wage but bed and board in.'

'Thanks, Nellie, I'll go and get my stuff and tell my landlady I'm moving out.' Frederick's grin showed lovely even teeth and as he turned to leave, he leapt in the air and clicked his heels together, no mean feat for a man of his size.

'I'll get his room ready then, shall I?' Nancy asked dryly.

'Ta, Nance, I've a feeling Fred will be really useful around here. He's like a big bear ain't he?' Nellie said with a laugh.

'Oh ar, let's just hope he doesn't snore too loudly,' Nancy murmured as she went to clean and air a spare room for their new staff member.

As Nancy ascended the stairs, she wondered if it might be as well to sort out the other spare rooms too. The saloon had eight upstairs rooms, five of which were already taken; now Frederick would be moving in.

Pushing up the sash window and wedging it open with a stick kept especially for the purpose, Nancy dragged the single flock mattress from the iron bedstead. Draping half of it over the window sill she picked up the trefoil shaped wicker paddle and began beating the dust from the flocking. Then, swapping the ends she began again, her apron held over her nose against the dust flying in all directions.

Pulling the mattress back to the bed she then drew a rag from her apron pocket and dusted down the old furniture. A chest of drawers, tallboy and dressing table. Once she had swept the floor she went to a cupboard on the landing and took out fresh bedding and made up the bed.

Happy with her efforts, she then did the same in the other two rooms but left the beds unmade. Another job which had badly needed doing was now complete.

Returning to the kitchen, she made a start on the evening meal. Covering grey maple peas with seasoned water she set them to boil before adding bacon and leaving them to simmer. Taking the groats she had soaked overnight, she added them to stewing beef, onion, salt and pepper. Covering them with water, she put the large pan to boil too. Groaty pudding and grey peas in hand, Nancy made a pot of tea to go with freshly baked scones as a treat for everyone.

Popping her head around the doorway she yelled, 'Tea up!'

Before she had returned to the table, Jack and Dolly rushed into the kitchen.

'Scones there, jam and as a treat, some cream. Tea's in the pot so, Jack, get it poured while I check this on the range.' Nancy said.

Ensuring the evening meal was not burning, she returned her attention to the two now enjoying their afternoon tea.

Nancy smiled, she loved these kids more than she could say and felt very lucky to be loved in return.

'Nell,' she called out, 'Get yer arse in 'ere and have a cuppa!'

Dolly's tea shot from her mouth as she laughed. 'I'm sorry,' she said as she mopped up the mess with a teacloth.

Nancy grinned, 'It don't matter, sweet'eart. Here, have another scone before smelly Nellie comes in.'

Jack and Dolly howled as the woman in question walked in.

'What's so funny then?' she asked.

'Nuthin' at all. Jack's poured you a drink so get it down yer neck.' Nancy replied.

One by one the staff all enjoyed high tea before returning to their respective jobs.

16

Afternoon tea with Sylvia Chilton did not go exactly to plan for Arthur as the daughter was also in attendance. Elizabeth Murray had no intention of leaving her grieving mother alone. She was rather an outspoken young woman; in fact, some would describe her as bossy.

On both of the occasions when Arthur had called previously, it was Elizabeth who had questioned him regarding his business. He had managed to think on his feet and divert her by saying he had a finger in a number of pies. He confessed to only having met Mr Chilton a few times and said he had been hoping to strike a business deal before the poor man's demise.

'I'm afraid I still don't understand why you continue to visit my mother, Mr Short,' Elizabeth said.

'Elizabeth! Don't be rude to our visitor,' Sylvia remonstrated.

'Oh, Mother! I simply asked what Mr Short hopes to gain—'

'Nothing, Mrs Murray,' Arthur intervened. 'It was merely

my intention to assure Sylvia she has a friend and if need be – a companion.' Turning to the woman in question he added. 'If you find yourself wishing to attend a function and not wanting to go alone, please feel free to call on me. I would be happy to escort you and deliver you home safely.' He smiled at Sylvia as she nodded.

'Mother won't be attending any functions, Mr Short. She is, after all, still in mourning. I'm sure it will be twelve months or more before she is in a position to accept invitations of any kind,' Elizabeth put in.

'Elizabeth dear, please don't try to organise my life, I'm not your child,' Sylvia said quietly.

Good on yer, girl, you tell her! Arthur thought as he fought to hide a smirk. Instead he cleared his throat.

'See now, you've embarrassed Mr Short,' Sylvia said.

'Gabriel, please.'

'Gabriel, please forgive my daughter. I know she only has my best interests at heart but—' Sylvia began.

'I'm here, Mother, in case you hadn't noticed!' Elizabeth snapped.

'Yes dear, you are, when you should be at home taking care of your husband!' Sylvia's voice was sharp in her reply.

'Ahem, Sylvia, maybe I should be leaving,' Arthur said, getting to his feet.

'Certainly not! Please sit, Gabriel.' Sylvia smiled before going on. 'This is my house and I will have as many callers as often as I wish.'

Elizabeth harrumphed and dropped into an armchair.

Sylvia turned to her daughter saying, 'Elizabeth, I'm grateful you wish to be with me, but to be truthful – I don't need you here. I'm perfectly capable of taking care of myself so I'd really rather you went home.'

'Mother!'

Arthur pulled out his pocket watch and checked the time. 'Oh my! If you'll excuse me, I have a business appointment and it seems I'm already late.'

Kissing Sylvia's hand, he bowed to Elizabeth. 'I will see myself out. Thank you for the tea. Good day, ladies.'

'Gabriel, please call again soon,' Sylvia called as he walked from the room.

Grabbing his hat and cane from the hall table he heard an argument begin to rage. With a smile, Arthur, alias Gabriel, was sure Sylvia Chilton's daughter would not be there on his next visit.

As he pulled the door closed behind him, he turned to look back at the house he had just left. Set on the corner of Bishop Street it commanded a lot of land but with no garden as such; Sylvia's flowers grew in urns dotted around the yard. The front door was flanked by stone pillars and had two steps which led to a large foyer. There was a parlour and kitchen, which were the only two rooms Arthur had seen. He guessed there would be at least four bedrooms, a living room and scullery.

The parlour was cluttered with expensive but mis-matched furniture and loaded with ornaments and trantle-ments. The rugs were of good quality but showing their age, and tea was always served in bone china cups and saucers.

As he walked home, Arthur wondered if the widow Chilton was actually worth the effort. He decided to make one more call on the woman to see if she would succumb to his charms. If not, then he would move on rather than waste his time.

Strolling beneath the viaduct bridge he turned his mind to Dolly. He had still not found a way to get to her. The Crown Saloon was like a fortress – locked up tightly at night, and the girl was surrounded by others during the day.

Throwing open the back door to his house, he slammed his cane onto the kitchen table. Today had gained him nothing and Arthur was very frustrated.

Going upstairs and changing into his old clothes, he decided a little thievery would ease his tension. He was going to chance his arm in the market again; having other people's money in his pocket would make him feel so much better.

* * *

It had been a busy evening over at The Crown Saloon and midnight saw the last customer thrown out and the doors securely bolted. Then Nellie joined the others in the kitchen.

Accepting the much needed cup of tea from Nancy, she said, 'Frederick Dell starts work here tomorrow shifting barrels and sorting out any fights that flare up. He used to work for Ezra Morton but he quit today.'

'We need the help,' Jack put in.

'We do, lad. Now, speaking of Ezra – he's got his eye on you, Poppy.' Nellie continued.

'Me?!'

'Yes. The fancy-dressed bloke you saw t'other day.'

'Oh, the handsome one,' Poppy said with a blush.

'Handsome! If I was a bloke, he'd have a face like a squashed tomato!' Nancy put in.

Nellie ignored her friend and went on, 'Listen to me, Poppy, he's out to win you away from here and it's Dolly's contention he will try to blackmail me into sacking you.' Nellie didn't try to gild the lily for the girl as she needed to understand exactly what Morton was like.

'How? Why?' Poppy asked.

Nellie related what she'd learned from Frederick earlier in the day and added, 'So you have to be aware of what's going on. He's after anything to use as a lever to blackmail me with – which brings me to you, Jack.'

'Me? What have I done?' Jack asked as he glanced around.

'Nothing, but there's something you need to know and it needs to come from me before Ezra finds out.' Nellie was afraid, for she had no idea how the boy would react.

'I need to speak with you – just us two,' Nellie said as she got to her feet. Leading her son to the little used living room, Nellie lit the gas lamp and sat down.

Jack took a seat, he was worried about what his mother had to tell him. Then the quiet became too much for him and he asked, 'What is it, Mum?'

'That's the thing, Jack – I ain't your mum.' There, she'd told him at last and, as Nellie waited, she felt a lump in her throat.

After a short silence Jack muttered, 'I don't understand.' Then, as the shock of the revelation began to slowly abate, he asked, 'Tell me, explain how it is I ain't your boy.'

'When you were a baby, somebody left you on my doorstep. Nancy and I took you in and we decided that I would raise you as my own,' Nellie confided.

'So, who is my real mother? Where is she? Why did she give me up?' The questions poured from Jack's lips as tears rolled down his young face.

He didn't wait for answers but ran from the room back to the kitchen, looking to Nancy for further explanation.

Nellie followed, feeling wretched. A tilt of the head from Nancy told her the others had heard and Nellie nodded. At least she wouldn't have to explain to them as well.

It was Dolly who went to comfort Jack. Wrapping an arm around his shoulder she said quietly. 'To all intents and purposes, Nellie is your mum, Jack. As for your birth mother, she must have had a very good reason for 'giving you up' as you put it. Also, she left you where she knew you'd be found and taken care of. At least she didn't take you to the orphanage.'

'It's all right for you – you knew your mother!' Jack spat.

No one said a word but they all saw the hurt in Dolly's eyes.

'Yes, I did,' Dolly went on bravely, 'but I lost her and now I have a new mum too in Nancy; Nellie is like my auntie and Poppy my big sister. You, Jack, are like the brother I never had. So, like the phoenix which rises from the ashes I have a wonderful new family around me – something you've had all along.'

Sniffs sounded in the quiet kitchen at the heartfelt little speech.

'But – I don't know who I am now!' Jack said in utter frustration.

'You are Jack Larkin. Why would you want to be anyone else? If in the future anything can be discovered about your real parents, I'm sure Nellie wouldn't mind.' Dolly paused to glance at the woman who nodded affirmation.

'Why didn't you tell me this before?' Jack asked accusingly.

'You were too little to understand at first, and then – I just couldn't find the right time,' Nellie said on a breath.

'Now it makes sense why you wouldn't talk about my dad – cos I ain't got one!' Jack snapped.

'I never married, Jack. When my parents died they left me the pub and I built it up into this place – with Nancy's help,' Nellie explained.

'But you said I had a dad who died of fever!' Jack wailed.

'I had to tell you something until I could find the right moment to explain it all.' Nellie's eyes flooded with salty liquid as she spoke.

Jack nodded, trying his best to understand. 'So, what do I call you now I know you ain't my real mum?' he asked scathingly.

Nellie closed her eyes but hot tears squeezed from between her lids. This was why she had not wanted to tell him. In an instant she had felt the change in him; the shift in their relationship and suspected he had too. He didn't know how to deal with it, so, like the child he was, his questions were blunt and seemingly harsh.

'Why should anything change? Nellie is still the same person – she's still your mum,' Dolly said.

'I s'pose,' Jack said as he looked at the woman who had taken him in, as she had with Poppy, then Dolly. 'I'm going to bed – I have a lot to think about,' he added as he ran from the kitchen.

'Dolly, you're a bloody marvel!' Nancy said.

Nellie nodded and then she added, 'That could have gone so much worse, but thanks to you, Jack took it better than I had expected.'

'He's very upset, Nellie,' Poppy ventured.

'I know, but he didn't run off into the night or—' Nellie began, but it was Nancy who finished her sentence.

'Or bounce anythin' off yer head!'

'Besides teaching me academics, my mum told me to look at situations from all angles. There is always a bright side if you look for it,' Dolly said with a smile.

'So, Jack being upset at Nellie not being his mum was turned around and made better by her taking him in!' Nancy said in a Eureka moment.

'Exactly,' Dolly confirmed. 'Nellie, I expect Jack might be a little off, shall we say, for a few days. He has a lot for his mind to process but once he gets to grips with it, I'm sure he'll be fine.'

With a hug for them all, Dolly retired to bed.

'Now we turn to you, Poppy,' Nellie said, still sniffing away her tears. 'You know as much as we do regarding Ezra Morton. Yes, he's a handsome bugger, charming, well off and powerful – but, think on it, gel. He would use you and throw you away like an old dish cloth. I'm only telling you like it is, sweetheart, cos I couldn't bear to see you out on the street, barefoot and pregnant.'

'Oh, Nellie, it wouldn't come to that even if—' Poppy tried to explain.

'Tell her about old man Pickles!' Nancy interrupted.

Nellie sighed and then began. 'An old fella by the name of Pickles who lived in a shack at the back of the railway borrowed some money from Ezra.'

'For his daughter's wedding,' Nancy piped up.

'Well, he was in his eighties and gathered wood—' Nellie continued.

'Sold it in bundles,' Nancy said eagerly.

'Do you want to tell her or shall I?' Nellie asked, exasperated by Nancy's interruptions.

'Sorry, Nell.'

'Anyway,' Nellie took up again, 'he was paying back a penny a week, until he got ill that is. Unable to sell his bundles meant he couldn't pay his debt.'

'What about his daughter, didn't she help?' Poppy asked.

'She couldn't...' Nancy put in, unable to stop herself.

With a glare at her friend, Nellie continued.

'No, she'd moved away with her new husband, something to do with his work I believe. After a couple of weeks, it's said Ezra went to visit Mr Pickles to collect his money. When the old man told him he had nothing to give, Ezra...' Nellie paused to take a deep breath. '... snipped off Mr Pickles' little fingertip with his cigar cutter!'

'Or so the story went,' Nancy added with a sheepish grin.

'Oh, my God!' Poppy exclaimed.

'It's also said he left the old man to bleed to death, but a heart attack from the shock got him first,' Nellie concluded her tale with a sad shake of the head.

'Is it true?' Poppy asked, her face ashen.

'Nobody knows but the doctor found the end of his pinky lying in his lap,' Nellie said.

'Now you know what Ezra Morton is like, Poppy, so be ruled by us and stay away from him,' Nancy begged. 'With a face as pretty as your'n he'd have your head hangin' on his bleedin' wall!'

'Nance, for God's sake!' Nellie chastised. 'You're frightening her. Poppy, just keep yer distance from him, that's all we ask.'

'I will,' the girl said as she tried to pour herself more tea, but her hand shook so badly it slopped all over the table.

'Don't worry, lass, if we all stick together, we'll be safe enough,' Nellie said.

'And tomorrow we'll have big Fred on our side too,' Nancy added.

Silence descended as they drank their tea and thought about poor old Mr Pickles and the dastardly Ezra Morton.

17

Jack lay in his bed with his mind in turmoil. For ten years he had thought Nellie was his mother, and now in a matter of moments his world had been turned upside down. He had no idea who he truly was, where he came from, or even who his parents were.

He had been given a name by Nellie but what was his birth name? Did he have one? How could he find out? Would anyone else know? Why had Nellie not tried to seek out his natural family?

Over and over the questions formed in his brain until his head ached with it all. One thing was for certain – he would get no sleep for worrying about it.

The more he thought on it, the more his emotions threatened to betray him, until at last they won out and he burst into tears. Turning his face into his pillow he sobbed at the sudden confusion which had affected his life.

Eventually he began to pull himself together and look at the situation logically. He had a mum, albeit not his birth mother; he had a relatively good home, a bed to sleep in and food in his belly. He should consider himself very fortunate rather than fretting about questions he couldn't answer.

That being so, the best he could do now would be to get on with life as usual, as hard as that might be.

Down the hall in her own room, Nellie was also having a bad night. All that had been said in the living room rolled through her mind like a set of moving pictures. She knew she should have told Jack long before but somehow day-to-day living got in the way. The longer she had kept her secret, the harder it had become to find the right moment to divulge it.

Now that it was at last out in the open, Jack was clearly mortified. Nellie prayed he would overcome the trauma soon and they could return to some sort of normality. In her heart however, she wondered if the whole structure of their relationship had altered so much that it would never be the same again. In that one moment she had seen the look in Jack's eyes. Sudden mistrust, disappointment, disbelief – all merged in a confusing jumble. She saw also a pleading for it not to be true, then sad acceptance when she confirmed that it was. Her poor boy was in turmoil, and so was she.

Nellie then thought of the man who was causing all this upset in her family. Ezra Morton! He had made so many people's lives miserable, and now it was her turn. Was it because she had bested him over repaying her loan? Or was he smarting over being humiliated in her saloon on his visit that day? Whatever the reason, Nellie knew she had to be on her guard. That man was capable of anything and keeping her loved ones safe was her main priority.

Turning over onto her side, Nellie resigned herself to being unable to sleep.

Dolly was sitting by the window looking up at the brightest star she could see. 'Oh, Mum,' she whispered, 'I've only just found these lovely people and now it's all going wrong for them! I want so much to help but I don't know how!' The star glittered but it gave her no answers. 'I thought it was best for Nellie to pay back her debt with the money from your necklace, but now I'm not so sure it was such a good idea. I'm afraid for Poppy and Jack, Mum. Surely there is something I can do to make things right again!'

With a huge sigh, Dolly stared out at the night sky, willing the answers to come, but deep in her heart she knew these were things she couldn't fix. Only time would tell how it would all work out and Dolly prayed it would be for the best all round.

The following morning, Jack eyed Nellie warily, still wondering why she had kept her counsel for so long about finding him on her doorstep. He was finding it difficult to come to terms with the fact that his real parents had dumped him onto someone else.

He knew the way he was treating Nellie was hurting her but he couldn't help himself. In a way he felt betrayed – as though she felt that he couldn't be trusted with the truth and only now, when Nellie felt threatened, had she revealed all.

Pondering the words Dolly had spoken helped a little and Jack knew he had to pull himself together and get on with life. He might never know who his birth mother was or why she'd abandoned him, but he did have Nellie.

In his way, he loved the woman who had taken him in, despite her harshness with him at times. He was certain she loved him back, otherwise why would she keep him around? He began to realise how unfair he was being to her by keeping his distance. They had barely spoken a word to each other, and Jack reasoned it was now time to grow up and take it like a man.

* * *

One by one everyone came in and sat around the kitchen table, bleary eyed from lack of sleep.

'I've been thinking...' Jack said as he watched the others nod – clearly of the same mind. 'Dolly said it ain't no use fretting about something you can't change. So, as far as I'm concerned, you're still my mum.' In a very much out of character gesture, Jack flung his arms around Nellie.

Tiredness and worry saw her in floods of tears as she hugged her boy tight. 'I love you like my own, you'll always be my son, sweetheart.'

'I've been thinking as well, Nellie,' Poppy said gently, not wanting to disrupt the show of familial affection. 'I ain't having anything to do with Ezra Morton – ever!'

'Thank God!' Nancy said on a breath. 'Now can we have some breakfast – I'm bloody starving!'

A banging on the door had everyone silent in an instant. Then Nellie said with a grin, 'That'll be Frederick Dell if I ain't mistaken. Best let him in before he bosts the door down.'

A moment later the huge man followed Nellie into the kitchen and plonked his suitcase on the floor. 'Oooh, just in time,' he said as he breathed in the aroma of bacon and eggs.

'Sit yerself down then,' Nancy said as she fetched more bacon from the cold slab. *This big 'un is going to take some feeding,* she thought as she saw him tuck into some bread and butter.

Nancy was right in her thinking for after two huge breakfasts, half a loaf and a pot of tea, Frederick's hunger was finally sated.

'I'd rather keep you a week than a fortnight,' Nancy said with a smile.

'That were the best!' Frederick said with a boyish grin. 'Right, Nellie, what's to be done?'

Led down to the cellar, he was set to work tidying and

shifting empty casks, replacing them with full ones. His loud cheerful whistle could be heard all over the saloon.

Around mid-morning a fight broke out in the bar and Nellie yelled for Frederick's assistance. Striding across to the two men rolling about on the floor, Frederick grabbed each by his collar and hauled them to their feet. Without warning he banged their heads together but held on to them whilst their senses returned. Then he stood them both facing the wall like naughty children and boomed, 'When you can behave, you can turn around!'

Nellie's laugh sounded loud across the cheer in the bar. 'Good on yer, Fred,' she called as she looked again at the brawlers. Slowly they turned around and shook hands with each other – and with Frederick.

Dolly and Jack giggled at the spectacle as they served diluted rot-gut gin to eager customers.

Frederick smiled shyly at Poppy as he returned to the counter and flushed scarlet when she patted his arm.

Nellie rolled her eyes – Oh blimey! Another who's fallen under Poppy's spell!

* * *

Ezra Morton was, at that moment, grinning wickedly at the cigar cutter in his hand, which had brought to mind Mr Pickles.

Poor old boy – and all for a tanner! Had you but known that was all that was left on your debt!

A tap to the door was heard before a head peeped in. 'Found out what you wanted to know, Guv'. The big man is working for Nellie Larkin.' The head disappeared and the door slammed shut.

Larkin! That woman again! Ezra threw the cutter on the

desk in a temper. Although Frederick Dell had left his employ of his own accord, Ezra felt slighted he had chosen to go to Nellie.

Something had to be done about Mrs Larkin – and soon! At every turn of events that one was besting him and Ezra felt enough was enough. It was time to take action and let her know who the boss was in this town.

Within the hour Ezra had a team of men out visiting every brewer and distiller in the town, to inform them it would be in their best interests not to trade with Nellie Larkin. Now he could sit back and wait. The Crown Saloon would soon run dry and with no way to replenish stocks there could be riots. Angry customers would most likely smash the place to bits, then that woman would well and truly be out of business. However, when that happened, he could be on hand to swoop in and offer a paltry sum to take the ruined building off her hands. He had more than enough money to rebuild it and make it grander that it was before.

The look on Ezra's face was one of pure evil as he pondered on the thought of getting his revenge on Larkin for the humiliation she had caused him.

18

'Mum, we're really low on stocks,' Jack said as he came up from the cellar where he'd been chatting with Frederick.

'Right. I'll go around the town and see what's on offer and compare the prices, then I'll organise a delivery for tomorrow.' Nellie said, before calling through the doorway, 'Poppy! Keep that bar running and take no nonsense! Call on Fred if you need to.'

Grabbing her bag, she hitched up her skirts and set off. Whistling for a cab waiting at the end of Gin Barrel Lane, she tapped her foot impatiently as it rolled towards her.

All morning was spent visiting every distiller and brewer she knew and all gave her the same answer. They could *not* help her. She had asked the reason and as lips remained sealed and heads shook, she guessed just what was going on. Clearly, they had been threatened – warned off doing business with her, and she knew precisely who was behind it all – Ezra Morton!

By the time she returned home, Nellie was furious. She stomped into the kitchen and threw her bag onto the table.

'Hey up, Nell, what's going on?' Nancy asked.

'That bloody man!' Nellie rasped.

'Who?'

'Ezra Morton! I can't get a gin supply from anybody, Nance – he's put a stop to it!'

'Christ A'mighty! What will you do?' Nancy asked as she dropped onto a chair, her hands on her cheeks.

Nellie paced the kitchen and shook her head. 'I ain't got a clue, Nance! Once we run out, I'm done for!'

'Why don't you ask Dolly?' Nancy asked.

'Dolly's only a kid!'

'Ar, but she's a clever kid, and is always ready with an answer of some sort,' Nancy said with a grin. 'Anyway, you'll have to tell the others what's happening.'

Nellie nodded before yelling for the girl.

'Did you want me, Nellie?' Dolly said a moment later as she hobbled in from the bar.

Listening carefully as Nellie explained, Dolly then said, 'There are distillers in other towns, why not order from them?'

'Why didn't I think of that?!' Nellie said as she slapped a hand to her forehead.

'I imagine you were too worried. You could visit first and once you've made your choice you could have it brought in by canal. You'll need to bring it from the wharf though so maybe Frederick could help with that,' Dolly said.

'If it could come to Snow Hill Wharf, then you'll just need to shift the barrels from there, up St Mary's Row and down Loveday Street,' Nancy said, trying to be helpful.

'I'll need to borrow a horse and cart then – or hire one,' Nellie said, her spirits lifting once more.

Dolly frowned and Nellie caught the movement. 'What?'

'We would have to keep it a secret – where the gin is

coming from, I mean, otherwise Ezra could threaten them too,' Dolly warned.

'Good idea,' Nellie concurred.

'Do you think they would use plain barrels?' Dolly asked.

'Why?' Nancy asked, wondering what the girl was getting at.

'If the distiller's name or marks are on the casks, anyone could see them and Ezra would immediately be informed – for a price, I suspect. If not, then the barrels and casks should be covered at all times.'

'Blimey, Dolly, you think of everything!' Nellie said with a laugh.

'I'm beginning to know how Mr Morton thinks and the trick is to try and have a plan ready so we can stay one step ahead,' Dolly answered.

'If we get this sorted out it will rile the hell out of him!' Nancy said.

'Yes, but what will he come up with next?' Nellie's face fell at the thought.

'Nellie, until he leaves you alone, it might be an idea to hire a couple of night watchmen,' Dolly suggested.

'Oh, my God! He wouldn't go that far, would he?' Nancy asked, suddenly afraid.

'We can't rule anything out, Nancy. To my mind he's out for revenge for Nellie besting him over that loan and losing his hold over supplying alcohol to The Crown. He's preventing us buying gin locally by threatening the distillers. He means business, so who knows how far he will go to see Nellie ruined? I just think it would make sense to have someone on guard at night so we can all sleep safely,' Dolly replied.

'Thanks, sweetheart. I'm so glad you came to us, it was meant to be,' Nellie whispered as she hugged the girl.

Dolly smiled warmly then went back to her work in the bar, leaving Nellie yelling Frederick's name.

Explaining her predicament and Dolly's suggestion, she asked for his help.

'I knew Ezra could be mean, but this...? You can count on me, Nellie. I know two young blokes – brothers – who would be glad of the work, I'm sure. I'll go and see them and ask 'em to come here where you can talk to them.' Fred's eyes moved to Nancy and he flushed as she gave him a big smile.

'Ta Fred, I appreciate it, would you be kind enough to see to it now please?' Nellie asked.

Fred nodded and Nellie watched the big man walk to the back door. She smiled as she thought, *with legs that long he'll be there and back in no time!*

An hour later two young men sat in Nellie's kitchen listening to her woes. Matthew and Noah Dempster were handsome boys with thick fair hair and twinkling blue eyes. Well-built with bulging muscles from manual labour, they were afraid of no one – not even Ezra Morton's men.

When Nellie had finished speaking, they simply looked at each other and grinned. No words were needed between them, it was as if they were of one mind.

'When do we start?' Noah asked.

'How does tonight sound?' Nellie answered with her own question.

'Grand,' Matthew said.

Agreeing a wage, Nellie then said, 'You'll have a meal with us then settle yourselves either in here or the bar. I'm trusting you to keep us all safe, and that means you an' all, as well as this place. Now, come with me and I'll show you around.'

Following their new employer, the Dempsters were agog at the noise that greeted them in the bar. They stared at the people pushing and shoving their way to the counter to be served. Then their eyes landed on Poppy and their grins appeared again.

Bloody hell! Not these two as well, Nellie thought with a shake of her head.

Back in the kitchen, Nellie asked the boys where they lived.

'We rent a doss-hole over in Slaney Street; a pigsty it is but it's cheap,' Matthew explained.

'Our dad was a miner so when he died we were turned out by the pit boss,' Noah added.

'Where's your mother?'

'She died when we were kids,' Matthew answered. 'There's just the two of us now.'

Nellie rubbed her forefinger beneath her nose as she considered her next words. 'I've a spare room here if you don't mind sharing, but I warn you now – I'll kick yer arses myself if there's any hanky-panky!' Nellie's voice was firm and they were under no illusions that she would not carry out her threat if they misbehaved.

'You don't even know us and you're inviting us to live in your house,' Noah said.

'True, but I'm offering you a job. Would you repay my kindness by stealing from me?' Nellie countered.

'No, we wouldn't,' Matt returned.

'Besides, it will save you the walk to work every day,' Nellie added. 'I took Fred in and he ain't let me down. And another thing – he vouched for you.'

Nodding in unison, the Dempsters spat on their palms and reached out their hand to seal the deal and Nellie shook each of them in turn.

'Fetch your stuff and you can get settled in right away.'

'Thanks, Mrs Larkin,' Noah said happily.

'Nellie's the name, use it – don't abuse it.'

Slapping each other on the back they scrambled out through the door, eager to be ensconced in their new home.

'It's a good job I cleaned them spare rooms when I did, ain't it? Nancy asked.

'It is. You must have known,' Nellie answered.

'P'raps I've got that second sight thingy like the gypsies,' Nancy went on.

'What, you think you'm a gypsy now, do you?' Nellie asked sarcastically.

'You never know, I could be. It might be that my folks way back were and it's come down through the family line.' Nancy said, a little excited at the thought of being of Romany descent.

'You ain't!' Nellie exploded.

'How would you know?' Nancy turned away grumbling under her breath as she saw to the mutton simmering on the range.

When the brothers returned, each held a bundle of clothes which was everything they owned. Nellie felt sad for them; all they had to show for a lifetime was a few old rags. She led them upstairs and left them to settle in, saying a cup of tea awaited them when they were ready.

Whilst they were collecting their belongings, Nancy had made up the two beds. Now she was serving up a meal of mutton stew with fresh bread.

A clattering of boots on the stairs had her smile turn to a laugh as the Dempsters jostled to be first through the doorway. Although in their twenties, they had a boyish charm which endeared them to everyone they met. There was no doubt Nancy would sleep better knowing these young men were on guard duty every night.

Nellie closed the saloon for two hours whilst everyone ate together and was introduced to each other. The customers complained loudly but Nellie laughed it off saying they would be open again shortly.

As they ate, Nellie glanced around at her expanding family, for that's how she saw it.

First her friend, Nancy, had come to her after the loss of her husband and baby. Then she had taken in Jack as a baby. Poppy had turned up starving and alone and was drawn in. Dolly had found her way to them almost as though she'd been led by an invisible thread. Frederick Dell had come next and now the Dempsters. Nellie felt in her heart it was meant to be; that a higher force was looking out for them.

She enjoyed the chatter going on around her and the giggling as Noah Dempster teased Jack and Dolly with a 'magic' trick. Frederick's deep belly laugh boomed across the kitchen as he joined in the joviality but his eyes never strayed from Nancy for long.

Nellie knew then, that each time she had brought someone into her home it had been the right decision. She just prayed she would not be proved wrong in the future.

After a couple of hours of light-hearted frivolity, Nellie opened the saloon doors and allowed folk to pour inside and rush to the counter like they were dying of thirst.

Tomorrow, she decided, she would visit Darlaston to find a distiller who would be in a position to supply The Crown Saloon with much needed cheap gin.

19

It was mid-morning when Arthur Micklewhite entered The Crown, his cap pulled low over his eyes. Served by Poppy, he moved to the side of the room where he could keep an eye out for Dolly. Sipping his gin, he almost choked; the liquid felt like it had burned the skin off his throat. He leaned against the wall away from the jostling crowd and scowled at anyone who dared to look his way.

Not entirely sure what he would do if he saw the girl, Arthur continued to wait. He needed to assure himself that she was still living there. About to take another sip of his drink, he winced and thought better of it.

Then suddenly there she was – behind the counter, serving drinks like she'd been born to it. Arthur's eyes never left her for a moment and he debated what to do next. So involved in considering whether to approach Dolly or not, he unthinkingly took a gulp of gin and instantly regretted it. Coughing hard, he bent forward, one hand on his knee. Someone clapped him on the back but he couldn't straighten up to thank them. His throat was aflame and he felt the burn of the fiery liquid as it made its way to his stomach. Gasping for breath, he wiped the tears from his eyes and tried to focus on the people around him.

How do folk drink so much of this stuff?! he wondered as he blinked hard. A woman next to him laughed as he sniffed and wiped his eyes a second time. Seeing her glass was empty, he tipped the remainder of his drink into it and received a beaming smile in return. He didn't dare hang on to it for fear of drinking it again by accident.

Bringing his attention back to Dolly, he watched as an old woman leaned in to speak to her. He had no idea this was Aggie and she'd had eyes on him from the moment he walked in.

'Dolly, my wench,' Aggie called as she bent forward over the counter. 'Don't look now, but there's a bloke by yonder wall watching you like a hawk.'

'Thanks, Aggie. Nellie says all help is to be rewarded,' Dolly smiled as she gave Aggie a free tot.

Aggie's toothless grin was quickly hidden by the rim of her glass.

It was all Dolly could do not to look towards the wall and the man who was supposedly watching her. Serving another customer, she then glanced around the room as though assuring herself no one else was waiting. It was then that she saw him and her heart sank – it was her step-father and he had found her!

Fear swept through her as she turned and hobbled out of the bar as fast as her weak leg would allow.

'Dolly – whatever is the matter? You look like you've seen a ghost,' Nancy said.

'Not a ghost, but my step-father. He's in there right now and he knows I'm here!' Dolly exclaimed, throwing an arm in the direction of the bar.

'Oh...' Nancy was at a loss for words.

'Nancy, what am I to do?!' Dolly was in a blind panic and clearly unable to think straight.

'You don't need to do anything,' Jack said as he came rushing through. 'Aggie told me – for a free gin of course.'

'She had one from me too; she's on to a good thing there. Jack, I'm scared. What if Arthur has come for me? He might insist I go home with him – can he do that?' Dolly asked, feeling her heart beating out of her chest.

'No, of course he can't! You don't need to be frightened of some trumped-up little squirt!' Nancy assured her.

'What's occurring?' Frederick asked as he emerged from the cellar.

Nancy explained quickly and the big man laid a huge hand on Dolly's tiny one. 'You're safe here, I'll make sure. Now take a squint around that door and point him out to me.'

Dolly did as she was bid and Frederick nodded. The two then returned to the bar and Dolly had the pleasure of watching Frederick escort her step-father outside – by the scruff of his neck.

'Time you left, fella!' Fred said as he bundled Arthur out of the door.

'Why? I ain't done nothing wrong,' Arthur protested.

'You ain't wanted in here. Besides, you weren't drinking.' Fred turned Arthur around and pushed him in the back.

'You're a bully!' Arthur yelled as he backed away.

'You have no idea,' Fred said quietly.

A cheer went up as he came back indoors and he grinned widely, tipping an imaginary hat to Dolly, before work went on as usual.

Arthur was fuming at being thrown out of the saloon but he couldn't exactly argue with the giant. Stamping his temper out on the cobbles, he marched home puffing and blowing out his anger. He wasn't sure why he had been ejected, and so indignantly too, but he knew he couldn't go back now. They would be watching for him. He had been about to approach Dolly and tell her she had to come home, but in the event, he was rather glad he hadn't. God knows what the big man would have done to him if he had.

Dolly and that necklace were proving virtually impossible to get his hands on, and Arthur began to wonder if both were completely lost to him. Should he give up and concentrate on the widows? Was he ready to concede defeat? He pondered these questions as he stared out of the kitchen window.

* * *

In the meantime, Nellie had travelled to Darlaston, a little town not too far away, having hired a cab for the whole day.

Looking through the window, Nellie saw that companies had sprung up everywhere. They manufactured bolts and nuts which were sold all over the country as well as abroad. Travelling up the wide thoroughfare known as Darlaston Road, the cab was kept to the left; the tramway taking up the centre.

Nearing the Bull Stake, Nellie peered out, leaning forward for a better view as they rolled over the bridge. Below was the London and North West Railway line which cut the town in half.

The cab drew to a halt and she heard the driver call out, asking for directions. She smiled as she heard the reply from an exasperated woman surrounded by a gaggle of noisy children. 'Yow goo up theer, right to the top.'

'Thanks very much, missus,' the cabbie yelled back and once more the carriage moved on.

King Street was lined with dirty houses and Nellie thought it was much like any other Black Country street. Industry had covered all brickwork with a layer of grime added to by household chimneys.

The monotony of soot-blackened houses was broken briefly by a patch of green where the imposing St Lawrence's church stood. *You work hard all your life and that's where you end up!*

At the top of Church Street, they came to a little school behind which sprawled the buildings of the brewery. Nellie took a good look at the red brick structure as the cabbie pulled into the yard. Jumping down, the driver opened the door and helped Nellie alight. Instantly she could smell the hops being turned into beer and she wrinkled her nose.

'I wonder how folk live with this stink all the time,' she said.

'I s'pose they'm used to it, Mrs Larkin,' the cabbie replied.

Nellie's eyebrows shot up as she realised the man had recognised her.

He grinned. 'Everybody knows about what Ezra Morton has done regarding your deliveries. I'm guessing that's why we're here. They also know about the kindness you show to others.'

To cover her embarrassment she said, 'I hope I won't be too long in there,' tilting her head to the building she was about to enter.

'Good luck,' the cabbie said as he tipped his hat.

Nodding, Nellie strode towards the entrance.

Shown into the office by a secretary, Nellie was then asked to take a seat. The man behind the desk smiled warmly as he spoke.

'I'm Ned Burton, how can I help you?'

'Nellie Larkin,' came the answer. She then explained that

she ran a gin palace in Birmingham and was looking for a new distiller.

Nodding, Mr Burton went to a sideboard and pointed to a decanter half full of clear liquid.

Offered a tot to try, Nellie feigned horror. 'No, thanks, I only sell it – I don't drink it!'

Mr Burton, the brewer, howled with laughter. He was an older man, having been in the business since he was a boy and he had liked Nellie the moment he met her.

'I don't drink it either. May I ask why you've come to me? Surely it would be less expensive to buy your gin in your home town?' he ventured as he returned to his seat.

'I'll be honest with you, Mr Burton. I'll tell you my problem, then you can decide whether you wish to deal with me.' After laying everything on the line she watched the man as he thought about what she'd told him.

'It could be dangerous for you, Mr Burton,' she warned him.

Mr Burton answered with, 'I don't mind a bit of danger, Mrs Larkin, it adds spice to an otherwise boring existence.' A grin spread across his face as he held out a hand.

They shook hands and the deal was done – Nellie's order would be delivered the following morning by dray cart. The plain barrels would be covered by a tarpaulin and the Shire horses would pull the cart into her yard where they would be unloaded away from prying eyes.

Nellie was delighted. She'd had to pay for delivery, of course, but overall it was not too much more than she'd paid Ezra. Placing an order for a regular supply, Nellie travelled home a distinctly happier woman. She had found a brewer who also distilled gin and at a reasonable price.

'How did you get on?' Nancy asked eagerly as Nellie walked in through the back door.

'Blimey, let me get in first!' Nellie said with a laugh, then proceeded to tell her friend about her meeting with Mr Burton. 'He's delivering by cart so we won't have to worry about it coming via the cut.'

'I bet that cost you,' Nancy answered.

'Not that much more, Nance, and certainly less than it would have been moving it by barge,' Nellie said.

Pouring Nellie a glass of home-made lemonade, Nancy was relieved to hear they would stay in business. She then informed Nellie about the debacle of Dolly's step-father being removed from the premises by Frederick.

'It was Aggie who noticed him first off,' Nancy said.

'That don't surprise me,' Nellie said with a little smile.

'Ar, got eyes like a shit-house rat has that one! Anyway, Dolly pointed him out to Fred and before we knew it the bloke was being rejected through the door arse end first!' Nancy said with a grin.

'Ejected, Nancy,' Nellie corrected gently.

Nancy waved a hand to dismiss both error and correction as she went on hurriedly, 'You should have seen it, Nell, Fred almost lifted him off his feet!'

Seeing Nellie's frown which told her Nellie thought she might have been shirking her work, Nancy quickly added, 'I popped me head round the door to see what was going on.'

Nellie nodded.

'What was he after?' Nellie wondered aloud.

'I don't know, but I don't think he'll be back if he knows what's good for him,' Nancy answered.

'We need to watch out for that little 'un, Nance,' Nellie said with a frown.

'Fred will look after her if you ask him.'

'Good idea. I'd best get my tail end in the bar and give the kids a break.' Nellie finished her cool drink and walked through the open doorway.

A moment later Jack and Dolly appeared, more than ready to enjoy a glass of lemonade and a freshly baked scone with jam.

'How are you feeling now, Dolly?' Nancy asked.

'I'm all right, thank you,' Dolly answered quietly but it was plain to see she was still afraid.

'Don't you be worrying any more, Fred's going to look out for you.'

'And I will,' Jack mumbled through a mouth full of crumbs.

'Did Nellie sort out a delivery?' Dolly asked, wanting to change the subject.

Nancy explained what she'd learned from Nellie and was pleased to see Dolly smile again.

Later, Jack helped Frederick to move the empty casks out into the yard and clear a space for the new ones due the following day.

Dolly returned to help out in the bar as Nancy got the evening meal underway. The Dempsters went to get some sleep in readiness for their night shift on guard, and Poppy had a well-earned break before starting again behind the counter.

Nellie was like a new woman. She served customers with the energy of a girl and her smile stayed in place for the rest of the day.

Tomorrow she would see the cellar fully stocked and as far as she was concerned, Ezra Morton could go to hell and take his lousy gin with him!

20

The house on the corner of Bishop Street was more of a small mansion and had many rooms both up and downstairs. Sylvia Chilton had little idea of style but she knew what she liked and her parlour was a hotchpotch of designs and colours. An English oak sideboard was flanked by two delicate spindle-legged chairs. Chintz curtains hung at the windows and a huge Ormolu clock took centre position on the shelf above the fire. Large rugs covered the highly polished wooden floor and small tables were dotted between armchairs and sofas.

Now Sylvia lived alone, only one of the six bedrooms was used, above which the servants' quarters were reached via a set of back stairs; these lay dormant and dusty. On the ground floor, as well as the parlour, was a dining room – again unused as Sylvia ate in the kitchen. The drawing room door was never opened and the butler's pantry was also closed off. The scullery housed cleaning materials and a tin bath hung on the wall.

Sylvia had let her daughter in and eyed her as they now sat opposite each other in the parlour.

'Mother, what is wrong with you that you can't see what Gabriel Short is doing?!' Elizabeth Murray spat nastily.

'Elizabeth, it really isn't any of your business,' Sylvia replied. 'You are my daughter – not my keeper!'

'Oh, for goodness sake! He's only after your money!'

'I don't agree. In my opinion, Gabriel is a gentleman,' Sylvia was trying to keep her temper in check.

'Gentleman! He's a gigolo, Mother, and at your age you should know better!' Elizabeth snapped. She was so wrapped up in her own anger, she didn't see the hurt in her mother's eyes.

'I'm concerned he will ingratiate himself into your affections before taking your money and leaving you high and dry.'

'I've heard enough!' Sylvia barked. 'Just go home, Elizabeth, and leave me to live my own life.'

Taken aback by the sudden outburst, Elizabeth sniffed loudly and flounced from the room.

Sylvia sighed as she heard the front door open, then slam shut. In the silence that followed, she couldn't help but wonder if her daughter was indeed correct in her thinking. Was she doing the right thing going against Elizabeth's wishes regarding a man she barely knew? What if Elizabeth was proved right in the end and Gabriel Short was only after her money? Was this man worth falling out with her daughter for? After all, she had only known him but a few weeks.

If she was honest with herself, the thing that irked Sylvia the most was how Elizabeth thought she knew what was best for her mother. Living alone now did not mean that Sylvia had lost all reason. She was still capable of making her own decisions and, right or wrong – she only had herself to answer to.

Feeling weary, Sylvia pushed herself out of the easy chair and went to the kitchen to make tea. The house was silent and empty and suddenly loneliness wrapped itself around her and held her tight in its grip. Covering her face with her hands, Sylvia Chilton wept for her dead husband, her overbearing daughter, but mostly for herself. The thought of feeling this way for her remaining years had her cry like her heart was broken.

* * *

Elizabeth Murray had no intentions of letting that man dupe her mother out of her money. She would find a way to prevent it happening if only for the fact that it was her inheritance.

Travelling home in a cab, her mind worked rapidly as to how she could expose Gabriel Short for the man she suspected he truly was. His sweet words and his bowing and scraping had no effect on her whatsoever, in fact it made her dislike him all the more. It all seemed so false. She was confident that she had hit the nail squarely on the head – the man was a charlatan. Although her eyes had stared out of the window on the journey, Elizabeth registered nothing. She didn't notice the men standing in the bread line, as they did day after day, in the hope of finding work. Nor did she see the bedraggled women chatting in the street as they kept an eye on their wilful children. All she could focus on was that dreadful man and what he was putting her mother through.

Once home, Elizabeth sat in her own parlour and pondered. She could let her mother have her own way regarding Mr Short, but that could prove an expensive lesson for Sylvia to learn. Or, she could find a way of discovering whether Short was the man he claimed to be.

Trying to recall his answers to her questions, Elizabeth frowned. ... *fingers in many pies* he had said. Mr Short had not revealed exactly what business he was in, which was suspect in itself, and would make it difficult for discreet enquiries to be made. However, Elizabeth would not give up, she would find a way to prove her point – that Gabriel Short was a perfidious liar and cheat. Knowing there was no time like the present, Elizabeth grabbed her parasol and once more left the house. She was going to visit the foreman of her late father's carriage works. Maybe he could shed some light on the mysterious Mr Short.

* * *

Over in Bailey Street, Nellie watched with glee as one full barrel followed another into her cellar; the draymen helping Frederick to unload and roll them into the spaces made available.

Doffing their caps for the tip Nellie gave, the draymen went on their way.

'That's it, cellar's full to bursting,' Frederick said as he walked into the kitchen.

'Ta, Fred. I'd like a word so sit you down. That fella you chucked out t'other day – he was Dolly's step-father.' She was unaware that Nancy had explained all to him previously.

'Oh, I'm sorry Nellie, if I made a mistake...' Frederick replied. He was feeling wretched and his eyes darted to Nancy hoping she wouldn't hold his error against him.

'No, you did the right thing,' Nellie assured him. 'Look, let me explain. Dolly's mum left her a necklace which she sold. She gave the money to me and that was how I could pay Ezra off. Now, I suspect her step-father thinks she still has the necklace and he wants it. I'm worried he might try to take off with Dolly. She's scared stiff of him Fred, and I need...'

'I'll do it! I'll look after her, Nellie. I swear I won't let her out of my sight,' Frederick said quickly.

'Thanks, Fred, I knew I could rely on you,' Nellie said with a smile.

'Me an' the Dempsters will keep everybody safe, Nellie.' The big man's voice was quiet but the promise in his words gave Nellie the reassurance she was looking for.

'Cup of tea, Fred?" Nancy asked now that was settled.

'Ooh, lovely. Can I have a bit of your smashing cake an' all please?'

Nancy grinned and nodded with a blush to her cheeks.

Taking a seat, Frederick rubbed his hands together in anticipation of the culinary delight.

Just then Jack and Dolly tumbled in through the doorway to join Frederick at the table and he immediately began to tease them.

'No, you gotta say it quick like,' Fred said. 'Try again. I chased a bug around a corner, I'll get his blood he knows I will.'

It took a moment for it to sink in precisely what was being said and the children laughed heartily as they realised they had actually been swearing.

'Try this one – red lorry, yellow lorry,' Fred suggested.

This tongue-twister caused howls of hilarious laughter as everyone gave it a go.

'I know one an' all,' Nancy said as she collected her thoughts. 'She sells sea shells on the sea shore.'

Again, shea sells were being shold on the shea sore which had Fred's booming voice bouncing off the walls.

Nellie watched them for a moment. It was like having

three children, albeit one being much bigger than the other two.

Frederick was not academically inclined but he knew right from wrong. Nellie revelled in the laughter echoing around the kitchen, which was interrupted by Poppy calling for some help in the bar. Nellie duly obliged, leaving the others to enjoy their break time.

* * *

The Chilton Carriage Works stood at one end of a long street named Cheapside. The horse repository was spread out around it and inside men worked long and hard putting together many different styles of carriages. Landaus, cabriolets, phaetons, traps – all were constructed here and sold on to those who could afford to buy them. The loud banging of hammers on metal echoed around the massive space as men knocked in bolts. Grunts sounded as others forced large springs into place and whistling could be heard from the upholsterers as they stitched together the leather for the seating.

Elizabeth had arrived and immediately headed towards the foreman's office. The man apologised for being unable to help Elizabeth regarding her questions about Gabriel Short at that precise moment. However, he assured her he would make enquiries himself and inform her of any outcome.

She had also confided in her husband who had agreed to help in her quest. After all, when his mother-in-law passed on, the carriage works would come to Elizabeth and himself so it was in his interests to keep it safely within the family.

There was nothing more Elizabeth could do but sit back and hope someone could give her more information about Short.

With regards to her mother, Elizabeth was in a quandary. Should she apologise for her behaviour and hurtful words and hope to be welcomed back? Or should she just leave Sylvia to her own devices and pray all turned out well in the end? Elizabeth pondered the dilemma until she could no longer think straight. In the end she decided to do nothing and wait for her mother's call for help – which she guessed would surely come eventually – sooner rather than later, she hoped.

21

The following weeks were extremely busy for everyone, and the slow change of season went unnoticed for the most part. The heat of the summer gave way to a chilly morning mist which swirled through the streets in a ghostly manner. Jackets and mufflers were donned, and women wrapped their shawls tight around their shoulders. The silver lacework of spiders' webs covered in dew hung in nooks and crannies and between the stalks of fading flowers. People no longer strolled in the sunshine; instead they rushed along as if in a hurry to prepare themselves for the oncoming winter. Jams were being made and stored to last the months when fruit would be expensive and hard to come by. Jars of pickled onions and vegetables stood in rows on most shelves in Birmingham kitchens and sculleries, and recipes for time honoured traditional stews were brought out in readiness.

Arthur Micklewhite considered his visits to the widows over breakfast. It was all taking far too long and he wanted to be a man of means sooner rather than later.

Making a decision, he shrugged into a jacket, wrapped his

muffler around his neck and slapped a cap on his head, then he stepped out into the cold yard. Slamming the door shut behind him, he strode purposefully down Rea Terrace.

He was on his way to The Crown Saloon – it was time to confront Dolly Daydream about that necklace. It was a long way and he thought as he walked, realising he would have to look out for the big man who had ejected him previously. He guessed the fellow was all brawn and very little brain so his best bet would be to confuse him with words.

An hour later the saloon came into view and Arthur stopped. Rubbing his chin, he ran through the different scenarios in his mind before he carried on.

Pushing an inebriated woman out of the doorway, Arthur ignored her grumbles of protest and entered the saloon. He grimaced at the number of drunken folk – even at this early hour of the morning.

Shoving his way to the bar he banged his fist on the counter.

'You'll have to wait your turn,' Poppy called out as she cast a reproving glance at the impatient man.

'I need to see Dolly!' Arthur yelled.

'Do you now? Well, you still have to wait your turn,' Poppy returned.

'You fetch my daughter – NOW!'

'I won't tell you again!' Poppy snapped as she continued to pour gin and take money.

'Dolly! Get yourself out here!' Arthur shouted at the top of his voice.

The noise in the bar quietened somewhat as everyone, eager to hear what was about to take place, stared at the irate stranger.

Dolly hobbled through, followed closely by Frederick.

When she spied her step-father, her face lost all colour and she moved closer to her big protector.

'Right, madam, it's time you came home with me!' Arthur yelled.

'No,' Dolly replied with a shake of her head.

'You don't belong here; your place is with me!' Arthur tried again to push his point.

'You can't make me – you're not my father!' Dolly's voice was like breaking glass as she struggled to keep control of her emotions.

Arthur sighed loudly as he looked around him at the faces watching the contretemps. 'Do you believe this? My step-daughter refuses to come home!'

Some heads shook, clearly feeling the man was hard done by, whilst others moved closer to the counter, showing their support for the young girl.

'Don't you come into my place shouting the odds!' Nellie finally intervened.

'She shouldn't be in *your* place!' Arthur spat nastily.

'She's better off here with us than with you!' Nellie growled.

'She's family! So—' Arthur began.

'So that gives you the right to abuse her, does it?' Nellie was furious now.

Murmurs sounded as people stepped away from the man accused.

'What I do is none of your business!' Arthur snapped.

'It is when it concerns you trying to fill your dead wife's shoes with this young 'un, you dirty bugger!' Nellie's patience was all but gone.

Oohs and ahhs told Arthur exactly what the crowd thought of him now.

'That one has something that belongs to me! She stole it!' Arthur tried a different tack.

'I did not! I have nothing of yours,' Dolly shouted, finding courage from the support around her.

'You're a liar!' Arthur snapped.

'Now she's a thief and a liar – is that what you're saying?' Nellie asked, a smirk on her face.

'Yes! I want my property right now. I'm entitled to it.' Arthur searched the crowd for backing.

'What you want – if I'm not mistaken – is for Dolly to keep yer bed warm!' Nellie raised her voice so all could hear.

A woman standing next to Arthur gave him a push saying, 'You filthy swine!' Her words were echoed by others standing close by.

Arthur ignored her and kept his attention on Nellie. 'That's slander! I'll get the police on to you and they'll shut you down!'

'I'm breaking no laws so they can't,' Nellie replied, hoping no-one would inform on her not closing her doors at the appointed time.

'I'm not going to stand here arguing with you, I have things to do!' Arthur shot back.

'Go and do them then, but I tell you now – you even think about coming near Dolly again and you'll regret it,' Nellie said forcefully.

'Are you threatening me?' Arthur turned to the folk around him. 'Did you hear that? She threatened me!'

Heads shook. The possibility of being banned and so being unable to drink their beloved gin was uppermost in their minds and helped to keep their mouths shut tight.

Poppy and Jack were still serving drinks whilst the argument raged on. Nancy stood in the doorway with her hand covering her mouth, a worried look on her face.

'I've had enough of this,' Fred boomed out as he walked towards the end of the counter and pushed his way through the little gate. 'It's time you left, mister!'

'I'm not going without her!' Arthur yelled jabbing a finger in Dolly's direction.

Now at the other side of the bar, Fred grabbed Arthur's arm and swung him around. Face to face it was Fred who growled, 'You, get out – NOW! I'll tell you summat else an' all, if you bother our Dolly again – they'll never find yer body. That is a threat as well as a promise.'

A loud cheer went up from the crowd as Fred physically removed the man from the saloon. Out on the street he spoke quietly into Arthur's face as he held onto him. 'What you had in mind for that young wench is disgusting, and it ain't gonna happen. Now, if you know what's good for you, you'll get yerself off and don't ever think about coming back.'

'She's got a piece of jewellery that's mine!' Arthur spat in frustration.

'She hasn't – it's gone,' Fred said before quickly realising his mistake. He shouldn't have told the man that, it was Dolly's business.

'She's sold it? That bitch!' Arthur fumed.

That was all it took for Fred's fist to shoot forward catching Arthur squarely on the jaw.

Staggering backwards, Arthur landed hard on the cobbles and his hand went to his face where pain lanced up towards his temple. 'I'll have you for that!'

Fred shook his head and with a grim smile asked, 'Can you swim?'

'What?' Arthur answered with a frown, still rubbing his sore jaw.

'I'd stay away from the canal if I were you, pal,' Fred said with a grin.

Arthur paled visibly as he realised the significance of the statement. Jumping to his feet and spinning on his heel he walked swiftly away, muttering as he went.

Fred returned to the bar to be greeted by yet another cheer. Going to the kitchen where Dolly was being hugged by Nancy he said, 'He's gone, and he won't be back.'

'Thank you,' Dolly said with a warm smile.

'No more worries now, you'm safe with me,' Fred said, returning the smile.

'Ta, Fred,' Nancy added shyly, a blush rising swiftly to her cheeks.

Dolly caught the look that passed between Nancy and Fred and her smile turned to a grin. She had a feeling that look would turn into something more before too long and the thought pleased her immensely.

'Dolly, I'm really sorry but your step-dad riled me to such an extent I told him the necklace was gone.' Fred's head hung in shame.

'It doesn't matter. The important thing is he's gone now. Besides, he probably won't believe it. Don't worry about it any more, Fred, I just want to thank you for stepping up and help-ing.' Dolly said.

Fred nodded and they shared a warm smile.

'Right, I'd best get back down the cellar,' he said.

'That was a lovely thing to do, Dolly, cos the big man was fretting there for a minute,' Nancy said.

Dolly grinned and said, 'Back to work for me too, other-wise Nellie will be cursing.'

22

The chain of ragamuffin boys employed by Ezra Morton were stationed on every street corner from The Crown Saloon to the brewery site.

Each was promised a tanner, six whole pennies, when they reported in relay that Poppy Charlton had left the gin palace for any reason.

Stepping out into the street, Poppy had no idea that she was being watched. With a basket over her arm she strolled down the street towards the market. Normally it would be Nancy who did the shopping, but she was up to her armpits in pastry and so Poppy had volunteered to go.

The message was passed from boy to boy and then on to Ezra – Poppy was headed for the market, judging by the basket.

'Her's just left The Crown, Mr Morton, sir!' the boy said as he wiped a dirty hand beneath his nose.

'Good lad. Which way?' Ezra questioned.

'Down Gin Barrel Lane, towards the market 'all,' he said,

trying to catch his breath. He had run all the way from his post on the corner of Ryder Street.

'Here, make sure the others get theirs, mind,' Ezra said as he gave the boy the money to be shared with the others in the chain. Grabbing his hat and cane he strode out of the office.

Stepping out, Ezra's excitement mounted at the prospect of meeting the girl again. He knew he would have to be careful not to frighten her away by being too forward. It must seem as though they had met by chance and he would have to ensure he was as charming as he could be.

Then he spotted her, blonde curls bouncing among a sea of dark haired people. Increasing his pace, he walked behind her, admiring the sway of her hips. He knew he must have her for he was sure it would strike directly at the heart of Nellie Larkin.

The news of that woman paying off her loan had travelled like wildfire. Everyone knew each other's business in this town – nothing was kept secret for long. He guessed Nellie had broadcast her news far and wide, letting others beholden to him know what she had achieved. He was still unaware of how she had come by the money and he'd bet no-one else knew that either. Somehow Larkin managed to keep *her* business to herself and only trumpeted what *she* wanted known. How did she manage to do that?

Deliberately bumping into Poppy, he turned as she looked around. 'Miss Charlton? It is you, is it not?' Ezra asked as he doffed his hat.

Poppy stared at the man addressing her.

'It is, Mr Morton,' Poppy said, flushing to the roots of her hair.

'I see you are off to the market,' he said, pointing to her basket with his cane.

'Yes, I needed to get some air; it's so stuffy in the saloon at times,' she answered before turning to walk on.

'I can imagine. If you don't mind my saying, it's no place for a lady such as yourself.'

Poppy blushed at his compliment and concentrated on putting one foot in front of the other. 'Forgive me, Mr Morton, but I really must get on with my shopping.'

'Allow me to assist you, Miss Charlton,' Ezra said, moving to take the basket from her arm.

Poppy gasped and looked around at the faces staring at them. It was unheard of for a man to carry a basket or help with the shopping. 'I can manage, thank you.' Poppy moved the carrier to her other arm.

Ezra smiled and touched his hat with the silver topped cane to the people now muttering quietly.

'Mr Morton, people are talking,' Poppy said, taking a step forward.

'Let them, Miss Charlton, I'm not worried by a little gossip.'

Poppy sighed and continued to glance around as she walked through the throng of people.

Seeing her discomfort, Ezra smiled in an effort to comfort her. 'My apologies, Miss Charlton. It was not my intention to subject you to tittle-tattle.' Cupping her elbow, he moved them further into the market.

'Mr Morton, I'm not sure it's such a good idea to be seen with you,' Poppy began.

'Why ever not?' Ezra feigned a hurt look.

'Well, I've heard – there are stories...' Poppy was trying to dissuade him from accompanying her although her efforts were half-hearted. In truth, she was enjoying being with him, and the jealous looks of the women they passed. She felt important walking by this man's side and loved the way the crowd parted to allow them through.

'Ah yes, I've heard them too,' Ezra said with a beaming smile. 'It's all a tissue of lies, Miss Charlton.'

'What about poor Mr Pickles?' She was unable to hold her tongue and her question was out before she realised what she'd said.

'Let me tell you about that dear old man. Mr Pickles' daughter was due to wed so he borrowed some money from me. After the wedding I learned the old fellow had become ill so I went to call on him.' Ezra was looking Poppy directly in the eye and he saw she was hanging onto his every word.

'So I heard! And that's not all – it's said you cut...' She raised her hand and her fingers and thumb moved in a pincer movement.

'I did, Poppy,' Ezra said, daring to use her first name. 'I did cut – his debt in half.'

'Oh!' Poppy's cheeks burned with embarrassment.

'All these tales about me are not true. However, I cannot deny it helps when collecting debts, but make no mistake – my men are courteous and helpful, I absolutely insist upon it.'

Poppy felt relieved and was now more inclined to believe that the stories she'd heard about this handsome man were indeed all lies.

The conversation halted while Poppy bought some vegetables and then she moved on, Ezra close by her side.

'Miss Charlton...' Ezra began.

With a gentle blush, she turned to face him.

'Miss Charlton, would you do me the honour of having dinner with me sometime soon? We could visit the theatre and dine at our leisure.'

'I'm afraid I don't have much time off from my work, Mr

Morton,' she replied, trying to recover quickly from the shock of his inviting her out.

'I'm sure Nellie would give you an evening off if you asked her,' he pursued.

'I doubt it. The saloon is extremely busy just now,' Poppy said with a sad look.

'I understand, but I have to say I'm very disappointed. I was hoping to have the pleasure of your company, but I see I will have to eat alone – again.' Ezra was pushing harder now for he desperately wanted her accept his invitation.

'I suppose I could ask – but I can't promise anything,' Poppy relented.

'Excellent! You can get word to me at the brewery. There's always an urchin ready to earn a copper, which I will pay for of course. Thank you, Miss Charlton, you've made me a very happy man.' Ezra silently congratulated himself as he bundled Poppy and her full basket into a cab. Kissing her hand, he then paid the driver to take the lady home.

Ezra Morton had a spring in his step as he walked back to the brewery. The smile stretched across his face as he thought about the evening he felt sure he would be soon spending with Poppy Charlton.

Nellie would be furious about Poppy agreeing to step out with him which pleased him immensely. It would most likely cause an enormous row between the two women and could possibly lead to Poppy quitting her job and walking out. In turn it would mean Nellie would lose a good barmaid and he would be held responsible. Then, when he'd had his fun with the girl, he would send her packing. Would Nellie take her back? A young girl used and tossed aside, one who would be unable to find a husband after he had finished with her. Could he do that to Poppy? Ezra grinned, knowing full well he could.

Poppy alighted from the cab outside the saloon and thanked the driver before stepping inside. She was excited at the prospect of having dinner with a notorious man like Ezra, but she was also worried about what Nellie would say. She was certain Nancy and Nellie would warn her off the man yet again, but Poppy felt it was time now to make her own decisions. She was eighteen years old after all and a lot of girls her age were already married with children of their own.

Unpacking the shopping in the kitchen, Poppy didn't hear the banter between Jack and Dolly – her mind was on Ezra Morton and what he could do for her. He could take her from the back-breaking work at the saloon; maybe he would set her up in her own little house somewhere. He might even propose marriage and then she wouldn't want for anything if she became Mrs Morton.

Making tea without thought for what she was doing, Poppy then considered the other side of the coin. Nellie Larkin had taken her in off the street when she was starving. She had been given a job and a place to live and drawn into the small family unit without question. Could she go against Nellie's advice which would surely hurt the woman who was like a mother to her? Could she risk the possibility she would be alienated by the others just to have an evening out with Ezra?

Then again, it would just be the theatre and dinner.

All she could do was ask Nellie for the night off. She didn't have to say why, or where she was going, or who with. Poppy made her decision – she would make her request at the end of the night when the saloon had closed up.

At midnight, everyone sat around the kitchen table supping tea. Matthew and Noah Dempster joined them before taking up their night guard work.

'Nellie, I'd like an evening off,' Poppy said in a rush before her confidence left her. She had deliberately asked in front of everyone in the hope they would support her request and so make it more difficult for Nellie to refuse.

'What for?' Nellie asked with a tired sigh.

'I want to get out of that bar for a few hours. I'm sick of seeing the same gin-sodden faces and hearing the same old drunken songs – I need a break,' Poppy answered, ignoring everyone watching the exchange.

'Poppy, I understand, but we're so busy right now, I ain't sure I can spare you—' Nellie began.

'I'm entitled to a night off – even if it's only once a year!'

Nellie stared at the young woman, wondering what had sparked the outburst.

Poppy raged on. 'I never go anywhere – like the music hall or theatre! As much as I love your cooking, Nancy, it would be nice to eat out on occasion!'

Suddenly Nellie knew – Poppy had been invited out by a young man. With a smile she asked, 'Do we know him?'

'Who?' Poppy asked.

'The young fella who's asked you out,' Nellie qualified.

'Bloody hell! It's like the Spanish Inquisition here! It's my business, Nellie, and I shouldn't have to share it with all and sundry!'

Nellie's face fell. 'Oh, Poppy – please tell me it ain't who I think it is.'

'I can go out with whoever I want, Nellie, I'm old enough now.' Poppy stood her ground.

'Yes, you are, Poppy, but – Ezra Morton? For God's sake have you forgotten what we told you?!' Nellie was exasperated.

'It's all lies, Nellie, he told me so!' Poppy's bravado began to crumble as she spoke.

'When did you speak to him?' Nellie demanded to know.

'In the market today,' Poppy answered.

Nellie dragged her hands down her face and sighed audibly. 'I can see you're determined so I'll say this. Go out with him if you must, but be careful. Just know, if it goes wrong, we'll all be here for you.'

'Oh, thank you, Nellie!' Poppy said, giving the woman a hug. Then she said her goodnights and skipped off to her bed.

'Nell, I'm worried for her,' Nancy said.

'So am I, Nance,' Nellie concurred.

'Nellie, can I make a suggestion?' Noah Dempster asked, his blue eyes twinkling in the gas light.

'Yes, lad, go ahead,' Nellie said.

'One of us,' he jerked his thumb between himself and his brother, 'could follow Poppy – discreetly of course.'

'I could do that!' Fred said sharply, feeling a little pushed out.

'No disrespect, big man, but with your size you'd be spotted right away,' Noah replied.

'Besides, Ezra knows you,' Nancy said, laying a hand on his arm.

'Oh, yeah,' Fred said with a little grin.

'I don't know...' Nellie began.

'Have a think about it and let us know,' Noah said, 'for now we have a job to do. Come on, brother – time to check doors and windows.'

They left Nellie pondering the suggestion as they ensured the building was locked up tight.

23

Ezra Morton was in a good mood having sent a note via the string of urchins to Poppy arranging to meet her later. Sitting in his office sipping his morning tea, he was looking forward to her reply.

After a quick knock, the door opened and one of Ezra's men strode in. 'There's nothing to be found on Nellie Larkin, boss.'

Ezra frowned. 'Nothing?'

The man shook his head.

'What about a husband?' Ezra asked.

'No sign of one. Maybe he was sent to the Crimea and died there,' the man suggested.

'Maybe, but where was he before that?'

'Nobody knows, boss.'

'Nellie has a lad – ten years old – no husband that can be found...' Ezra paused, running a thumb nail over his bottom lip as he thought out loud. 'It's all very suspect if you ask me.'

'Yes, boss,' the man said, then at the flick of Ezra's fingers, he turned and left the office quietly.

Thinking over what he knew about Nellie, Ezra was puzzled. Left the pub by her parents, she and Nancy – a widow of many years – began the restoration of the place with money borrowed from him. Nellie quite suddenly pays off her loan so – where did the money come from? She takes in waifs and strays, as well as the unemployed, and he thought of Fred. She has no husband but has a son. How old was Nellie? Whatever her age she must have had that boy late in life.

With a frustrated sigh, Ezra determined he would quiz Poppy later to see what else he could learn about the enigmatic Nellie Larkin.

Over at The Crown Saloon, Fred was re-arranging the cellar in readiness for the next delivery of gin. Poppy and Dolly were working the bar with help from Jack, and Nellie was having a conversation with Nancy in the kitchen.

'I'm going to ask one of the Dempster boys to follow Poppy,' Nellie said.

'Thank Christ for that! It's a good idea, Nell,' Nancy concurred.

'Bloody Ezra Morton! That man will be the death of me!' Nellie rasped through her teeth.

'I'm worried for Poppy – she's so innocent. Pound to a penny he'll turn her head; she'll fall for him, Nell, and then God knows what will happen!' Nancy was twisting her apron in her fingers, and her eyes held fear.

'I know, Nance, but I don't know what we can do about it. She says he's taking her out tonight and she's very excited about it,' Nellie said, finishing with a long drawn out sigh.

'Of all the men in the world – it had to be him!' Nancy snapped as she threw her apron away from her.

It was then that Jack joined them saying, 'I just found out – it's Dolly's birthday on Friday, she'll be fourteen!'

'So I take it we should have a little celebration?' Nellie asked with a smile.

'Can we? I wish I could buy her a present,' Jack said dreamily.

Nellie reached into the table drawer and drew out three pounds and passed it to Nancy. 'Get some bits and pieces – and will you bake her a cake?'

Nancy nodded as she took the money.

'Give Jack five bob so he can get her a gift.'

'Ooh ta, Mum, I thought I'd get her a book,' Jack enthused.

Nellie nodded. 'Nance, see if you can get her a coat – from all of us – cos winter will be here in no time.' Turning to Jack she said, 'You go with Nance and I'll tend the bar. Let's keep all this a secret from Dolly until Friday.'

Jack gave a whoop and headed for the back door.

The weather was sunny but the autumn chill managed to wrap itself around Jack and Nancy as they walked briskly to the market. The sun glinted off the morning dew which layered the cobblestones in the road, giving them a glassy sheen, and the brightness made Jack squint. The air was damp and seemed to force itself through their clothes, making them shiver. In the Old Square a brazier was burning and was surrounded by men warming their hands. These were the unfortunates – the ones with no jobs, and every day, come rain or shine they stood waiting for someone to give them an opportunity to earn a wage. It was known as the bread line and these queues of men could be seen on street corners everywhere – such was the poverty in certain areas of the town.

With his five shillings in his hand, Jack sped off after arranging to meet Nancy later, back at the entrance. With that much money he could buy Dolly lots of books and he knew just what she'd like.

The market was set out in rows with small aisles between them and Jack's eyes darted this way and that as he hurried along. As he went, he heard the calls of the vendors over the hubbub of shoppers. There was a smell of flowers as he passed a stall full of colourful blooms, which was replaced by the odour of fresh fish further along.

Jack halted to listen to the banter taking place between a man selling meat and a woman in the crowd.

'A pound of sausages and I ain't even asking a quid,' the man shouted as he laid them on a huge set of scales.

'I should bloody think not!' the woman yelled back.

'Indeed, missus. Add to that a pound of bacon.'

'Still daylight robbery!' the woman heckled again.

'Ar, but what if I slapped a bit o'steak on the top, eh? That would be worth a quid of anyone's money,' the butcher said.

'Stop clarting about and give us a price for yer trotters,' the woman called.

'Me trotters are me own, but I do have some pigs' for you right 'ere.' A ripple of laughter ran through the throng of women standing waiting in the hope of a bargain, and Jack smiled before he set off in search of a book stall.

Further down he heard gasps from another crowd gathered and he stopped to investigate. A man was catching dinner plates thrown by his assistant and laying them along his outstretched arm. Tea plates came next, followed by saucers, and the man swung his arm for all to see. Tilting his hand down, the crockery slid into a neat pile which he laid down on the stall. Cups came sailing over which he deftly caught, building them into a tall stack which he deliberately wobbled before placing them down.

Jack grinned at the vendor's antics and tore himself away from the amusing spectacle.

At last he found what he was looking for, a stall covered with books. Now he could take his time, he wanted to get just the right thing to please Dolly.

Nancy raked through the clothes on the stalls searching for a coat for Dolly, but there was nothing that was nearly good enough.

'Don't maul the goods if'n you ain't gonna buy!' the vendor shouted.

'Goods! This is a load o'rubbish!' Nancy yelled back and nodded as others around her mumbled their agreement.

'I d'aint ask you to come and shop on my stall!' the woman said.

'No, and I won't be coming no more! That ain't no way to treat perspective customers!' Nancy retaliated.

Few realised the word she should have used was prospective but they kept their counsel as they watched the contretemps continue.

'I can do without customers like you and that's a fact!'

'Well, you'll bloody well have to now, won't yer? I'll tell you summat else an' all – I'm gonna let everybody know what a nasty bugger you am! I'll mek sure the market inspector 'ears about this as well, you mark my words!' Nancy harrumphed and turned to face the crowd. 'If you'll 'scuse me I have money to spend elsewhere.'

Remembering there was a little shop close by, she strode away to investigate what was on offer. The shop was a front room affair, run by the woman who lived there.

Nancy stood staring at the window display. A red woollen coat with an attached shoulder cape was on show. The collar, buttons and cuffs were black and a wide brimmed hat accompanied it.

Stepping inside, Nancy asked to see the item which had captivated her. The woman reached it from the window and Nancy felt the quality between her fingers. Good and thick, she knew it would fit Dolly a treat. She had a surprise when the woman lifted the short shoulder cape and fastened it at the front with a button so it acted as a muffler.

'How much?' Nancy asked.

'Two pounds, ten shillings,' the woman replied.

Nancy blanched. 'Blimey! It would have to be med of gold for that much!'

'It's worth it,' the woman said.

'Ar well, you'd have to say that to get the sale,' Nancy replied. The woman made to put the coat back in the window but stopped when Nancy spoke again. 'I'll take it!'

The woman smiled warmly and folding the coat carefully she placed it in a box which she tied with string. Finding a small round box, she packed the hat.

Nancy left the shop feeling very pleased with her purchase. Now all she had to do was tell Nellie how much she'd paid and hope she didn't get her head bitten off.

Striding back to the market, Nancy saw Jack waiting for her and he was carrying a pile of books, also tied together with string.

As they walked home, Jack and Nancy excitedly planned Dolly's surprise birthday party.

* * *

Whilst Jack and Nancy's shopping spree was underway, Elizabeth Murray had decided to visit her mother. She was dressed in a long navy blue coat and matching silk organza hat adorned with feathers, an umbrella and leather gloves completed the ensemble.

'I wondered how long it would be before you came back,' Sylvia Chilton said.

'You don't have to be so churlish, Mother,' Elizabeth returned.

'Elizabeth, I'm treating you in the same manner that you treat me.'

'Well, I'm here now.'

'You are indeed. What do you want, Elizabeth?'

'I don't want anything, Mother! I merely came to see how you are!' Dropping into a chair, Elizabeth snatched at the hat pin and removed her large feathered hat.

'Shall I make tea?' she asked.

'Later – when my visitor arrives,' Sylvia said, bracing herself for her daughter's reaction.

'So, he's still calling, is he – Gabriel Short?' Elizabeth asked with a scowl.

'He is.'

'Mother—'

'Don't, Elizabeth! Please let's not go into this again.' Sylvia really didn't want to argue further with her daughter on the matter.

Elizabeth sighed audibly and rolled her eyes as the knocker rapped.

Sylvia smiled and went to answer the door. A moment later she was back with Gabriel in tow.

'Mrs Murray, so nice to see you again,' he lied.

'Mr Short, still visiting, I see,' Elizabeth responded sharply.

'Take a seat, Gabriel, whilst I make tea,' Sylvia simpered.

Complying with her request, Arthur felt uncomfortable under Elizabeth's glare.

'I know what you're up to, Mr Short,' she said, leaning forward in her chair.

'I'm sure I don't know what you are referring to,' he said amiably.

'Please don't treat me like an idiot! You are trying to inveigle your way into my mother's affections in order to get your grubby hands on her money!'

'Mrs Murray! You do me an injustice! Your mother and I – we are friends.' Arthur's discomfort increased with every passing moment.

'Friends!' Elizabeth spat. 'You expect me to believe that? Well, I don't, Mr Short, and I warn you now, I will expose you one way or another!'

'Here we are,' Sylvia cooed as she carried in the tea tray.

Arthur got to his feet and relieved her of her burden.

'Thank you, dear,' Sylvia gushed as she retook her seat.

'For goodness' sake,' Elizabeth muttered under her breath and rolled her eyes again, not even trying to hide her disgust. Accepting the cup and saucer from her mother, she sat listening to the conversation taking place. There was no effort made to draw her into the discussions and Elizabeth began to feel like a third wheel.

Sylvia was explaining that the carriage works was running smoothly under the keen eye of the foreman, and Arthur was nodding in all the right places.

'I must be going, Mother, but I will visit again next week,' Elizabeth interrupted rudely.

'All right, dear,' Sylvia said as she watched her daughter don her hat.

Ignoring Arthur completely, Elizabeth left them to it.

Walking to the end of the street she waited. Gabriel Short would emerge before too long, and when he did, she would follow to see where he would lead.

An hour later, Elizabeth was tired and frustrated. The cold nipped her fingertips even through her gloves, and she rolled her toes inside her boots to try to increase the blood flow and warm them. Then at last she saw him – smiling and waving as he left the house.

Strolling along, she kept him in her sight. Fortunately, the streets were busy and she was able to hide herself in the crowd. Following him along Sherlock Street, Elizabeth held a handkerchief to her nose as she passed the slaughterhouse and meat market. The smell wafted on the air and she increased her step, wanting to be away from it as soon as possible. On they went around the Bull Ring, past the statue of Nelson and down Bell Street before her quarry turned into the extensive market hall. Slowly and carefully, Elizabeth tailed Gabriel and by the afternoon she knew far more about him.

Leaving the market the same way she had entered, Elizabeth looked both ways for a cab. Raising her rolled umbrella she waved it to attract the cabbie's attention. Tipping his hat in reply he flipped the reins and the horse walked on. As the carriage drew to a halt, she climbed aboard, calling out the address before closing the door. Elizabeth was going home; she had a lot to think about.

For his part, Arthur had left Sylvia and he concluded that the whole situation was becoming tiresome. Making his way to the market, he wondered again if the widow Chilton was worth the time he was spending on her.

Despite still being dressed in his good clothes, he needed to replenish his coffers, so he decided a little thievery would rectify that particular problem. It would also make him feel better. He had made the decision previously to stay away from this particular area, but the danger of being caught was pumping adrenaline around his body as he wove his way between the market stalls.

Having lifted a few wallets and purses, Arthur emptied

and dropped them before striding out for home. He had no idea that whilst he was stealing from those less fortunate, he was being watched closely. So intent was he on keeping an eye out for the police, he did not notice Elizabeth Murray shadowing his every step.

24

The autumn chill began to take hold and the leaves on the few trees dotted about turned to gold and copper. The weak sunshine held no warmth and folk donned thicker clothing as they went about their business. Winds picked up debris lying on the streets and blew it into piles. More household fires were lit and the smoke plumed from chimneys all over the town. The rain was cold as it pattered down from the heavens, soaking everyone to the skin.

In the cellar of The Crown, Jack and Dolly were busy filling bottles with diluted gin when Jack suddenly asked, 'Do you miss your mum?'

'Yes. Every day,' Dolly replied sadly.

Jack nodded.

'What is it, Jack?'

'I'm still confused about my parents,' he admitted after a short silence.

'I can understand that,' Dolly whispered.

'I keep wondering who they are. Why did they give me up like they did? Are they still alive? What sort of person dumps a baby on a doorstep and walks away?' Jack shook his head in disbelief.

'Lots of questions and no answers.' Dolly gave him a sympathetic smile. 'Have you thought about this in a more methodical way?'

'How do you mean?' Jack frowned as he passed her a half-full bottle.

'Well, taking it from the beginning, your mum had you. Now, was she married or not? Was she too poor to be able to keep you? Also, and I'm sorry to say this, Jack, but were you what is considered an accident?' Dolly paused, allowing the boy to digest her words. 'Going a step further, why did she choose to leave you on Nellie's doorstep? Did she know Nellie or Nancy?'

'Blimey! I never thought of that!' Jack said on a breath.

'It doesn't necessarily follow that Nellie or Nancy would know your mum though,' Dolly added.

'I s'pose.' Jack's sudden excitement at possibly having a lead to his parentage dissipated in a cloud of disappointment.

'On the bright side though, your mum didn't leave you at the workhouse or the orphanage.' Dolly was trying to lift the boy's spirits after she saw his body sag.

'You've got a birth certificate, ain't you?' Jack asked and when Dolly nodded, he went on, 'I wonder if I ever had one.'

'Possibly not, but it would depend on your mum's circumstances.' Dolly bit her bottom lip, not at all sure she was helping.

'I've tried not to think about it all, Dolly, but it won't leave me alone!'

'It's the not knowing that's the worst I'm sure, but it might be that one day you'll find out.'

'Until then I'm left wondering,' Jack said sadly.

'Jack, look at the other side of it more a moment. You were

found and taken in by Nellie. For your whole life she brought you up as her own. She fed you, taught you and kept you safe. You have a home and family who love you.'

'You make it sound like I landed on my feet,' Jack said, passing over another bottle.

'You did. Considering what could have happened, you are very lucky,' Dolly replied with a warm smile.

'Like you, Poppy and Fred,' Jack said.

'Yes, and Matthew and Noah Dempster – Nellie has brought us all into the fold rather than turning us away,' Dolly added.

'We're all in the same boat then.' Jack gave her a small grin.

'Yes, maybe that's why we are like a big family.'

'Speaking of Poppy, what do you make of her stepping out with Ezra Morton?' Jack asked.

'I'm worried for her, I just hope—'

'She's got her head screwed on,' Jack interrupted.

'I know that, Jack, but love knows no bounds,' Dolly said on a sigh.

The bottle filling continued in silence as both got lost in their thoughts.

It was then that Fred, who had heard their conversation as he smoked a cigarette by the outside door to the cellar, walked quietly into the kitchen.

'Cup of tea, Fred?' Nancy asked.

'Hmm,' came the reply.

'Summat on yer mind?' Nancy probed as she passed over the cup and saucer.

Fred related the exchange he'd overheard between Jack and Dolly.

'The poor little bugger doesn't know if he's coming or going. I always said Nellie should have told him long before now. I wonder if he'll ever come to terms with it.' Nancy said as she settled herself on a kitchen chair. 'It's Poppy I'm worried about now though.'

Fred nodded. 'I don't like it, Nancy, she shouldn't be seeing someone like Ezra.'

'Are you sweet on her, Frederick Dell?' Nancy asked with a teasing grin.

'No! Don't get me wrong, she's a nice girl but not for me – or Ezra either. He'll use her, Nancy, then toss her away.'

'I said the same, but she's a grown woman now and can make up her own mind, I suppose.' Nancy sipped her tea silently, wishing Poppy would tell Ezra to clear off and leave her alone, but knowing in her heart it wouldn't happen.

Fred watched her from the corner of his eye and he flushed as her eyes met his.

'One of the Dempsters is going to follow her and make sure she gets home safely.' Nancy said at last. She smiled as she saw Fred relax a little. He was clearly glad Nellie had agreed to Noah's suggestion, now he wouldn't have to worry.

A screech from the bar had them both look at each other.

'Sounds like you're needed,' Nancy laughed.

Fred nodded and got to his feet. Giving her a wink, he marched towards the door.

Nancy blushed and laid a hand on her chest in an effort to slow her fast beating heart. It had been a while now since she realised she had feelings for this big man, and she had hoped they might be reciprocated. Was that wink a confirmation of her dream of a budding relationship? Her stomach gave a little flip as she returned to her work.

In the bar Fred looked to Nellie, then followed the tilt of her head. Two women were screaming obscenities and beating a man with their fists while he giggled as he relieved himself in the corner.

'Hey, fella,' Fred boomed, seeing the man now fastening his trouser buttons. In an instant Fred was at his side and tore the shirt from the man's back, then used it to mop up the mess. Cheers sounded when he slammed the soggy shirt into the man's chest and marched him from the premises. Then he fetched a bucket of water loaded with soda crystals and a mop. Satisfied the area was clean, Fred left the bar to deafening applause.

'My God! If he can do that in here, what must his home be like?' Poppy yelled over the noise.

'I dread to think,' Nellie shouted back. 'What time you out tonight?'

'Seven,' Poppy answered with an excited look in her eye.

'Best go and get ready then,' Nellie said, 'I'll get Jack to lend a hand here.'

Poppy ran lightly from the bar to wash and change. She had replied to Ezra's note accepting the invitation earlier in the day.

Nellie called for Jack and as he came through, she said, 'Fetch the Dempsters down then tend the bar with Dolly while I have a word.'

Twenty minutes later, it was agreed Noah Dempster would track Poppy that evening and Matthew would stand the usual guard duty.

'I'm sorry I have to ask you, Noah, because it all feels so – sneaky,' Nellie said.

'Better that than... She'll be fine, Nellie, I'll look out for her. Any sign of trouble and I'll whisk her away and bring her home.' Blue eyes twinkled in a reassuring smile.

'Ta, lad, you'll have a bonus apiece come the end of the week,' Nellie said with a nod.

* * *

At seven on the dot, Ezra Morton entered The Crown Saloon dressed in his best suit; top hat and walking cane in hand. Threading his way through the throng, he tapped the silver knob on the counter.

Nellie glanced at him then continued with her work.

Ezra smiled. She's trying to ignore me, he thought. Just then Poppy came through dressed in a bottle green velvet dress that fit where it touched. It was something she'd found on a market stall and had bought it with a few coppers borrowed from Nellie. The bodice was in a cross-over style which gave a deep neckline which was not too revealing, and it was nipped in at the waist. The skirt fell straight at the front to her black boots. At the back it was gathered into gentle ruffles which lay over a small bustle. Her blonde hair was piled high in curls and fastened with a feathered comb. Long black gloves covered her arms and over one of which she carried a black woollen cloak.

Oohs and ahhs sounded as Ezra took the wrap and draped it around her shoulders. Then hooking an arm, he led her out into the street where a cab waited.

Noah Dempster leaned against the wall of The Castle pub directly across the street having a smoke, his cap pulled down low over his brow. The couple didn't see him as they climbed aboard the carriage.

Hearing the address called to the cabbie, Noah waited for them to leave then he whistled for a cab of his own. Directing the driver to follow, Noah waited to see where they would end up. Before long Ezra's cab halted in Lower Priory and the couple alighted then stepped into a hotel across from the Grand Theatre. Noah, who had paid his cabbie handsomely, waited patiently inside the carriage now standing on the corner of the crossroads between Lower Priory and Dalton Street.

Poppy was breathlessly excited by being treated like a princess. 'I've never been to a hotel before,' she whispered as Ezra removed her cloak, passing it to an attendant.

'You should eat in places like this every day of your life, Poppy,' Ezra smiled.

'Not much chance of that,' she replied as he cupped her elbow and led her to the dining room.

'Ah, Mr Morton, so nice to see you again. Good evening, Miss,' the Maître d' said with a slight bow to Poppy. 'Your table is all ready for you, sir.' Snapping his fingers, he beckoned to a waiter. 'Show Mr Morton and his guest to their table.'

Poppy stared at all the cutlery and glassware as Ezra pulled out a chair for her.

Once they were both seated, the waiter poured them each a glass of water.

Poppy glanced up at him, a worried look in her eye. She had no idea about such hifalutin table etiquette, and a flick of the eyebrows told her he understood her concern.

'Would sir care to see the wine list?' the waiter asked as he tapped a white gloved finger against a wine glass. He smiled at Poppy, endeavouring to help her surreptitiously.

'Yes please,' Ezra said.

Poppy nodded and smiled at the young man for being so helpful.

In a matter of moments wine was ordered and the menus presented.

'Goodness, such a lot to choose from,' Poppy said, 'how much does it cost?'

The young wine waiter was at that moment uncorking the wine at their table when Ezra replied from behind his menu.

'My dear girl, top class hotels do not display their charges. It's tantamount to discussing money – it's vulgar.'

Poppy flushed scarlet with embarrassment but couldn't help but give a small smile when she caught the waiter pulling a face behind Ezra's back. Quickly she covered her mouth with her hand.

Pouring a small amount, he said, 'Your wine, sir.'

Ezra tasted it and then nodded.

The waiter skirted the table to serve Poppy first, then topped up Ezra's glass. Standing the wine in its cooler on the table, he grinned at the pretty girl before walking away.

Poppy squirmed in her seat as she stared at the French words she could not read. Her eyes roamed over the list as she tried desperately to pick out words she might know, but failing in the attempt made her heart sink.

Glancing around the room she began to wish she hadn't come. She felt so out of her depth she wanted to cry.

'Have you decided, m'dear?' Ezra asked, lowering his menu to peep over the top.

'Erm, no not yet,' Poppy said with a croak.

'What do you like – meat, fish?' Ezra pursued.

'Either,' Poppy answered in a whisper.

Poppy glanced around the room again before her eyes alighted on the wine waiter chatting to a colleague who looked her way. They were discussing her! Were they laughing at her? The food waiter nodded and gave her a beaming smile. What was going on between those two?

She quickly found out as the waiter stepped smartly to the table.

'She hasn't made up her mind yet,' Ezra said curtly.

'If I may be so bold – could I help the lady to decide?' the waiter asked.

'Please do, I'm famished!' Ezra's attention returned to his own menu.

'The Dover sole with its lemon sauce is particularly good here, madam.' The waiter pointed to the entries on her menu card as he spoke. 'Or perhaps you might prefer venison in red wine gravy, with potatoes and vegetables.'

Poppy said quickly, 'I like the sound of the sole.'

'Very good, and would madam like a starter?'

Closing her eyes tight she sucked in a breath.

'I could recommend the pâté, it comes from Brussels,' the waiter said quietly.

'That sounds lovely, thank you,' Poppy smiled her thanks with pure relief.

Turning to Ezra the waiter asked, 'And for sir?'

'Prawns then venison,' Ezra snapped, handing the menu into the waiter's outstretched hand.

'It's posh here,' Poppy said as the waiter left their table.

'It's not bad,' Ezra replied.

They didn't have to wait long for their starter to arrive and the waiter picked up Poppy's cutlery and gave it a quick wipe on a spotlessly clean cloth, indicating which she should use, before replacing it on the table.

Poppy nodded her thanks and cast a smile to the wine waiter standing by the doorway. They had not been laughing at her at all. They had guessed she was struggling with the menu and cutlery order and were in cahoots in trying to give her little clues which only she would see. Poppy was immensely grateful.

'Nellie was gracious enough to let you out then,' Ezra said sarcastically.

'She was kind enough to give me the night off, yes.' Poppy's words were sharp as she eyed the man sat opposite her.

'I'm so sorry, m'dear, that was rude of me,' Ezra said as he picked up on her pique.

'Nellie is a lovely lady – she took me in when I had nowhere else to go,' Poppy said quietly.

'I understand, please forgive me.' Ezra said insincerely between bites.

Having finished their starters, the waiter appeared and lifted her plate from the table before rearranging the knife and fork to be used with the main course. Another subtle sign.

'Thank you,' Poppy told him with a smile.

'You don't have to thank him, that's what he's paid for,' Ezra said, then drawing her attention back to himself, went on, 'tell me, Poppy, why do you work at that saloon?'

Poppy felt the waiter glance at her before removing Ezra's plate, and again her face burned with humiliation.

'It's a perfectly decent place, Ezra, and it's a good job albeit being hard on the feet.'

Ezra detected the note of protective loyalty in her voice. 'What I meant was, you shouldn't be working at all. You should be a lady of leisure, taken care of and spoiled.'

Sipping his wine, he realised he had been yelling orders at his men for so long, he had quite forgotten how to speak to a woman.

'I would be bored to tears without my work,' Poppy said with a little laugh.

'I see Nellie has found a new supplier,' Ezra said pointedly.

'Yes.'

Ezra watched as a warm plate filled with hot food was placed in front of her and then himself. 'Care to tell me who it is?'

'Care to mind your own business?' Poppy flashed back. She saw the waiter grin and flick his eyebrows.

Ezra laughed but it sounded hollow even to his ears. 'Can I ask where Nellie's husband is?'

'I'm afraid you will have to ask her about that,' Poppy answered firmly.

'I hear Fred is working for Nellie now,' Ezra said.

Poppy ignored the statement and continued to eat.

Ezra looked up from his plate saying, 'Well, is he?'

Clamping her teeth together, Poppy nodded. She had expected Ezra to try to seduce her on their evening out together and she had been prepared to repel boarders. If this was his idea of wooing then he was failing miserably. Where was the discreet touching of fingers? There were no long lingering looks or words of endearment. She felt like she was being pumped for information about Nellie and the dinner was her reward. She could feel the waiters' eyes on her, knowing they were aware she was not enjoying herself one bit. They consulted each other quietly each time Ezra spoke and Poppy concluded that they could hear every word.

'Nellie's lad should be in school, not working in that fleapit!' Ezra snapped, annoyed that he was getting nowhere. He had been sure Poppy was so enamoured of him she would tell him all he wanted to know, but she appeared to have other ideas. He pursued his line of questioning with mounting frustration.

'It's not a fleapit! It's my place of work and my home!' Poppy fired back. In her peripheral vision she saw the waiters nod their agreement with a grin.

'Yes, well, you couldn't do much worse,' Ezra said unthinkingly as he slurped his wine. 'It seems to me that Nellie takes in waifs and strays off the street.'

The waiter had stepped up to refill his glass just then and

his mouth formed a small 'O' in disgust. Walking around the table with the wine bottle, he waited for Poppy to accept or refuse another drink.

'You're right. She took me in off the street and I'm very grateful to her!' Poppy's wrath flushed her cheeks.

'I didn't mean—' Ezra began.

'Yes, you did. I was in the workhouse, Ezra, and when I signed myself out at fifteen years old I lived on the streets until Nellie found me!' Poppy's voice was even as she spoke but her eyes glared a black anger.

Ezra glanced at the waiter who coughed politely.

Dragging her smouldering eyes away from Ezra, Poppy looked up and smiled at the young man proffering the wine bottle.

'Thank you, no more for me,' she said, calmly covering her glass with a gloved hand.

Inclining his head, the waiter moved away, a smirk etching his face.

With each passing moment, Poppy was feeling more disillusioned. All day she had looked forward to her evening with Ezra and now she was beginning to see why he'd asked her out. He was quizzing her about Nellie and her business. He wasn't interested in her at all, just the information she could give him.

Suddenly her appetite deserted her and she pushed the food around on the plate before laying her cutlery down.

'Not hungry?' Ezra asked.

'I've had enough,' she answered.

Ezra continued to eat and Poppy glanced around the room at all the people talking and laughing. She was hurt and angry and she wanted to go home.

She watched Ezra finish his food, dab his mouth with a

napkin, then sip his wine. Flipping a fob watch from his waistcoat pocket he checked the time.

'We should be going soon otherwise we'll miss the first performances at the theatre,' he said. Raising a hand, he snapped his fingers.

The waiter moved forward in response.

'The bill,' Ezra ordered.

'Certainly, sir,' the waiter said and hurried away.

The Maître d' attended to the matter while the waiter helped Poppy from her chair. She jerked her head round as she felt something pushed into her hand. It was a small piece of paper.

Glancing at the paper she glimpsed the words *Bellyache for him tomorrow!* and hurriedly pushed it into her glove as she pulled it higher up her arm, desperately trying to hold back her mirth. Clearly disgruntled by the way Ezra was treating her, they had somehow arranged to have his food tainted with something to give him an upset tummy.

Adjusting her other glove, she looked up at the waiter standing by the door. Grabbing the seat of his trousers he pretended to run. Covering her mouth daintily with her hand, Poppy stifled a laugh.

Walking towards the pair who had given her a smile or two she stopped. 'Thank you, gentlemen,' she said with a huge grin. Then she turned to Ezra and waited.

'What? Oh yes, of course,' he mumbled as he drew some coins from his pocket to tip the waiting staff.

'I think I'd like to return home now, Ezra, I have a blinding headache,' she said.

'As you wish, my dear,' he answered. The evening had not gone as planned, but it would be better next time, he thought. It might be that on the next occasion, Poppy would answer his questions, in which case he would take her to see his home and show her how and where she could be living, albeit temporarily, if she played her cards right.

Outside, Noah saw them leave the hotel. They climbed into a cab and set off. Noah banged his feet twice and felt the carriage lurch into motion.

When they stopped again he was surprised to find they were back at The Crown. Seeing Poppy go inside, Noah watched to ensure Ezra left, then thanking his cabbie, he too went indoors.

25

Friday morning rolled around and Jack was excited. It was Dolly's birthday; today she turned fourteen. He sat at the kitchen table impatiently, waiting for his friend to rise from her bed.

'Anybody would think it's your birthday the way you're bouncing around,' Nancy said with a humorous smile.

'I wish she'd hurry up, I'm dying to see her face when I give her this,' Jack said as he tapped the books he'd wrapped in brown paper begged from the butcher in the market.

'She'll love them, lad, don't you worry, now for God's sake sit still, you look like you've got St Vitus' dance!' Nancy responded. 'I'll be able to make a start on her cake once you lot are out the way.'

Jack nodded, then his eyes returned to the doorway.

'A watched kettle...' Nancy began but at that moment Dolly entered the kitchen.

Grabbing the package, Jack jumped to his feet and rushed around the table. 'Happy birthday, Dolly!' he said as he thrust the parcel into her hands.

'Thank you!' Dolly breathed, overjoyed Jack had remembered.

One by one the others wished her many happy returns as she sat to open her gift. 'Oh Jack! Thank you, these are beautiful!' Dolly stroked the atlas and the books containing stories of myths and legends.

'I'm glad you like them, I picked 'em special like,' the boy said with a blush.

'Just what I would have chosen for myself. I love them!' Dolly replied.

Nellie passed a box across the table. 'This is from all of us,' she said.

Dolly was aghast as she lifted the red coat from its resting place. 'Oh my! Oh... it's... Nellie – everyone, thank you!' Dolly stood and slipped the coat on to show how well it fitted.

'There's this an' all,' Nancy said, sliding the round box towards her.

'Nancy – a hat! I've never had a hat such as this before! Thank you so much!' Dolly fitted the hat before giving a twirl, enjoying the attention as everyone applauded.

'Right, breakfast,' Nancy stepped to the range to begin what she considered to be the best meal of the day.

The Dempsters produced a large bag of boiled sweets as their gift and Poppy gave her ribbons for her hair. Then Fred presented Dolly with a little box.

'I know it ain't yer mum's but I thought you might like it.'

Dolly's eyes filled with tears as she took out the gold chain with its tiny locket. 'I'll treasure it forever,' she whispered and instantly fastened it about her neck. 'I'll just put these in my room...' Whirling around, she snatched the books from the table and limped from the kitchen.

Fred looked at Nellie, questions written all over his face.

'She's a bit overcome, lovey, give her a few minutes and she'll be down again.'

Fred nodded, satisfied with Nellie's explanation.

A good breakfast was enjoyed by all before work began. Poppy started cleaning the bar, and Nellie took the time to quietly quiz Noah about the goings-on of the evening before. She was relieved to learn nothing untoward had taken place between Poppy and Ezra Morton.

'Jack, Dolly – get yourselves wrapped up warm and go spend some time in the park. Come back at dinner time mind.' Nellie clapped her hands twice and ushered them out from under her feet. She smiled at the whoop of glee from the children as Jack raced off with Dolly limping behind.

Fred went to work in the cellar and the Dempsters retired to their beds, leaving Nellie and Nancy to converse over more tea.

Two minutes later, Jack and Dolly appeared with hats and coats on ready for their jaunt.

'Here,' Nellie said handing Jack some money, 'for a treat each.'

'Ta, Mum,' he said and with a grin he tipped Dolly's hat over her eyes and took to his heels.

'Hey!' Dolly yelled as she chased after him.

The two women laughed at the youngsters' antics and settled down to hot tea and a good chinwag.

'What did Noah say then?' Nancy asked once they were alone.

Nellie updated her friend before adding, 'I hope it's the first and last time she sees that bugger, Nance.'

'Me an' all,' Nancy agreed, then with a sigh she pushed herself to her feet. 'This birthday cake won't make itself. Here, Nell, have you noticed how we've been concreting with each other lately?'

'Don't you mean concurring?' Nellie asked, trying not to laugh.

'What's that mean?' Nancy asked, her back to Nellie.

'Agreeing.'

'Ar, that,' Nancy muttered.

'Yes, strange ain't it?' Nellie pursed her lips to prevent herself from laughing out loud.

Then, getting to her feet she went to the bar to help Poppy with the cleaning and restocking the shelves.

'So how went your evening out?' she asked tentatively.

'Well, it's something I won't be doing again,' Poppy bristled.

'Oh, why's that, then?'

Poppy stopped sweeping the floor and turned to walk to where Nellie was polishing the counter. 'It wasn't how I'd imagined it would be. He treated me like I was one of his men, Nellie. Like I was a dolt!' Poppy said on a dry sob.

Nellie rounded the bar and wrapped her arms around the girl. 'We tried to warn you but we knew you had to discover it for yourself.'

'Thanks, Nellie. How do you find a good man in this town?' Poppy's little laugh was empty.

'I don't know, I never managed it myself,' Nellie smiled.

'But you were married...' Poppy began.

'No, I've never wed,' Nellie's voice held a sadness. 'I found Jack on the doorstep as you already know, and when Nance and I decided to raise him it seemed a better idea for me to pretend to already be a married woman. Fewer questions that way.'

'I'm sorry, Nellie,' Poppy replied.

'What for?'

'For your never having married, for me not listening to

you in the first place,' Poppy's eyes glistened with tears as she spoke.

'Look, lovey, we're a family here and that means we don't always do the right thing. We care about each other so we poke our noses into other's business. I love you like a daughter so naturally I worry about you, especially when it comes to folk like Ezra Morton.' Nellie sniffed away her own tears.

'I love you too, Nellie, and I promise to take heed in the future.' Poppy gave the woman a squeeze before letting go.

'Right, now as it's Dolly's birthday we must keep a happy face on, agreed?'

Poppy nodded.

'I've sent the kids to the park for the morning. They'll be back at dinner time and Nancy's baking a cake for the little lass,' Nellie said with a smile.

'We'd better get on then,' Poppy said, picking up her besom once more.

'That's my girl,' Nellie grinned. 'Oh, and about finding a fella – why not look a little closer to home.'

Poppy frowned and Nellie laughed loudly. 'The Dempsters,' she said, 'the problem there is which one to choose.'

As she saw the penny drop, Nellie roared with laughter at Poppy's naivety.

Whilst Poppy was pouring her heart out to Nellie, Jack and Dolly strolled down the street towards Park Street Gardens chatting happily. There was a chill in the air but both were glad to be out of the fug of the bar, if only for a few hours.

Hearing the call 'any old rags' they stepped to the side allowing the tatter's horse and cart to pass by. Dolly wrinkled her nose as the horse left a deposit on the tramway, then her eyes widened in disbelief as a woman with a bucket ran to the spot. Scooping up the manure with her bare hands she plopped it into the bucket. Dragging her dirty hands down a filthy apron, the woman scuttled away with her prize.

'I hope she washes before she eats,' Dolly said with a grimace.

Jack grinned his agreement and they moved on. 'She'll sell that to an allotment owner,' he said by way of explanation.

As they passed St Bartholomew's Church, Dolly stopped and peeped through the trees. 'My mum's in there,' she said as a tear formed.

'Shall we go and say hello to her?' Jack asked tenderly.

Dolly nodded and they entered the churchyard silently. Jack followed along as Dolly found the right plot. There was a small headstone in the form of a cross to mark the place where Avril Micklewhite lay. Dolly gazed down at the spot and her tears flowed down her face and dropped off her chin.

Jack felt her pain and slipped her hand into his while Dolly's eyes remained glued to the cross, although she squeezed his fingers in recognition of his thoughtfulness.

'Hello, Mrs Micklewhite, it's nice to meet you.' Jack spoke in hushed tones, showing respect for all those laid in the holy ground.

Dolly caught her breath for his words had taken her by surprise.

Jack pulled a handkerchief from his back pocket and passed it to Dolly. 'My name is Jack and I'm Dolly's friend. We thought we'd drop by for a visit as it's your girl's birthday.'

Dolly sniffed and smiled. 'Hello, Mum,' she whispered. The two chatted away to the burial plot like they were talking to a live person. Then saying their farewells, they left the cemetery.

'Jack, that was so nice of you,' Dolly said as they entered the Gardens.

'I'm a nice bloke – d'aint you know?' said Jack with a grin.

Dolly gave him a push and burst out laughing before she tried to take to her heels but loped along with her uneven gait. Jack chased after her, yelling that he would get his revenge. The two made their way down the pathway revelling in their freedom as only children could.

Coming to a bench they plopped themselves down, thoroughly out of breath.

After a minute Jack said. 'We could come and visit your mum whenever we get the chance if you like.'

'I'd like that,' Dolly said before they both lapsed into silence, listening to the crows cawing in the treetops.

'Jack,' Dolly said after a while, 'can we go to the market?'

'Yes, what do you want?'

'I'd like to get some flowers for your mum, as a thank you for all she's done for me,' Dolly answered.

'She'd love that. Come on, we'll go now.' Jack pushed Dolly off the bench and she just managed to keep her footing. 'Gotcha back,' he grinned.

After a visit to the market stall they headed home, a large bunch of flowers in Dolly's arm, her cane in her other hand supporting her.

Nellie was in the kitchen with Nancy, both enjoying yet another cup of tea when the children arrived. The aroma of baking cake filled the room making everyone's mouth water.

'Hey up, you two,' Nancy called out.

'Nellie, these are for you – from both of us,' Dolly said as she glanced at Jack. Passing the bouquet to Nellie she went on, 'It's to say thank you for everything.'

Nellie took the flowers, a look of astonishment on her face. 'Oh, Dolly, I ain't never had flowers before. Thank you.

Oh, Nance… look!' Burying her face in the blooms, Nellie sobbed with delight.

Nancy dashed away a tear as she searched the kitchen for a vessel large enough to hold the flowers. Finding an old jug, she filled it with water and stood it on the table.

Nellie painstakingly arranged each stem carefully in the jug, and at last she stared at the blaze of colour. Dragging her eyes away from her beautiful gift she opened her arms, calling the children to her. As Dolly and Jack came to her, Nellie folded them in a loving embrace.

'You're the best children a woman could ever wish for, ain't that right, Nance?'

Nancy nodded, not trusting herself to speak, then moved to join the little group to enjoy a hug too.

Fred had watched the scene from the doorway. Silently he stole away back to the gloom of the cellar where he could let go of his own emotions in private. He felt lucky to be part of this wonderful family, and silently he thanked the Lord for his good fortune.

* * *

Over in Drury Lane, not far from his brewery site, Ezra had not had a restful night. He had groaned throughout the long dark hours, his stomach threatening revolt. Whatever he had eaten it was having a profound effect on his health and this morning proved no easier as he dashed to the privy. Queasiness rolled over him causing him to sweat, and eventually he returned to his bed feeling thoroughly miserable. He determined he would be having words with that hotel – once he began to feel better.

26

Two days later, Elizabeth again followed Arthur discreetly as he left her mother's house in Bishop Street. Feeling the first spots of cold rain, she opened her umbrella and tilted it slightly to hide her face. The sky began to darken and the raindrops pattered on the cobblestones. In the far distance a faint rumble of thunder heralded the forthcoming storm. Elizabeth ignored the inclement weather and pushed on through the streets after the man she knew as Gabriel Short. Where was he going now? Would he be returning home – maybe to a wife?

The town was busy with people hurrying to avoid the downpour, grumbling as they went. Elizabeth was jostled as she wove her way down one road and along the tramway. Turning into a side street, she halted at the corner then took a few steps, fearing she might lose sight of him. She stopped abruptly as she saw Gabriel knock on the door of a property a little way ahead. She watched as an older lady welcomed him and he kissed her cheek as he stepped inside.

I have you now! Elizabeth thought as she crossed over

and, shaking the water from her umbrella, she entered a shop. Her mind was in turmoil as she slowly browsed the nick-nacks. Who was the woman who had welcomed Gabriel so warmly? Could it be the man had a sister? Or was he canoodling with another woman? What was he up to? Was it all to do with money as she believed it to be?

Keeping an eye on the building through the window, Elizabeth inspected every item on the tables, chairs and in the cabinets. She had no idea how long Gabriel might be in that house, or if he would emerge at all.

Feeling the saleswoman's eyes on her, Elizabeth gushed, 'So many pretty things to choose from!'

The woman nodded and smiled as her eyes followed the customer around her shop.

Knowing she would have to buy something to avert suspicion, Elizabeth picked up a small bowl garishly painted with bright colours. 'Oh, how lovely – I'll take it,' she said, passing it over to be wrapped. Then she continued to scan more objects.

Over the next half an hour Elizabeth bought a basket and filled it with bric-a-brac, all of which would be confined to the midden on her return home. She was paying for her purchases, thinking it was time to leave, when she caught a glimpse of movement through the window. Gabriel Short was on the move again.

Waiting to be given her change, Elizabeth watched Gabriel pocket what she surmised was money before he stole a kiss, one that would most certainly not be given to a sister.

Thanking the saleswoman, Elizabeth picked up her basket and left the shop, again opening her umbrella for shelter from the rain as well as from being seen.

Right, Mr Short, where to next?

Eventually Elizabeth saw the man she'd followed most

of the day enter a small house in Rea Terrace. So that's where you live is it?! Instinctively Elizabeth knew this was the home of Gabriel. A two up, two down property in an area badly in need of renovation. Cold and soaking wet, Elizabeth trundled away in search of a cabbie looking for a fare.

With her umbrella down now against the rising wind, Elizabeth heard the voice before she saw the person.

'Watch where you'm going with that bloody thing!'

Moving the rain protector to the side Elizabeth saw the woman who spoke. 'I'm so very sorry,' she said.

'Ar well, this bleedin' weather is making everybody run for cover,' the woman returned.

With a glance at the basket Elizabeth said, 'I was about to dispose of these little things and I didn't see you.' She manoeuvred the umbrella to shield them both.

'Oh, don't you want 'em then?' the woman asked, peering into the carrier.

'No. Would you like them? I don't want anything for them,' Elizabeth said, hoping the woman would take her up on the offer just so she could be rid of them.

'Ooh, ta! That's nice of yer.' The woman grabbed the basket held out to her. 'Thanks very much,' she said as she hurried away in case the benefactor changed her mind.

Elizabeth smiled and turned to go on her way. At the end of the street she looked around for a cab and sure enough one came towards her.

'Cab, missus?' the driver called out.

'Yes, please,' Elizabeth said. Not waiting for the driver to jump down and open the door for her, she scrambled inside herself.

Calling out the address of her destination she settled down, her mind dwelling on Mr Short and his dubious visit.

Early the following morning, Elizabeth called on her mother yet again.

Sylvia couldn't help but wonder why her daughter had arrived at such an early hour as she made tea for them both.

Sat in the parlour now it was Sylvia who spoke first. 'Whatever it is, it must be important for you to be here at this time in the morning.'

'It is, Mother. I've been doing some investigating and on two occasions now, I have followed Gabriel Short and—'

'You did what?!' Sylvia was shocked by the revelation.

'Calm down, Mother, please, and listen to what I have to say,' Elizabeth said. 'He's a thief and a liar. I watched him steal from people in the market, Mother. I saw him visit another woman who he kissed as they stood on the doorstep. Before you say anything – it was not a kiss one would give a relative. I'm sorry, Mother, really I am.'

'I bet you are! I imagine you gloated, thinking me a silly old woman!' Sylvia was furious, both with her daughter for meddling and herself for falling for Gabriel's charms.

'Mother! How could you think such a thing? I was only trying to protect you.'

'I see, but what have you gained by all this cloak and dagger behaviour? Nothing! Save hurting me, that is.'

'I never meant for you to be hurt, besides it's *that man* who has caused all this,' Elizabeth said, feeling dreadful.

'Are you quite sure about what you've told me?' Sylvia asked.

'Yes, I'm sorry to say I am,' Elizabeth answered quietly.

Mother and daughter stared at each other, then at length Sylvia dropped her chin onto her chest and nodded. 'I am too. I'm afraid I rather fell for Gabriel like a silly schoolgirl.'

'He was very charming to you, but he disliked me from the off. He knew I could see right through him and that made him wary of me and me wary of him,' Elizabeth said gently, not wanting to make matters any worse than they already were.

'Why though? What was his intention?' Sylvia asked, but in her heart she knew the answer.

'Money, Mother – yours to be precise.'

'Oh, Elizabeth, I feel like such a fool!' Sylvia said on a sob.

'Mother, you clearly are not the only one to be taken in by his lies; the lady he visited is another. My question is, are there any more?' Elizabeth watched as Sylvia's eyes filled with tears.

'Whatever shall I do?' Sylvia sniffed. A melange of feelings raged in her mind. She was angry with Gabriel for what he had done and was hurt by him seeing another woman whilst promising Sylvia she was the only one for him. She felt foolish for believing him over her daughter, and ashamed for treating Elizabeth so badly throughout the whole debacle.

'First of all, you mustn't let that man into the house again. If he gets wind that we're on to him, goodness knows what he might do. Then I suggest you and I visit this other friend of his to see how the land lies with her.' Elizabeth waited whilst Sylvia brought her emotions under control.

'What if she is a relative or a dear friend? We could have this all wrong, Elizabeth,' Sylvia said, twisting her handkerchief in her fingers.

'I don't think we have, Mother, but either way we need to find out.'

Sylvia nodded. 'Can you remember where she lives?'

'Yes, I made a note of the address. Come on, let's go now and get it over and done with.'

With a sigh, Sylvia got to her feet. Grabbing her coat and umbrella, the two left the house.

The cabbie who had transported Elizabeth from home was waiting patiently. He helped the ladies into the carriage and tipped his hat when Elizabeth gave the address to be visited.

As the cab pulled forward Sylvia muttered, 'I hope we're doing the right thing.'

'We are, Mother, trust me,' Elizabeth said.

I may not be able to call a halt to your nefarious lifestyle, Mr Short, but I can put a spoke in your wheel regarding my mother and your other lady friend!

* * *

Arthur had had no idea he was being tailed by Elizabeth Murray when he called on Ann Bradshaw. It was a spur of the moment decision and he was pleased to have been welcomed so warmly.

A quick cup of tea, a few words of his undying love for her and Ann had handed over some much needed cash.

She had begged him to stay a while longer but he'd told her he had business to conduct. He had promised to visit again before the week was out saying he was finding it impossible to stay away from her.

He smiled as he sat at his kitchen table enjoying a leisurely breakfast. His best clothes were hanging on an airer to dry out after being caught in the deluge yesterday. It was of no importance, he hadn't planned to venture out today anyway. He banked up the fire in the living room and slouched in the easy chair watching tiny orange flames lick around the black coal nuggets. The crackling fire was mesmerising and before long he began to doze. With a full belly and the heat in the small room, he fell into a deep sleep.

But a few hours later Arthur was rudely woken by a

banging on the back door. Rubbing the sleep from his eyes he grumbled his discontent as he pushed to his feet.

'All right, all right! I'm coming – hold your bloody horses!'

Opening the door Arthur gasped at the three women stood facing him.

'Oh, bugger!' he muttered.

'Indeed!' Elizabeth Murray replied.

27

It had taken Ezra two full days to recover from his illness and return to work. Once there he summoned one of the street urchins in his employ.

The boy stood before him dressed in rags and smelling like he'd never had a wash in his life. His hair was long and matted and his hands and face were black with ingrained dirt. He was barefoot and his toenails were long and filthy. He sniffed loudly as he awaited instructions.

'Take this note to Poppy at The Crown Saloon and wait for an answer,' he said, before dismissing the lad with a wave of his hand.

A short while later he read her reply and gasped. His note had said he would collect her that evening at seven o'clock but, much to his consternation, her reply had read, 'Don't bother'. What was going on? Why had she not accepted his offer to step out with him again? He had thought she'd enjoyed their last outing and would be eager to repeat it. Obviously not, but the reason escaped him. Maybe Nellie had put a stop to it by making Poppy work and refusing the girl permission for another night off.

Screwing up the note, he pondered. Should he write another, asking her to explain herself, or should he visit her in person? He knew he would possibly not be welcomed at The Crown now, but with his henchmen around him he'd be safe enough.

Throwing the ball of paper into the fire, Ezra sat at his desk debating what to do next.

Pretty much all over Birmingham, Ezra Morton was known as a man not to be crossed. It wouldn't be long before people speculated about his relationship with Poppy, and if it ever got out that she had spurned him he would be the laughing stock of the town.

There must have been talk already about Nellie paying off her loan too, because his employees were struggling to collect monies owed. Folk were not paying up, saying they would inform the police if any bully-boy tactics were used. The townsfolk were suddenly aware that if they stood together against him, Ezra could do nothing.

What had sparked this peasant revolt? Who had initiated it? Would this come to a war between his workforce and the men of the town? If so, how would it play out? Fighting in the street perhaps, or would his money collectors be ambushed and beaten senseless?

Ezra felt the cold finger of fear crawl up his spine. The possibility of losing his position of power terrified him. Now, after all the years of hard work building up the reputation of being a man not to be trifled with, Ezra felt it slipping away.

He banged his fist on the desk in utter frustration. No matter how he looked at this, he was sure Nellie Larkin had to be at the bottom of it, and even if she wasn't – he needed someone to blame.

Ezra scowled as he gave his mind to that woman being a well-respected member of the community. She had lived in the town all her life and was loved by a great many folk. Was it because she provided their favourite tipple? No, she was admired for who she was – a woman with a backbone and a wise head on her shoulders.

Jumping out of his chair, Ezra marched from the office. 'You and you, come with me,' he said to two of his suited employees. Glancing at each other, the men trailed behind their boss as he stomped from the brewery.

'Where are we going, gaffer?' one asked.

'The Crown Saloon,' came the gruff answer.

The men's eyebrows shot up as they exchanged a surprised look.

He took a cab the short distance to the glittering gin palace, and Ezra stopped outside the front door. He scowled as his minders bumped into him.

'I have business in there so mind yourselves. I don't want any trouble unless it cannot be avoided – understand?'

'Yes, boss,' the men chorused.

Ezra nodded and turned back towards the door just as a fellow came hurtling out and landed hard on the cobbles.

Shaking his head, Ezra sighed before pushing his way through the folk packed into the bar room, his men close behind him. His eyes searched the length of the counter for Poppy but she was nowhere to be seen.

'Well now, here again, Ezra? And John and Jim Jenkins – it's been a while. You were only kids when I last saw you.' Redirecting her attention back to Ezra she asked, 'What can I do for you this time?' Nellie's voice sailed above the noise of arguing customers.

'I'm not here to see you,' he replied curtly.

'Fair enough. You come here to drink then?' Nellie asked

with a grin, all the while knowing exactly why he was visiting.

'Where's Poppy?' he asked, ignoring her taunt.

'She ain't here,' Nellie said, her hands resting on her hips.

'Where's she gone?' Ezra pushed.

'It ain't none of your business.' Nellie then banged her booted foot twice on the floor.

Ezra frowned wondering why she was stomping the floor-boards. A moment later he was rewarded with an answer as Frederick Dell appeared from the cellar.

'Look, Nellie, I'm not here to cause a ruckus, I just want to speak to Poppy.' Ezra nodded towards Fred as he spoke.

'She don't want to talk to you, Mr Morton,' Fred said respectfully.

'Now, Fred, this has nothing to do with you so why don't you go back to your work?'

'Sorry, Mr Morton, Nellie's my boss now which means you can't tell me what to do.' The big man stood his ground and then he noticed Ezra's companions. 'Hey up, fellas, nice to see you!'

The two grinned and nodded at Fred who had been their friend when they all worked together.

Ezra turned to look at his men and saw their smiles quickly disappear. 'This isn't a bloody works outing – you're supposed to be working!' he snapped.

'You said—' John began but at a look that could burn him to a crisp, the man clamped his mouth shut.

'Having trouble with your staff, Ezra?' Nellie asked before her booming laughter caused everyone to take note of the confrontation.

The noise in the bar turned to some low voices asking what was going on and others saying they didn't know.

Aware of the sudden quiet, Ezra kept his eyes on Nellie. In

his peripheral vision, he saw Jack drag Dolly up the bar towards his mother. Then two young men appeared from the back room. These would be the brothers he'd been told about if he was not mistaken.

'Everything all right, Nellie?' Noah asked.

Nellie nodded as the room now held an eerie silence.

'Mr Morton has come to visit Poppy but as you know she don't want to see him.' Nellie saw Ezra clamp his jaws together in frustration as she spoke.

'You've made your point, Nellie,' Ezra said through clenched teeth.

'Not quite, Ezra. You see this here is a gin palace, so if you ain't drinking then maybe you should leave.' Nellie tilted her head towards the door. Fred and the Dempsters stepped forward in a show of unity.

'You've not heard the last of this!' Ezra ground out and as he spun on his heel he knocked into his bodyguards. 'Get out of my way!' he yelled, pushing them aside.

'Hey!' Nellie called out and Ezra stopped. 'If you two blokes fancy a change of employment, I could do with some help.'

The two men grinned but Ezra scowled as he dragged them from the place.

'Think they'll come to work for you Nellie?' Fred asked.

'I've a feeling they might,' she answered with a smile.

Poppy, in the meantime, had been kept in the kitchen by Nancy. They had heard the raised voices and therefore knew exactly who was out in the bar and why.

Now the room was back to its usual noise level with shouting and singing as more gin was consumed rapidly. Some were discussing the conversation between Nellie and Ezra, delighting in the prospect of passing on the gossip once they left The Crown.

'Oh, Nancy, I knew this would happen. I should never have gone out with Ezra in the first place!' Poppy wailed.

'No, you shouldn't. That Ezra bloody Morton! He's a *swine!* We tried to warn you against it but you wouldn't listen,' Nancy replied sharply.

'Don't be too hard on her, Nancy, she has to learn, same as we all do,' Fred said quietly as he walked into the kitchen.

Nancy nodded. 'Ar well, what you need is a nice young man to be walking out with then...'

'Like me!' Noah laughed as he pushed his head around the door.

'Or me!' Matthew said, jostling his brother out of the way.

Poppy couldn't help but smile at their antics.

Fred sat down at the table next to Poppy and took her hands in his. 'You don't have to be afraid, cos me and Noah and Matt will look out for you.'

'I know, Fred, and I thank you, but I feel like I'm in gaol! I daren't go out in case I bump into him and I can't live my life cooped up in this place!'

'I understand. That's why when you do go out, one of us will come with you.' Fred said with a comforting smile.

'Fred, you can't babysit me forever!' Poppy retorted.

'True and one day we won't have to. There will be a time when your own young man will protect you, but until then – we are your bodyguards,' Fred answered with a quiet force-fulness.

'That said, you lot bugger off out of my kitchen cos I've work to do!' Nancy put in, her grin belying the sharpness of her words.

It was then that Nellie came through followed by Jack and Dolly. Nancy rolled her eyes. *Now what?*

'I've shut up shop for an hour,' Nellie said, 'we need a meeting.'

Nancy sighed as she set the kettle to boil, at this rate she'd never get their lunch prepared.

When all were sat at the table with tea mashing in the huge brown pot, Nellie eyed her family.

'Right. Something has to be done about Ezra Morton – and soon!'

28

'Are you going to invite us in?' Elizabeth Murray asked, seeing the colour drain from the face of the man calling himself Gabriel Short.

'I—'

'We can always discuss our business out here on the doorstep if you prefer,' Elizabeth said before he could answer.

Standing aside, Arthur in his guise as Gabriel, held the door open and the three women stepped into the untidy kitchen.

Arthur was thinking rapidly, questions rolling through his mind one after another. How did they find him? Were they all friends? Did they know what he was up to? What did they want with him? Should he come clean and admit to his shortcomings? Would they call in the constabulary and have him arrested?

'Now then, Mr Short, if that is indeed your real name, I think you have some explaining to do!' Elizabeth snapped.

'I'm sure I don't know what you mean,' he answered

tentatively. Arthur knew if he was to come out of this unscathed, he had to play the innocent. His best bet was to turn this around and lay it all at the feet of the interfering Elizabeth Murray.

'Come now, we are all aware of what you've been up to,' Elizabeth responded with a look that would sour milk.

'Mrs Murray, if you would care to explain what it is you think I've done—'

'Mr Short! Don't play games with me, sir!' Elizabeth's temper exploded. 'You have courted these two ladies at the same time. You have taken goods and money from both—'

'Gifts, Mrs Murray,' Arthur cut in.

'You cajoled Mrs Bradshaw and my mother into giving you those gifts, sir, with – in my opinion – a view to getting your hands on their businesses and fortunes!' Elizabeth was beside herself with anger as she saw he planned to wriggle out of the situation he found himself in.

'In your opinion,' Arthur repeated, his confidence beginning to grow. 'However, that opinion is quite wrong.'

'Gabriel, you said you loved me,' Ann Bradshaw said, her eyes misting over.

'And you said the same to me too,' Sylvia added.

'And I do, I love you – both of you.'

'Oh, for God's sake!' Elizabeth's voice rasped like a glede under a door.

'Mrs Murray, it is possible for a man to be in love with two women at the same time.' Arthur was playing for time in the hope the women would tire and leave his home.

'You are a charlatan, Mr Short, and I for one do not believe a word of it!' Elizabeth spat.

'That is your prerogative, madam. Now, what passes between myself and these fine ladies is none of your concern so I'll thank you to leave my property before I fetch a constable.' Arthur was on the attack now and saw the change in Elizabeth's demeanour.

'I saw you in the market, Mr Short. I watched you steal from those poor people,' Elizabeth countered.

'You are mistaken, madam. I have not been to the market for some months.'

'I most certainly am not mistaken! I saw you with my own two eyes!' Elizabeth felt him getting the better of her and she knew it was her word against his.

'Mrs Murray, I say again you have mistaken me for someone else. Now if you have quite finished invading my home and privacy, I would ask you to please leave – NOW!'

Elizabeth took a step backwards at the outburst she clearly had not expected.

'Pigsty more like! Come, ladies, I don't think we will get any further with this lying cheat. I warn you though, Mr Short, if I find you anywhere near my mother again, I will see you in gaol for the rest of your days!' Elizabeth cupped the elbows of Ann and her mother and marched them away from the house.

Arthur closed the door and slumped down on a kitchen chair, sweat pouring down his face. That was a close shave and now because of that damned woman he would have to find yet another wealthy widow to court. Picking up a dirty cup from the table he threw it against the wall in a temper.

* * *

Whilst Arthur was facing his accusers, Ezra and his men had returned to the brewery works. At his desk once more he fumed with disgust at Nellie's treatment of him in the bar. Something would have to be done about that woman and her gin palace. Rubbing his top lip with a forefinger, Ezra breathed heavily. He could burn the place down with them all inside – but no, Poppy lived there too. If he was to take such a drastic measure he would have to entice her out first and there was no chance of that now she was surrounded by her minders. Besides, he had set his sights on finding a way to acquire The Crown for himself.

With a huge sigh his hand left his face and landed on his desk with a thud. Tapping his fingers, his brain wound spirals trying to find a solution to the problem of Nellie Larkin.

She had embarrassed him yet again in front of his men as well as the dregs of society who frequented the place. Nellie showed him no respect and he could not let that pass. The woman must be made to understand that he – the great Ezra Morton – still ran this town.

Although unsure how he would achieve this as yet, he was certain he would eventually bring Nellie to heel.

Meanwhile, the two men who had accompanied Ezra to The Crown were now off duty and on their way home. John and Jim Jenkins were the sons of Joan and Joshua. They had a sister called Juliet and another by the name of Janice. Jonah and Jocelyn were the young twins. The family had been the laughing stock of the street because of the names the mother had chosen until the eldest boys had begun to work for Ezra. Only then did the gossip and teasing cease.

'I'm fed up with being treated like dirt,' John said as they strolled along the street.

'Me an' all. Bloody Ezra, he won't stop 'til he gets that wench in his bed,' Jim answered.

'It ain't just that though, brother, is it? I mean, all this threatening folk to pay back the money they owe,' John stated.

'It's hard enough for us, but imagine what's it's like for them as has to pay. I've no idea what it must be like to be poor enough to have to borrow money from a man like the boss,' Jim replied.

'Ar, I know, but Ezra don't give an inch. He don't give folk any leeway – remember old man Pickles?' John asked.

Jim shivered and nodded before he said, 'I think it's time to get out of all this, mate, what do you say?'

Both big lads, their suits fitted beautifully on their muscular bodies. With their dark hair and swarthy skin, they could have been taken for gypsies had they been dressed differently.

'I wonder what work Nellie was talking about when she called to us,' John picked up again.

Jim shook his head. 'I dunno, but I tell you what, it might be better than putting up with Ezra.'

'Money won't be as good,' John said.

'Peace of mind would be better and mum would be happier an' all,' Jim answered.

'What do you reckon then?' John asked.

'We can always ask. If we don't fancy it, we can say no thanks and not be any worse off.' Jim shrugged his shoulders.

'As long as Ezra don't find out,' John said out of the side of his mouth.

'He'll have to if we go to work for Nellie,' Jim answered with a little sigh.

Veering off down Vauxhall Street, the brothers crossed Gin Barrel Lane and headed for The Crown Saloon. They thought it a good idea to strike while the iron was hot.

Inside The Crown, everyone was sitting at the kitchen table waiting to hear what Nellie had to say.

'Now then,' she began, then rolled her eyes at a bang on the front door. 'Fred, lovey, go and tell whoever it is that we'll be open in an hour. Say – we're just putting on a new gin they can try.'

Fred grinned as he left the kitchen.

'Jack, remind me to change the label on the Ladies Delight. We'll put White Satin on instead.'

'I'll do it for you now, Nellie, while we wait for Fred, then it won't be forgotten,' Dolly said as she grabbed her walking cane.

'Ta, sweetheart.' Nellie watched the young girl hobble out to the bar. In a moment she was back followed by Fred and the two men in smart suits.

Nellie squinted at them as she wondered what message Ezra was sending now – so she asked.

'What's Ezra after this time?'

'Nothing, Mrs Larkin, he don't know we're here,' Jim answered.

'You said as how you might have work for us if we quit Ezra,' John said.

Nellie nodded.

'Well, we was wondering what sort of work...' Jim began.

'And how much money?' John interrupted.

'Same work as you're doing now in a way. Bodyguard, thrower-out and helping Fred in the cellar shifting barrels. Anybody misbehaving, you chuck 'em out; any of us going anywhere – you come along. You'll earn same as Fred here and I have one spare room left at the back of the house if'n you need it. I expect Joan will be glad of two less mouths to feed if you take me up on my offer.' Nellie grinned. She'd known the Jenkins family for years and had watched John and Jim grown into fine, strapping young men.

'Would it be all right to let you know tomorrer, Mrs Larkin?' John asked respectfully.

'Certainly, lads. Talk it over between you cos I'm sure the money will be less than you're earning now. Weigh it up – will the change of job be worth the cut in wages?' Seeing them exchange a glance she added, 'Think about it then and I'll await your answer.' Nellie turned her attention to Fred who was hovering in the doorway. 'Fred, when you see 'em out, tell 'em what they'll be earning – same as you're getting.'

'Fred chatted with his old friends as he saw them off the premises and returned to the kitchen and the meeting.

'Right, let's try again, shall we?' Nellie said as everyone quietened down.

29

The following morning Nellie sat in the kitchen recalling the discussions which had taken place the previous day and had brought forth no answers. There was no way the little band could put Ezra out of business, that was for sure.

Fred answered the persistent banging on the front door and returned with John and Jim in tow once more.

'Hey up, lads, come to a decision, have you?' Nellie asked.

The young men nodded. 'We'd like to join you,' John said. When do we start?' Jim asked.

'As soon as you've told Ezra you've finished with him. It's only polite after all. Then if you want, you can move in here with us,' Nellie replied.

'Thanks, Nellie,' John said with a grin.

'Our mum says to tell you hello and thanks very much for taking us on,' Jim added.

'I bet she's glad you won't be working for that toe-rag any more,' Nancy put in.

'She is,' they chorused.

They left and chatted and laughed with Fred on the way

out. With a sigh, Nellie returned to the thoughts that were swirling in her brain before she was interrupted. Poppy was adamant she would be having nothing more to do with the man and was grateful they were all looking out for her.

The coterie had grown by two more now – the Jenkins brothers, and Nellie wondered if any more would defect. If so, how could she employ them and could she afford to do so? Certainly, she couldn't house them as all the rooms were now taken.

'Nellie, there's a public house across the street and it ain't doing much business,' Fred volunteered as if reading her thoughts.

'How do you know?' Nellie asked.

'John Jenkins just told me. It seems they went for a beer the other night and the place was empty. The landlord is proper fed up an' all.'

'Well, I haven't the money to buy it if that's what you're thinking, Fred,' Nellie answered.

Fred nodded his understanding.

'You could though, with a loan from the bank,' Dolly said quietly.

'It ain't likely they would loan me money, gel. Besides, why would I need another property?' Nellie said kindly.

'They might if you took Mr Sharpe with you,' Dolly went on.

'That solicitor fella?' Nancy asked.

'Yes. He would know the right questions to ask and the correct answers to give. It might be worth discussing it with him. Then, if any more of Ezra's men come calling, you can employ them at the new place.'

'Do you think any more will detect?' Nancy asked.

'I can't just up and buy a pub on the off-chance Ezra's men *defect*,' Nellie emphasised the word as she glanced at her friend, 'and come looking for work with me! It would be a hell of a gamble and I ain't sure the risk is worth it.' Nellie was weighing everything up in her mind as she spoke.

'It wouldn't be simply to employ Ezra's men, it would be a sound investment,' Dolly said. 'Two places – twice the takings.'

'And twice the wages,' Nellie replied.

'Yes, but offset outgoings against earnings and you'd come out on top.'

'Another question – what makes you think we could make a go of it? Fred's already said it ain't doing so well.' Nellie wanted as much information and discussion as she could get before even thinking about it.

'If it's kept as a pub, I believe it wouldn't do any better than it does now, but if it was turned into a place like this...' Dolly spread her arms, 'it would be a roaring success, I'm sure.'

'What, two gin palaces opposite each other? You must be kidding! There wouldn't be enough business to keep both running,' Nellie said but her brain was already considering the idea.

'Nell, I think Dolly could be right. You know yourself how busy it gets in here, especially in the summer. It's so packed they spill out into the road to drink that bloody awful cack!' Nancy put in.

Jack and Dolly laughed at the expression, then Nellie spoke again.

'That's true, but anyway we don't even know if the pub is for sale,' Nellie said.

'I could go and ask. You never know – for the right price it could be, especially if the landlord has had enough,' Fred put in.

With her chin in the air, Nellie ran her fingers down her

neck as she pondered. Then, after a pause, she added decisively, 'Right, what harm can it do. I'll pop along and make an appointment with Mr Sharpe, hopefully he can help.' Getting to her feet she added, 'No time like the present.'

'If you get it, what will you call it?' Nancy asked.

'Bloody typical of you, Nance, lace curtains up before the floorboards are down!' Nellie boomed but in a kindly manner.

'Maybe, but you have to give it a bloody name, don't you?' Nancy replied with a grin.

'True. I'll think on it. Noah, can you come with me to Sharpe's. Poppy, get the bar open and let's get some White Satin sold!' Nellie grabbed her shawl from the nail in the back door and they set off.

Once Nellie and Noah had gone, Nancy and Fred sat with a cup of tea, while the others were going about their work.

'I wonder if she's thinking of taking on too much,' Nancy said quietly.

'No, I'm sure Nellie can cope. Besides, she has all of us to help.' Fred laid his massive hand gently on Nancy's and saw the blush rise to her cheeks. Squeezing her fingers, he was emboldened when she returned the gesture. 'Nancy, I've taken a real shine to you,' he whispered shyly.

'I have to you an' all,' Nancy replied, feeling her heart flutter.

'Nancy, can I ask you summat?'

Nodding, Nancy flushed a deeper shade.

'How would it be if you and me got wed?' It was a clumsy proposal but it was the only way he knew to ask.

Very little had passed between the two other than the odd wink and smile but Nancy had secretly hoped Fred was feeling the same as she. Now she was sure.

'I think it would be very nice,' Nancy replied as her heart hammered in her chest.

'Right then, should I pop out to see the vicar? There'll be stuff to sort out.'

'Ar, you go and mek an appointment for us to see him to discuss the arrangements,' Nancy said with a smile.

Fred stood, then lifted Nancy to her feet. Wrapping his arms around her he was careful not to crush her. The kiss they shared was chaste and as their faces parted Nancy whispered, 'I'm gonna need to get a new frock!'

Fred's laughter boomed out. 'I'll see when the vicar is free then, shall I?'

'Yes, that would be bostin',' Nancy said on a breath.

Gently laying his lips on hers again, Fred felt exhilarated. He placed butterfly kisses on her nose and eyes before he let her go. Then, with a whoop, he was out of the back door.

Nancy smiled as she heard his happy whistle as he left the yard.

Waiting for the clock to tick around to opening time, Jack and Dolly stood behind the bar.

'How do you know about all these things, Dolly? You know, books and solicitors and that?' Jack asked.

'My mum taught me. I think she knew somehow that one day it would be useful to me. Like the necklace, she made sure it came to me legally and my step-father couldn't take it.'

'Your mum must have been a clever lady,' Jack said with a warm smile.

Dolly nodded. 'She was and I miss her.'

'I'd miss mine an' all, even though she ain't my real mum,' Jack said.

'Does it bother you that much, Jack?'

'Not now. It did to begin with, but after I thought about it a lot, I realised how lucky I was that Nellie took me in. She raised me, fed me, taught me stuff – not the things you know, o' course, but about this place and how to look after myself out there,' Jack pointed a finger towards the street.

'Life lessons – very important,' Dolly agreed.

Opening the doors, Poppy rushed back behind the counter as the hordes pushed their way inside. She glanced at Jack and Dolly briefly.

'Oi, you two, less chin-wagging and more serving!' Poppy called out.

Jack lifted his cap and scratched his scalp. 'Slave driver!'

All three laughed before settling into selling the gut-rot gin graced with a fancy label.

Across at the brewery, Ezra's mouth dropped open. 'You what?!'

'We quit,' John Jenkins said simply.

'Why?'

'Cos we've got work somewhere else,' Jim answered, looking to his brother for support.

'Don't tell me – Nellie Larkin!' Ezra boomed.

The brothers nodded.

'Christ almighty! Just get out, the pair of you!' Ezra yelled.

Turning, John and Jim fled the office, happy to be still breathing.

Ezra shook his head as he considered the situation; two more of his men gone. Nellie was recruiting his workforce a couple at a time. At this rate he would have no-one left. He felt the anger burn as an image of Nellie formed in his mind. This latest incident would be around the town in no time and his reputation as a hard man would suffer even more because of it.

* * *

A couple of hours later, John and Jim Jenkins were moving their few belongings into the room allocated to them. Matt Dempster was lending a hand and Nancy was busy preparing a meal for everyone.

'Mum sez hello, Mrs Sampson,' Jim called as he passed through the kitchen towards the stairs.

'Next time you go home for a visit, let me know and I'll give you a cake to take with you,' Nancy replied.

Nellie and Noah returned with news that Mr Sharpe would see her the following day.

Fred rushed into the kitchen filled with excitement at having set a date with the vicar for his marriage to Nancy.

'Well, I never thought to see the day, Nance! You and Fred getting wed – I'm really pleased for you both,' Nellie said as the news was shared.

'Ta, Nell, we'll both need new frocks as well as Poppy and Dolly,' Nancy replied.

'Everyone will need new outfits but I warn you now, Jack will still wear his cap!' Nellie said with a grin.

Just then the young man in question walked into the kitchen and asked, 'For what?'

Nancy explained, 'Me and Fred are getting wed,' and as Jack gave her a hug she asked, 'Would you give me away?'

'Me?' he asked as he glanced around at the faces watching him.

'Yes, lovey – you.'

'I'd be honoured,' Jack said drawing himself up to his full height. With grins all round, work resumed in The Crown.

The following morning Nellie was readying herself for her visit to Mr Sharpe. 'Right, shawl, bag... I'll be off then.'

'I think Mr Sharpe will want to see your books, Nellie, so

he's able to calculate how much you can ask the bank to lend.'

'Oh, blimey, yes. Of course!' Nellie ran to her room and returned with the ledger which she shoved into a shopping bag. 'Ta, Dolly, I would never have thought of that.'

'You want me to come as well?' Noah asked.

'No, lad, you get some sleep, I'll get a cab,' Nellie answered.

'Nell,' Nancy called as Nellie was about to leave, 'good luck.'

'Ta, Nance, fingers crossed, eh?'

Everyone began their daily chores like automatons as their thoughts were with Nellie. Each watched the clock, eager for her return.

Two hours passed before Nellie walked in through the back door with the news that Mr Sharpe was happy to act on her behalf regarding purchasing the pub should it prove to be for sale.

That night after lock-up, Nellie addressed the little congregation around the table.

'Mr Sharpe reckons the next thing to do is to find out whether The Castle could be for sale, so, Fred, that's a job for you tomorrow.'

Fred nodded, feeling honoured to be given such a very important task.

'Once that's done, I suppose we'll have to approach the bank and ask for a loan,' Nellie added.

Dolly watched quietly from the doorway, her mind on the five hundred pounds Nellie had returned to her and the money she had left over from the sale of her mother's necklace. There was nowhere near enough to buy the property of course, but it would go some way to helping out. Would Nellie accept it if she offered? It would leave her with nothing, but then she didn't need much. A roof over her head, food in her belly and a bed to sleep in was all she wanted. Dolly was sure her money would be more useful to Nellie but she would have to approach it in a way which would not offend the woman she'd come to love.

30

The weather had changed rapidly and the colours of autumn were lost as winter began to make itself known. It was early one frosty morning and Jack was out sweeping the street of the detritus left by revellers the night before.

Wrapped against the cold with two pairs of woollen socks, a jumper over his shirt topped by a jacket, Jack pulled the muffler closer about his neck. Icy fingers pinched his nose as he breathed air so cold it burned his lungs. The onset of winter had come fast and threatened to be a hard one.

Looking at the window of The Crown Saloon, Jack saw white lacy patterns slowly creeping up the glass. His eyes travelled up to the guttering and caught sight of clear stalactites of ice hanging there.

He gave a shiver and continued sweeping, his back to the road. Suddenly there was a shout as a horse slipped on a patch of black ice. A woman watched in horror as the cart it was pulling skidded sideways before taking Jack clean off his feet.

The boy flew through the air to land with a sickening

thud as the iron rimmed cart wheels slid to a halt. A woman screamed and the carter jumped from his seat to run to the child who lay unmoving.

Nellie rushed outside to find out what all the noise was about. Seeing the carter bent over a figure lying on the freezing ground, she quickly moved to offer assistance.

But, seeing it was her boy lying prone, Nellie let out a low groan which rose to a high pitched keening as she knelt down beside the child she loved with all her heart.

'It ain't my fault... I... the cart...' the man was gibbering.

'Somebody fetch the doctor!' Nellie yelled at the top of her voice, 'NOW!'

Returning her attention to Jack she called his name softly. 'Jack, son, can you hear me?'

The woman who had screamed picked up the flat cap and held it out to Nellie. Nodding her thanks Nellie held it to her chest and looked around at the crowd beginning to gather.

'A bloke's gone for the doctor,' the woman said and Nellie could only nod again as she gently pushed Jack's hair from his closed eyes.

The carter whipped off his greatcoat and draped it over Jack while another man rolled up his jacket and pushed it beneath the boy's head with care.

It seemed to take forever for the doctor to arrive and Nellie's tears fell like rain. 'Jack, oh, bab, open yer eyes for me, lad,' Nellie blubbered. 'Come on, sweetheart, wake up!'

'Doctor's here,' someone called out and the crowd parted to allow him through. He then checked Jack's pulse and felt him all over for broken bones. Lifting the boy's eyelids, he looked into his eyes then said, 'Right, let's get him indoors so I can examine him thoroughly.'

'Is he—?' Nellie began.

'No, he's not dead, so don't be fretting too much.'

The carter and the man who had rolled his coat for a pillow very gently lifted Jack and carried him inside. Careful not to jostle him they took him upstairs to his bed and left the doctor to do his work.

Meanwhile, Nellie was trying to explain to the others in the kitchen what had happened. Fred was furious and all set to beat the carter to a pulp.

'It ain't his fault, Fred, the wheels hit the ice and our Jack was in the way of it.' Nellie explained what she'd been told by onlookers.

'Fair enough.' Fred then turned to the Dempsters and said, 'Rake the ashes out of the fires and spread 'em on the road.'

Matthew and Noah jumped to it and Nancy rushed to add salt to the mixture which would help clear the ice.

So busy were they that no one noticed Dolly in the corner crying silently.

The carter sat at the table with Nellie. 'I ain't half sorry, missus, but there were nothing I could do!' His hands shook as he accepted the hot sweet tea Nancy passed to him.

Nellie nodded her understanding as she wiped her tears on the corner of her shawl. Her eyes constantly darted to the stairs door as she awaited the appearance of the doctor.

Poppy glanced around the kitchen and saw Dolly quietly sobbing. Rushing to the girl she wrapped her arms about the slim form. 'He'll be all right, you'll see,' she whispered.

Everyone stood around the kitchen in a state of shock, not knowing what to do or say.

Finally, the sound of footsteps on the stairs had all look to the doorway.

'Well, his arm is broken so I've set it, bandaged it and put a sling on. No other injuries as far as I can see but – his head took a nasty bang,' the doctor said as he placed his Gladstone bag on the table.

Nancy passed him a cup of tea and then Nellie asked, 'Will he be all right?'

'There's no knowing until he wakes up, I'm afraid. I understand it's not what you want to hear but I'll tell it straight. There could be some brain damage...'

Nellie cried out and covered her face with her hands.

'*Could* be, Mrs Larkin; then again the lad could be fine. We'll just have to wait and see. I'm sorry it's not better news. Stay with him and keep him warm and I'll call back this evening,' the doctor said picking up his bag.

Nellie paid him and Fred saw him out before returning to fold a sobbing Nancy in his arms.

Nellie sat staring into space and her adoptive family exchanged glances as Poppy tried to talk to her. Nellie did not respond, but continued to stare into the middle distance, concentrating on something no one else could see.

With everyone consumed with comforting Nellie, the Dempsters took over serving at the bar, and no one saw Dolly slip away and quietly climb the stairs.

Tiptoeing into Jack's room she dragged a chair to the bedside and sat down. Silent tears streaked down her face and dripped off her chin.

'Jack,' she whispered, 'you have to get well. You're my brother now and I need you. I love you, Jack Larkin, so come back to me.'

A little while later Nancy popped her head around the door and asked, 'How is he?'

'No change as yet,' Dolly answered.

'I brought you a cup of tea. I told Nellie you was here. I popped up quietly a little while ago and peeped in when we couldn't find you earlier. Bloody hell, it's cold in here, I'll get one of the boys to light a fire.' Taking a spare blanket from an ottoman in the corner, Nancy draped it around Dolly's shoulders.

'Thank you. How's Nellie?'

Nancy just shook her head and left the room. Moments later John Jenkins was building a fire in the grate before leaving Dolly to her silent vigil.

Watching Jack's chest rise and fall evenly, Dolly's eyes then moved to his face. His complexion was pasty and his eyes were still beneath their lids. In her mind Dolly prayed for her friend's recovery. Over and over she asked God to make him well again.

For want of something to do, Poppy and Fred joined the Dempsters in the bar while John and Jim watched from the side lines for any trouble brewing, ready to intervene if needed.

Nancy busied herself in the kitchen, keeping a close eye on the still form of her friend and she kept up a constant chatter in the hope Nellie could hear her.

'The lad will be fine, Nell, you'll see. I thought Fred was gonna paste the life outta that carter though. Poor bugger was shaken to his bones; couldn't even hold the cup of tea I gave him. It ain't surprisin' though, I bet it was quite a shock for him.'

Later, Dolly was startled when the doctor entered the room; she'd not noticed the grey daylight slipping away.

'You should get some rest, m'dear,' the doctor said as he examined Jack.

'I'm all right, but thank you for your concern,' Dolly whispered.

'Well, he's no worse so that's good news.'

'Will he wake up soon?' Dolly asked.

'I don't know, chick, and that's the truth. I'm hoping by the morning he'll be asking for his breakfast.' The doctor gave a wan smile as he lifted his bag.

'Can he hear me if I talk to him?'

'Some in the profession don't think so, but I believe he can. It's my contention that familiar voices help in circumstances such as this. It assures the patient he's not alone. Talk to him, read or sing to him – he'll hear you, I'm sure.' The doctor patted Dolly's shoulder and left the room to check on Nellie who, he had been told, hadn't moved a muscle all day.

Dolly threw more coal on the fire and turned up the gas light the doctor had lit. Returning to her seat she pulled the blanket around herself once more.

'Right, Master Larkin, in the words of your mother – open yer eyes and get yer arse out of that bed!'

31

The gin palace was closed for the night and all went to their respective beds except Nellie and Nancy. The women sat in the kitchen and every now and then a dry sob escaped Nellie's lips. Nancy was very concerned for her friend; afraid Nellie had lost her mind with grief.

'Nell, you have to understand, Jack ain't dead. He's only hurt and you sitting there like that is not bloody helping!' Nancy knew the only way to snap Nellie out of her trance-like state was to act as normal as possible, and the norm for these two was swearing and yelling at each other.

Nancy sighed heavily when she saw her words had made no difference. It was then she feared the only thing to bring her friend back would be for Jack to ask for her.

'Please, God, make that little lad well so Nellie will come back to us,' she whispered into the quiet of the kitchen. Then to Nellie she said, 'That little wench has sat with your boy all day so I'm taking her a hot drink. I won't be but a minute.'

Nancy left the kitchen and as she opened the door to Jack's room, she heard Dolly's soft voice. By the dim gas light, she was reading aloud and Nancy swallowed the lump in her throat.

'You'll need this with all that reading, sweet'eart,' she whispered.

'Thank you, Nancy. The doctor suggested I read to him, he said it would help,' Dolly said as she accepted the tea.

'Good on yer, but if you need a break, I can watch over him.'

'No, I'm fine. I'd rather stay here with Jack. Nellie...?'

Nancy shook her head. 'Ain't moved a muscle since it all happened. I'm that worried—!'

'It's the shock,' Dolly interrupted. 'It affects some people that way. Oh, Nancy – what about the bar?!'

'Poppy and Fred will open up in the morning and Matt and Noah are lending a hand,' Nancy assured her.

'Wasn't Nellie going to see the bank manager tomorrow with Mr Sharpe?' Dolly asked.

'Yes, she was going to make the landlord of that pub an offer then go to the bank afterwards. I suppose we'll have to let Mr Sharpe know what's happened and postpone everything now,' Nancy replied.

'No, I'll go with Mr Sharpe in Nellie's stead.'

'But Nell will have to sign the papers, won't she?' Nancy queried.

'Yes. I reckon Mr Sharpe will bring the papers here for Nellie to sign when she feels better. However, we could put a deposit down on the pub if Nellie agrees,' Dolly explained.

'Where are we going to get the money from for that though?' Nancy asked.

'Leave that to me,' Dolly answered with a smile. 'I know exactly what to do.'

Nancy nodded and left the room saying, 'I'll tell Nellie you're still here and reading to him.'

On into the night Dolly read Jack's favourite story of Leonidas and the 300 Spartan warriors who defended their Greek homeland against Xerxes and his Persian army. Jack had been enthralled when she had told him the tale of the battle to defend the pass at Thermopylae. He loved the courage of the warriors and their sword fighting skills.

Feeling her eyelids drooping, Dolly closed the book and placed it on the bed. 'I'm a little tired now, Jack, so I'm going to have a nap, but I'm here if you need me.' With a gentle sigh, Dolly closed her eyes and slowly her head lowered as sleep claimed her.

A murmuring in the early hours had Dolly wide awake in an instant. The fire was dying down and she felt the chill in the air. In the dim yellow glow of the gas light she saw Jack was restless.

'It's all right, Jack, you're safe now,' she said.

'Dolly...' It was barely more than a whisper, but she had heard it and her heart soared.

'I'm here, Jack,' she said as she took his hand.

'Mum...'

'I'll fetch her right away.' Dolly grabbed her cane and hobbled from the room.

'Nellie! Nellie, Jack's asking for you!' she called, walking swiftly into the kitchen.

Nellie seemed to be in a world of her own and Dolly wasn't sure she'd heard her.

'Nell...' Nancy tried. 'Dolly's been reading to your lad about them Greek warriors all bloody night!'

Dolly limped over to the woman and raised her hand. 'Look away, Nancy,' she said and brought her palm down in a resounding slap to Nellie's cheek. Nancy winced but heaved a sigh of relief when Nellie blinked and rubbed her face.

'What the bloody hell...!' Nellie cussed.

'Jack's asking for you,' Dolly repeated.

Nellie was up and gone in a flash leaving Nancy and Dolly hugging each other, tears of joy coursing down their faces.

'Mum...' Jack managed with a croak.

'I'm here. Now have a sip of water then you rest.' Nellie lifted the glass that covered the carafe and poured a small amount of cold water. Holding it to her son's lips she repeated, 'Just a sip now – enough to wet yer whistle.'

Jack swallowed then rested back on his pillow. 'Mum – what happened?'

'A bloody cart slipped on the ice and knocked you over!' Nellie thundered – but quietly.

'Oh, yes, I remember now.'

With another sip of cooling water Jack gave a little grin then winced. 'My arm aches.'

'It's broke the doctor says,' Nellie explained. 'You had a nasty bump on your head an' all. We all thought it was lights out for you.'

Jack gently shook his head and grimaced at the pain. 'Hard as nails us Larkins.'

'Ain't that the truth.' Nellie smiled and silently thanked God for his mercy.

'I'll build the fire up cos it's bloody freezing in here,' she said.

'I was dreaming about Leonidas and the 300,' Jack said wearily.

'That's the story Dolly told you last night, so Nance said,' Nellie mumbled.

Sitting by her son once more she said, 'Fred was all set to do the carter in.'

Jack grinned. 'Mum, I'm hungry.'

Nellie laughed and kissed his forehead. 'Nancy's got some chicken soup on the go, I can smell it from here. Fancy some?'

'Bostin! Mum, I love you,' Jack whispered.

'I love you too lad – more than life itself,' Nellie said tearfully.

32

Later that morning, the chain of ragamuffin boys had delivered the message to Ezra that Jack Larkin had been knocked down in the street.

Hastily donning his overcoat, Ezra left his office in the brewery and whistled for a cab. He was going to visit Nellie to ask after the lad's health although really it was also a good opportunity to see Poppy again.

Outside The Crown Saloon, Ezra instructed the cabbie to wait and he strode inside. Even at this early hour the place was filled to capacity and he thought to himself, *I'm in the wrong trade!*

'I'd like to see Nellie,' he called across the counter.

'She's busy,' Noah Dempster answered.

'Tell her I'm here!' Ezra demanded.

Noah nodded to Jim Jenkins who disappeared into the back room. A moment later he was back with Nellie in tow.

'What do you want?' she snapped.

'I've come to pay my respects and ask how Jack is. I heard

about his accident,' Ezra said as he cast a glance around for Poppy.

'Nothing gets past you, does it?' Nellie's words drew his attention back to her.

'I was sorry to hear the news.'

'I don't want your sympathy – in fact I don't want anything from you, Ezra Morton,' Nellie said loudly.

'Poppy not working today?' Ezra asked, completely ignoring Nellie's statement.

'Look, Ezra, you're not wanted here so why don't you just sling your hook!' Nellie was becoming angry; this little tête-a-tête was taking up time she should be with Jack.

'That's not very nice considering I made the effort to enquire after your boy.'

'You're being a nosy bugger, is all. Now, if you don't mind, I'm a busy woman.' Nellie turned and walked away, leaving Ezra among her laughing customers.

Ezra stomped from the premises full of thunder. *Blast that woman!* Yet again she had made him look like a fool. He supposed it served him right for going there in the first place. He was angry with himself for being such an idiot – would he never learn?!

'The brewery,' he yelled at the cabbie as he climbed back aboard the carriage and slammed the door shut behind him.

'Yes, your bloody highness!' the cabbie mumbled before clicking his tongue to the horse. *Some people have no respect for others*, he thought as the cab rolled away.

When Ezra left, Nellie returned to the kitchen and the conversation she was having with Dolly, regarding whether the pub would be for sale, before Ezra had interrupted them. Jack was sleeping peacefully so Nellie had left him to get his rest.

'I could accompany Mr Sharpe while you stay and take care of Jack,' Dolly said.

'I ain't sure, gel,' Nellie began.

'Nell, the lass knows what she's doing, let her go.' It was Nancy who spoke. Nellie nodded.

'I know that, Nance, but this is a big endeavour! What if I can't afford it?'

'Mr Sharpe has seen your accounts and he knows what you can and can't afford. He would also know roughly what the pub is worth, I would think,' Dolly said by way of assurance.

'All right, but don't agree to anything without my say-so,' Nellie relented.

'Of course I won't. Mr Sharpe will be here in a few minutes so I'd best get my coat on. When I get back, I'll read to Jack some more.'

'You're a good girl, Dolly. God bless you,' Nancy added with a smile.

It was a while later when Dolly and Mr Sharpe returned, and Nellie was eager to know the outcome of their visit. Tea and cake was served, then it was down to business.

'The bank are willing to extend a loan in the form of a mortgage facility,' Mr Sharpe said.

Nellie and Nancy exchanged an excited smile.

'What you have to decide now is how much you are willing to offer the landlord for his premises,' Mr Sharpe added. 'It's all there in my report, along with my recommendations regarding an offer to be made and repayment of the bank loan etc.'

'Ta, Mr Sharpe,' Nellie said as she took the papers being passed to her.

'Let me know what you decide and I can then act on your

further instructions. I thank you for the refreshments and I bid you all a good day.'

'Tarrar a bit,' Nancy called out as the solicitor left by way of the back door.

'We need to read this through carefully before we make a decision, don't you think?' Nellie asked.

'What's to think about? Get it bloody sorted!' Nancy said impatiently.

'Yes, I agree we should read the whole report, but I still think it would be a good investment,' Dolly replied.

'Right, let's have a look then,' Nellie said as she picked up the papers.

* * *

Across town in Rea Street and knowing nothing of what Dolly was doing, Arthur Micklewhite was thinking only of himself. That interfering Elizabeth Murray had most decidedly shoved a spoke in his wheel with regard to him getting his hands on some serious money. Now he was back where he started, with no cash and no prospects.

Arthur paced the kitchen, his anger mounting. He was reduced to stealing from the folk in the market yet again in order to live, and that would be dangerous. He had no doubt the police would be on the look-out for whoever was stealing from would-be shoppers.

His thoughts moved to Dolly and he wondered if what he'd been told by the big man at The Crown was true. Had she sold that necklace? Doubt began to creep into his mind. After all, Dolly Daydream had adored Avril and that piece of jewellery was the only link the girl had with her dead mother. Perhaps the big fellow had lied and only told him that in order to get rid of him.

He had tried to get Dolly back but she was too well protected, so where could he go from here? Arthur's next thought chilled him to the bone, but if he wanted those gems it was the only way left open to him.

Dressing in his best suit he donned his overcoat and picked up his hat. Smoothing a hand over the brim he placed it on his head and left the house. There was someone he had to see.

Whilst Arthur was getting smartened up, Ezra was working in his office in the brewery. A while later there was a rap to the door before it opened to reveal a face. 'Bloke to see you, boss.'

Ezra nodded and the door swung open, admitting a well-dressed man.

'Come in and take a seat,' Ezra said by way of welcome.

'My name is Arthur Micklewhite and I need your help.'

The two men discussed at length Arthur's predicament until Ezra said at last, 'I know the girl you speak of, but my question is – how do you intend to pay for my assistance?'

'Once the necklace is recovered and sold then I will be in a position to pay what you ask,' Arthur replied. His nerves were getting the better of him and he shuffled around in his chair.

'Mr Micklewhite – Arthur – do you take me for a fool? Let me explain. What happens if the necklace has indeed already been sold? And what if the money realised from the sale has been spent? I'm sure you understand that would put me in an awkward position as to how to claim my fee from yourself. Then, of course, you would be unable to pay. Am I correct?' Ezra's false smile flitted across his face.

'Yes, but—' Arthur began.

'Mr Micklewhite!' Ezra's retort was sharp before he

continued more calmly. 'I will need collateral – something to safeguard my investment.'

'I'm not asking for money,' Arthur said. He felt perspiration forming on his brow and a chill ran down his spine.

'I know that, but you see, I would be investing my time, my reputation and my men – who have to be paid. So, I ask again, what collateral do you have to put up against any losses I may incur?' Ezra steepled his fingers beneath his nose and waited.

It was clear the man was as poor as a church mouse despite his good clothes, which Ezra suspected were all he had. However, the train of thought uppermost in Ezra's mind was regarding that piece of jewellery. Had Arthur been clever, he would only have told Ezra he wanted his step-daughter home. Instead he had revealed all. What was there to stop Ezra getting the girl and the necklace? If it was as valuable as Arthur made out, then Ezra could have it sold in the blink of an eye, the proceeds paid into his bank account and Arthur would be none the wiser. All Ezra had to say was that the girl didn't have the gems, and if she chose to argue the point – well, young girls went missing quite often in these difficult times.

Ezra's hands moved to rest on the arms of his chair, denoting he had waited long enough for an answer.

'I... I have a small house in Rea Terrace,' Arthur said quickly.

Ezra nodded and said nothing. It was up to Arthur to offer up his dwelling, that way Ezra could not be accused of coercion.

'I'll put the house up,' Arthur said finally. He knew he had no other choice if he was to deal with this man and come out alive.

Ezra drew out a sheet of paper from the desk drawer.

Dipping a pen nib into the inkwell he scratched out a contract. Ezra would endeavour to return Dolly to her stepfather for a sum of money to be paid once they were reunited. Should Arthur fail to pay said sum, then his dwelling would be forfeited.

'If, as you say, the necklace was left to the child legally, then it would be unwise to incorporate it into our contract. I'm sure you don't wish to find yourself in gaol for theft and neither do I. Therefore, I suggest we keep that snippet of information between ourselves. Agreed?' Ezra asked.

Arthur nodded.

'You must understand I cannot kidnap the girl or force her to come home to you,' Ezra emphasised.

'But you said—' Arthur began.

'I said, and it states here, that I will do my utmost to have Dolly returned to your care. It's the best I can do for you, Mr Micklewhite, take it or leave it.'

Arthur quickly weighed up the options. He could sign the contract and hope Morton could deliver Dolly to him, or he could remain as he was with no chance of retrieving the girl or the necklace.

With a curt nod, Arthur signed the paper Ezra had slid across the desk. He watched as Ezra also signed before placing the contract in his desk drawer.

Ezra stood and extended his hand. He felt the sweat on Arthur's palm as they shook. 'Nice doing business with you, Mr Micklewhite. You will be hearing from me before too long.'

Arthur blew out his cheeks and rushed from the room.

Ezra took out a handkerchief and wiped his hand. Retrieving the contract, he nodded and smiled. It was like taking suck from a babby!

As he sat and pondered however, his thoughts soon

returned to Poppy and his mood darkened. Why was she avoiding him? Ezra had wondered about this often since their evening out and he had all but convinced himself that Nellie was at the root of it. It must have been she who had forbidden Poppy to see him again, he was certain.

With a sigh, Ezra suddenly realised that his interest in Poppy had shifted. His heart no longer beat a tattoo in his chest when he thought of her. Now, his blood boiled with anger at her treatment of him. He knew also that his men were laughing behind his back with regard to the whole debacle.

Maybe it was time to forget about Poppy and concentrate on the business of increasing his fortune. He had wondered whether he could get his hands on The Crown Saloon, but it would seem the chance of that happening had somehow slipped away. It was a shame, he would have liked that place. No matter, for now he'd be happy to take Arthur Micklewhite's house.

33

Nellie had sent word with Noah saying she agreed with Mr Sharpe's recommendations. A couple of days later, Dolly and Mr Sharpe returned from their business meetings, and she was delighted to see Jack up and about.

Nellie had refused to leave Jack until he was feeling better and so Dolly had accompanied the solicitor with Nellie's instructions.

Jack was still in some pain from his accident and his arm itched beneath its heavy bandaging. His hip ached from time to time where he'd landed hard on the cobbles, but it was improving with each passing day. It wouldn't be long before he would be back to normal which was a great relief to everyone.

Sat at the kitchen table, the solicitor began to speak. 'Miss Perkins and I made your offer to the landlord of The Castle across the road,' he tilted his head in the direction of the street. 'We also had a good look around the place, did we not, Dolly?'

Dolly nodded and Mr Sharpe continued, 'In addition to the lounge bar and public bar there is a kitchen and scullery downstairs. The lavatory block is out the back at the present time but there is sufficient space upstairs to house the WC. Also, there is living accommodation and six guest rooms.'

Nellie's eyes grew wide with surprise and she and Nancy exchanged a nod.

'Now, the place is in dire need of refurbishment. The windows are all intact but the building is damp and the plaster is crumbling in places. However, the current landlord is desperate to leave and would be willing to accept your offer.'

'Marvellous!' Nellie exclaimed. 'What did the bank say?'

'As you are aware, the bank manager is willing to loan you enough to buy and refurbish the property provided you can lay down a deposit on said building.'

'That's that then, cos I can't. I don't have enough saved, Mr Sharpe, as you well know,' Nellie said as her high spirits took a dive.

'I suspected as much from your accounts, Nellie, so Dolly came up with a suggestion.' The solicitor held out a hand, giving Dolly leave to speak.

'I still have some money left from the sale of my mother's necklace and there's the five hundred pounds you returned to me which could be used as a deposit,' she said.

'Oh, no! I ain't taking any more of your inheritance Dolly and that's final!' Nellie shook her head vigorously and folded her arms beneath her bosom.

'Dolly knew you would say that so this is what we propose. You use that money as a deposit for The Castle in exchange for Dolly having co-ownership.' Mr Sharpe paused to let the idea sink in.

'You do know she's only fourteen years old, Mr Sharpe?' Nellie asked.

The solicitor nodded.

'Nellie, many girls of my age are married,' Dolly protested.

'She's right, Nell, a lot of 'em up the spout an' all!' Nancy intervened.

The kitchen fell silent as Nellie considered the offer. She felt badly about taking the last of Dolly's money; it was left to her by her mother, after all. On the other hand, co-ownership would help them both out. Two premises – twice the takings, and more people in work.

Feeling the eyes of the others upon her, Nellie reached her decision.

'All right, I accept that but if I agree to it who's gonna run the place? I can't do both!' Nellie suddenly wondered now if this was such a good idea after all.

'I could run it,' Dolly said.

'What! You? It's business, Dolly...' Nellie was aghast at the notion.

'I know that, Nellie. I would have to hire some staff and Mr Sharpe has offered to help with the book-keeping. We would need to gut the place and dry it out before it's re-plastered and decorated. The money from the bank would cover all that – it would be on a mortgage facility which the bank manager explained to me.' Dolly was excited at the prospect of running a business and her keenness was infectious.

'It could work, Nell, if you trust her to do it,' Nancy put in as she too began to realise the potential of the old building.

'It would all be above board and legal with contracts drawn up and signed by all parties,' Mr Sharpe added.

Nellie studied the man, then asked, 'What's your opinion, Mr Sharpe?'

'I think it would be a very sound investment and you should do this with all due haste before someone else gets wind of The Castle being up for sale.'

'That someone else being Ezra Morton, you mean?' Nellie asked.

Mr Sharpe puckered his lips and nodded.

Quiet descended in the kitchen as Nellie thought hard about what she was about to undertake. Then suddenly she banged her hands on the table making everyone jump. 'Right! Let's do it!'

Applause sounded as everyone breathed a sigh of relief.

Mr Sharpe left with instructions to draw up the necessary paperwork which he, Dolly and Nellie would present to the bank as well as a contract of sale for the current landlord.

Jack and Dolly sat discussing the agreement made and Nellie joined Poppy and the Dempsters in the bar.

Old Aggie was singing and dancing as usual and Nellie grinned, feeling she'd love nothing more than to join in. She knew there was a lot of hard work ahead of them, but she was no stranger to that. Deep inside, Nellie felt the decision taken today was in everyone's best interests, and the thought warmed her heart.

She watched as John and Jim Jenkins helped a prone man to his feet and gently escorted him outside. It seemed she was destined to add to her family bit by bit and she wondered who would be next to turn up on her doorstep looking for work.

The Jenkins boys returned to the bar and saluted Nellie before taking up their stations by the wall once more.

And with that, a sudden thought took Nellie by surprise and she scuttled back to the kitchen.

'Dolly, I may just know who we could interview about working in the new place!'

* * *

The following day Mr Sharpe returned to The Crown Saloon with duly drawn-up documents ready for signatures.

'This one here – for the bank – only has my name on it,' Nellie said after reading the paper.

'That's because the bank manager would not consider lending such a large amount of money to a fourteen year old girl.' The solicitor gave Dolly an apologetic look before continuing. 'The mortgage would be in your name, Nellie, then this other agreement states that Dolly and yourself are co-owners of the property, which has nothing to do with your bank loan. Here is the contract of sale to be signed by yourself and the landlord of The Castle. I assure you it's all legal and above board, but please read everything through carefully – both of you.'

Nellie nodded and while Nancy provided tea and cake, she and Dolly did as they were bid and read every word on both documents, with Mr Sharpe explaining the legal jargon every now and then.

'Phew! I can't believe I'm doing this but – here goes!' Nellie said, then she put her signature in all the right places and Dolly quickly followed suit. Mr Sharpe and Nancy added their signatures as witnesses to the transactions. With the documents and Dolly's money securely locked in his briefcase, the solicitor set off for a visit to The Castle before he went to the bank.

Dolly and Nellie stared at each other, then they both burst out laughing.

'I hope we've done the right thing,' Nellie said eventually.

'Me too,' Dolly concurred.

But before they could celebrate, they heard a ruckus

coming from the saloon. 'Oh, bloody hell – now what?' Nellie said, her exasperated tone evident as she heard Poppy yell out for some help in the bar.

Jack was busy finishing his cake and Dolly watched him carefully. She was still checking for any ill effects from his accident. She was delighted that, other than his broken arm, there appeared to be none.

Nellie strode into the bar to see two huge men in neat dark suits standing at the counter. She sighed heavily, then plastered a smile on her face.

'Morning, gents, a little early for you ain't it?'

'Ezra would like a word,' one said.

'Would he now? Not again...' Nellie replied, her smile still in place.

'Yer!' the other man answered.

'What about?' Nellie asked, knowing full well these goons would not have been taken into Ezra's confidence.

'Dunno!' they answered in unison.

Nellie's smile grew wider as she thought, *these two ain't the sharpest – why has Ezra sent brawn instead of brain?*

'Well, gents, as you can see, I'm rather busy at the moment and so am unable to vacate my establishment at this precise time. Therefore, I suggest you return to your lord and master and relay my apologies and suggest that if he wishes to discuss certain matters with me, he perambulates the streets to my saloon.' Nellie then ran her tongue around her back teeth in order to prevent herself from laughing at their confused expressions.

'Eh?' the first spoke again.

'She says to bugger off and tell Ezra to get his arse down here if'n he wants to talk to her,' Nancy said as she wandered through with a cup of tea for Poppy.

'Oh, righto,' the man answered and turning to his mate he added, 'best go and tell the boss then.'

They left the bar to catcalls and whistles from its patrons, who then continued their singing, dancing, arguing and most importantly – their drinking.

'What was all that about?' Nancy asked.

'No idea, but I'm sure we'll find out soon enough,' Nellie answered. Turning back to her customers, she began to serve the mind-numbing liquid like the devil was chasing her.

Nellie, Poppy and the Dempster brothers were run off their feet all morning. It had been decided that as there no longer appeared to be a threat to the saloon, Noah and Matthew should help out in the bar rather than stand guard all night. Both were more than happy with the arrangement and worked like demons.

It was mid-afternoon when Ezra finally arrived, surrounded by four of his minders.

'I'd like a word in private, Nellie, if you please,' he said politely.

Nellie nodded with a feeling of self-satisfaction that he had come to her to ask a favour. Another feather in her cap.

He left the burly strongmen in the bar where they greeted the Jenkins brothers like long lost friends, and was invited by Nellie into the kitchen.

Nancy ushered Jack and Dolly upstairs and with a backward glance, quickly followed them.

'Now then, Ezra, before you begin, let me just say this. I ain't beholden to you no more so if you want a word in future, you come to me. Do not summon me like one of your lackeys.' Nellie glared at the handsome man now sat at her kitchen table.

'Understood,' Ezra replied with a small grin.

'Right, now what do you want?' Nellie asked pointedly.

Ezra began to speak and Nellie listened without interruption. When he had finished, she said quietly, 'You're a sly old bugger, Ezra Morton!'

34

Arthur Micklewhite sat in his filthy kitchen and considered his visit to Ezra Morton. He had been glad to leave with his skin intact but now he worried about whether he'd done the right thing.

It had been very risky approaching that man, but Arthur felt he'd had no other choice. If he wanted to get hold of that necklace, then Ezra was the only one who could help.

He chastised himself for offering up his house as collateral, but he had nothing else of value. Besides, it wouldn't matter once he had the proceeds from the sale of the jewellery. He would still have his property and money too – lots of it.

Arthur thought again about what the big man at the saloon had told him, that Dolly had already parted company with the gems. He didn't believe it for a second; the girl would never let go of that last link to her mother.

Rubbing his hands together, Arthur permitted himself a smile. Not long now and he'd be a toff of the first order.

His mind returned to Ezra and the contract they had both

signed. Mr Morton would return Dolly to her step-father who would then pay a sum agreed between them.

What if Ezra could not get Dolly to come home? Arthur would still have to pay for Ezra's services. It had been his intention to pay up out of the proceeds from selling the necklace, but if he didn't have it – what then?

A shiver ran down his spine as he pondered. He didn't have a penny to his name and he doubted very much that Ezra would wait for his coin. Somehow Arthur had to find the money to pay off his debt whether he got the necklace or not, and stealing from those frequenting the market would not cut the mustard. He had to gather enough to pay when Ezra came calling – but how?

His wealthy widows were of no use to him now, they had melted into the background of his life thanks to Elizabeth Murray. Arthur scowled at thought of the woman who had ruined his prospects of owning the widows' businesses. However, he had no time to dwell on that now. His immediate priority was to rectify his cash flow problem.

Arthur scratched his ear as he tried to force his brain to produce some good ideas, but nothing was forthcoming. Maybe he should sleep on it; by the morning he may well have the answer. Besides, there was no telling how long it would take Ezra to bring Dolly Daydream back to him.

Relaxing a little, Arthur felt sure he had a few days leeway at least. For now, he had no food in the larder, no coal in the grate and no money in his pocket.

'Right then, best get myself up the market,' he muttered as he donned his coat and left the house.

The weather took a turn for the worse as Arthur strode purposefully through the streets. The sky was heavy with the promise of snow and the wind whipped through his coat like a lash. Freezing rain began to hammer down and Arthur swore under his breath as the sharp droplets assaulted his face. Words from the Christmas carol sprang to mind as he trudged on. *In the bleak mid-winter.*

People scurried away like rats leaving a sinking ship, eager to be out of the awful downpour. Children splashed in the puddles beginning to form and mothers boxed their ears and dragged them home.

The tram screeched to a halt and Arthur was suddenly swamped by the alighting passengers, all pushing and shoving their way to their destinations.

Arthur cursed again as a woman elbowed him out of her way. Had he not been desperate for funds and food, he would never have ventured out. He ploughed on through the throngs of people, his chin on his chest against the howling wind and stinging rain.

Coming at last to the market, he was dismayed to see relatively few people ambling around the stalls.

'Bloody weather!' he mumbled.

'I agree with that, mate!' a woman said as she walked past him.

Slowly, Arthur patrolled the market, his eyes alert to any purse left unguarded. He walked twice round the stalls, all to no avail. There would be nothing doing today. His best bet now would be to scavenge what he could to make himself a meal of sorts.

Arthur's mood darkened as he filched foodstuff here and there; at least now he could eat. Deciding to call it a day, he set off for home. Leaving the market, he grumbled loudly as the rain turned to snow. Big fluffy flakes fell silently from the heavens and settled where they landed. In a matter of hours it would be white over and the dowdy landscape would be transformed in to a winter wonderland.

Although he knew children and their sledges would be

out having a wonderful time, Arthur just wanted to be home and in his bed with a full belly. He had a lot of thinking to do between now and when Dolly returned.

* * *

That evening when the bar was shut up for the night, Nellie called a meeting. The Jenkins brothers, Noah, Matt, Fred, Nancy, Poppy, Dolly and Jack all sat around the kitchen table waiting to hear what Nellie had to say.

'Some of you will know, but for those who don't, I'll explain. Dolly's step-father, Arthur Micklewhite, is after a necklace left to Dolly by her mother. Now what Arthur doesn't know is that Dolly sold the piece and gave me some money to pay off my debt to Ezra. Arthur has approached Ezra to return Dolly to him and promised to pay handsomely for the favour. So convinced was he that he was going to be rich, Arthur put up his house as collateral. We know Arthur is piss-pot poor...'

Jack and Dolly giggled at Nellie's expression and then with a smile of her own she went on. 'So, if Dolly is in agreement, we've hatched a plan to see Arthur Micklewhite remains that way.'

'What's the plan, Nellie? Cos I don't want our Dolly in any danger.' It was Fred's voice that filled the silence.

For the next hour, Nellie explained what they intended to do. The plan was discussed at length until the time came for Dolly to make her decision. Would she do what was being asked of her? For the longest time, Dolly considered whether she should agree or not.

Nancy busied herself making more tea, her nerves virtually frayed. The others sat quietly watching the girl trying to make up her mind.

'I'm not sure,' she said at last and everyone let out the breaths they'd been holding.

'Look, Dolly, that man is never going to leave you alone as long as he thinks you still have that jewellery. He won't believe you sold it, and even if he did – he'd want the money.' Nellie had laid a hand on Dolly's arm as she spoke.

'I understand that but Ezra—' Dolly began.

'Ezra won't touch him unless Arthur does something stupid, he promised me that,' Nellie said gently.

'But if Arthur has put up the house and he can't repay Ezra – he will be homeless!'

Nellie could see the girl was becoming agitated.

'Arthur knew what he was doing, Dolly. He knew he had no funds but he's avaricious. His greed for the necklace was all he could see.'

Dolly nodded her understanding. 'I see that but—'

'Have you forgotten what he had planned for you after your mum passed away?' Nancy intervened. 'He would have abused you then slung you out on the street, that jewellery safely in his pocket!'

'Nance!' Nellie retorted.

'What? It's the truth, ain't it? Don't treat her like a child, Nell, she's almost grown up now!' Nancy fired back.

'I can't argue with that,' Nellie relented.

'Please don't argue over me. I understand the implications and I've made up my mind – I'll do it!' Dolly said with conviction.

'Good. I'll contact Ezra tomorrow,' Nellie said, indicating that the meeting was at an end.

* * *

Whilst the discussions between Nellie and Ezra had been

taking place at The Crown Saloon, Elizabeth Murray – unbeknown to anyone else – was visiting the police station. She was there to report Gabriel Short for thieving in the market. His designs on her mother and Ann Bradshaw could not be brought to account as he had broken no law in that regard, but she would see him punished for robbery.

'How did you come to know this...' the desk sergeant glanced at his notes, 'Gabriel Short?'

'He was calling on my mother, Sylvia Chilton, with a view to getting his hands on her money – in my opinion.' Elizabeth answered calmly.

'I see, and you followed him to the market where you saw him stealing purses and wallets?'

'Yes, Sergeant. Then I tracked him to his home in Rea Terrace.'

'Then what did you do?' the sergeant asked, eyeing the woman who thought herself a sleuth.

'I went home, sir,' Elizabeth said politely.

'Why did you not come to us sooner?' the sergeant asked.

'I wanted to discuss it with my husband as I feared I might not be believed – being a woman, you understand,' Elizabeth played her helpless female card.

'Hmm. There have been a spate of thefts in the market place, so maybe this Mr Short is the man responsible,' the sergeant mused.

'Are you going to arrest him?' Elizabeth asked.

'We would need to interview him before any arrest can be made. Thank you, Mrs Murray, rest assured I'll be despatching a constable right away.'

Elizabeth nodded and left the police station with a feeling she had been dismissed like a naughty child.

Walking carefully on the icy ground, she made her way home, wondering whether Gabriel Short would indeed be taken into custody. She knew it was his word against hers and there was no evidence to show him to be guilty of the crime for which he was accused.

On the other hand, she could not stand by and allow him to get away with stealing from those who could ill afford to lose the little they had. He had not managed to steal from her mother, for which she was grateful, but that's not to say he wouldn't have had he been given the chance.

Stepping into the road, Elizabeth heard the thin ice on a puddle crack beneath her boot, and she quickly lifted the hem of her skirt to prevent it getting wet. Crossing the street, she kept a keen eye out for passing traffic having heard about a young boy who had been knocked down by a wayward cart.

She wondered if the police would bother to inform her should they apprehend Gabriel Short; somehow, she doubted it. One thing was certain though, if he wasn't caught by the constabulary, then she would definitely be paying that despicable man another visit.

35

It was mid-morning the following day when the young constable knocked on the front door of number twenty-seven, Rea Terrace. He had been instructed to interview the man living there – Mr Gabriel Short.

The door opened a crack and a pair of sleepy eyes peered out.

'Good morning, sir, I'm looking for Gabriel Short, would you be him?' the constable asked.

'No, officer, I'm Arthur Micklewhite,' came the answer.

'Does Mr Short live here, sir?'

'No. There's only me. I don't know anyone of that name, sorry.' Arthur had begun to sweat despite the freezing temperature.

'I see. Are you all right, sir? You don't look too well,' the policeman said as he took a step backwards.

Arthur forced a hacking cough and muttered. 'I have the influenza.'

The officer stepped back again and said hurriedly, 'Well, thank you for your time.' Then he marched away briskly.

Arthur grinned as he closed the door against the ice-cold draught. Lighting the range, he shivered, then pulled on his jacket which had been draped over a kitchen chair. Shaking the kettle to satisfy himself it held enough water, he slammed it on the range to boil for tea.

Dropping onto a chair, his mind was racing. So, the coppers were on the look-out for Gabriel. The only way they could have traced him here was if they had been told, and Arthur knew exactly who had informed on him. Elizabeth Murray. Now the question before him was – should he stay put or flee to safety? If he ran then Ezra wouldn't be able to find him, which meant he'd never own that necklace and he'd be out of pocket. He would still owe Ezra and he was sure the man would move heaven and earth to get his money. There would be nowhere he could hide from Ezra's men for he felt sure a man of such prominence would have contacts spread far and wide. That being said, if he did run, the police wouldn't feel his collar either for he guessed Elizabeth would be more than happy to lead them to his door once more. The other side of the coin was to remain where he was and risk another visit from the constabulary. He could hide; pretend he was out, but would they leave it at that? He doubted it. The coppers were like bloodhounds, they wouldn't give up until they had their man.

Caught on the horns of the dilemma, Arthur racked his brains for a solution.

'Bloody women!' he mumbled as he made himself a cup of tea with the last of the leaves. He took a gulp and grimaced; weak tea with no milk or sugar was not to his taste at all. Banging the cup on the table he ignored the dirty grey liquid that slopped over its rim.

What to do? He sighed explosively as he got to his feet.

Whilst he still lived in this house, he had to watch out for anyone coming down the path. The last thing he needed was to be caught on the hop.

Donning his overcoat, Arthur set out yet again, this time for the railway station where there were always good pickings to be had. He was desperate for money and supplies, otherwise he would go hungry. A quick foray, then home in case Ezra had kept his side of the bargain and come to deliver Dolly to her rightful place.

Arthur stomped his way through the snow laden streets seeing none of the beauty of nature's bounty. He was cold, hungry and mad as hell at Elizabeth Murray for causing him such grief.

As was Arthur's wont, he blamed everyone but himself for his misfortunes. It was Dolly's fault he was still a poor man, and Elizabeth had sent the police knocking on his door. He saw no wrong in helping himself to the odd few pounds he filched from the unwary. To his mind they should take better care of their money and belongings.

Strolling the platform, his eyes darted this way and that, looking for any Bluebottles lurking. It really wouldn't do to be caught red-handed by the police now.

Taking a wallet here and a purse there, Arthur then shot out of the station and to a little shop nearby where he bought some groceries with his pilf and rushed away home. He decided he wouldn't venture out again until it became absolutely necessary for him to do so.

Once indoors he relaxed a little. With food in his belly he sat staring out of the kitchen window. All he had to do now was wait for Ezra and Dolly Daydream, then all his problems would be over.

* * *

In the meantime, Elizabeth decided to take a detour on her way home and visit her mother.

'I thought to come and see how you are,' she said as she shed her outdoor clothing.

'I'm fine, dear,' Sylvia responded and headed to the kitchen with her daughter on her heels. 'I was just indulging myself with freshly baked cake.'

'Good for you, I hope there's some left for me,' Elizabeth said with a little laugh.

Sitting in the kitchen after tea was poured and cake sliced, Sylvia eyed the woman sitting opposite her. 'So why have you really come to visit?'

Taking a deep breath, Elizabeth explained about her visit to the police station.

'Was that truly necessary?' Sylvia frowned at her daughter, wondering when she had become such an interfering busybody.

'Yes, Mother, it was. That rogue would have taken everything you have, don't you see that?'

'Your inheritance, you mean,' Sylvia muttered over the rim of her cup.

'No – well, yes, I mean…' Elizabeth began to babble.

'Elizabeth, Gabriel Short would never have wheedled my fortune out of me, and I think deep down you know that to be true. He was a pleasant distraction, that's all.' Sylvia tried her best to hide the lie, for she had fallen headlong for the man's charms.

'Yes, well, it's up to the police to capture him now and put him in gaol. I hope they throw away the key!' Elizabeth snapped.

'You never did like him, did you? Why? What set you against him?'

'I saw right through him almost immediately, Mother. He's a charlatan; only out for what he can get! He lives in a two up, two down house; he thieves from other folk and it's my guess he targets people like you – wealthy widows!' Elizabeth was exasperated that her mother still appeared to be defending the man. 'Ann Bradshaw said she would be having nothing more to do with him when we came away from his hovel, do you remember?'

'Yes, dear, I do.'

'Well, then! Mother, please try to understand that I did this to protect you!'

'What you don't appear to understand, Elizabeth, is that I do not need your protection!' Sylvia threw the cake she was holding onto the plate. The sadness of losing her paramour and embarrassment at falling for his charms had fused together in anger. She was furious with her daughter for interfering, with Gabriel for duping her, and herself for being taken in by him so easily.

'Why will you not mind your own business? Clearly you don't have enough to do! You should have some children then you'd be too busy to poke your nose into my affairs!' Sylvia pushed back her chair as she stood.

Elizabeth gasped at the venomous outburst from her mother. Why was she being like this? Was it the passing of her husband, Elizabeth's father, which had turned her so bitter? Or did it have something to do with Elizabeth chasing away Gabriel Short? Something had happened to make Sylvia short-tempered and angry all the time.

'I can see I'm not welcome here at present so maybe I should go and leave you to your misery!' Elizabeth barked as she too, got to her feet.

'You can see yourself out!' Sylvia stamped from the

kitchen leaving her daughter alone, tears of hurt and frustration coursing down her cheeks.

A few moments later Sylvia heard the front door slam.
Closing her eyes and clamping her lips together she fought to
hold back her own tears. She lost the battle, and she crum-
pled onto a chair with great heaving sobs.

36

While Sylvia Chilton's heart was breaking over Gabriel Short, Ezra Morton was instructing his men concerning their visit to Arthur Micklewhite.

'You are to keep a very close eye on the girl – do not let her out of your sight! Do you understand?'

'Yes, boss,' the two chorused.

'You ask him for the money, but he won't give it to you,' Ezra continued.

The two men exchanged a confused glance.

'He won't have it, you dolts!' Ezra rolled his eyes at their stupidity. 'So, you tell him you can either take Dolly back to The Crown Saloon, or you can break his legs.'

Watching the grins cross their faces Ezra sighed. 'You don't actually have to do it, you just threaten it to frighten him.'

'Oh, right,' one muttered, a little disappointedly.

Ezra shook his head slightly, then said, 'When he doesn't come up with the cash you remind him about his contract with me. Then you take Dolly back to Nellie. Got it?'

The men nodded.

'Can't we just dislocate a few fingers?' the other asked hopefully.

'No!' Ezra snapped. 'Now bugger off and let me know how it goes!'

With heads hung low, the men left the office.

'Whatever am I doing, having blokes that daft working for me?' Ezra mumbled.

Leaning back in his chair, his mind formed an image of Arthur Micklewhite begging for mercy as the boys towered over him. Rubbing his hands together, Ezra grinned. By the end of the week he would be the owner of a house in Rea Terrace!

* * *

Over at The Crown, Nancy was quizzing Nellie about the deal made with Ezra.

'What's in it for you?'

'Ezra had to come to me so he could get that house, Nance,' Nellie answered as she accepted the plate of bread and cheese. 'He couldn't do it without Dolly and because she's in our care, he had to come cap in hand!'

'Even so, I don't like it, Nell, anything could go wrong!' Nancy wailed.

'It won't. Ezra assured me Dolly would be safe with his blokes and I don't think for a minute they'd hurt a kid – Ezra would never allow that. Besides, it's the house he's after.'

'Oh, Nell! I've come to love that little wench like she's my own flesh and blood!' Nancy dropped onto a chair with a sigh.

'I know, Nance, I've seen it happening. Don't worry, it will all work out nicely, you'll see.' Nellie was doing her best to reassure her friend as well as hide her own misgivings. She prayed she was right and Dolly would come back safe and sound.

'We should never have agreed to it, Nell!' Nancy clearly was not going to let the matter drop.

'If you're that worried, I'll send a message to Ezra and tell him it's all off,' Nellie said.

'I don't know...' Nancy wavered.

'Make your bloody mind up, Nance! Either we go ahead with it or we don't!' Nellie's temper rose at her friend's indecision.

'I'm frightened for her!' Nancy snapped back.

Nellie's anger dissipated in an instant on seeing her friend's angst. 'I'm sorry, lass, I didn't mean to snap at you,' she said in earnest.

'Me an' all,' Nancy answered. 'I just worry we're being drawn into Ezra's dirty world and I ain't happy about it.' Brushing away a tear, Nancy sniffed.

'Me neither, if truth be told,' Nellie confessed. 'I might have got a bit carried away with the idea of Ezra being beholden to me instead of t'other way round.'

'I can see that; you were in his debt a long time – until Dolly came along. Now it seems we're repaying her by putting her in danger.'

'I tell you what, let's have another word with her and see how she feels. What do you say?'

'Yes, let's.' Nancy smiled her appreciation at the thoughtfulness.

A little while later Dolly sat with the two women and heard their concerns.

'We're both worried for you, Dolly,' Nancy said.

'Surely I will be safe enough with Ezra's men there –

won't I?' Dolly asked as she began to feel her misgivings grow too.

'Yes, but after all you've done for us and as Nancy said, we could be putting you in danger,' Nellie answered, a frown creasing her brow.

Dolly sighed as she looked at each woman in turn.

'I know as well that you don't want to see Arthur out of house and home despite the way he treated you,' Nellie added.

'That's true, no one deserves to be pushed out onto the streets. It's no way for people to live, Nellie – I know, I did it.' Dolly shook her head as pictures flashed through her mind of when she had to beg and scavenge to survive; of sleeping in doorways frightened for her life, and the bitter cold in the winter months threatening to freeze her to death.

'Arthur is a greedy scoundrel who had disgusting designs on you, sweet'eart. He and Ezra are trying to get one over on each other and unfortunately you're stuck in the middle!' Nancy said with emphasis.

'I'm the catalyst,' Dolly mumbled.

Nellie and Nancy exchanged a puzzled look, having no idea what Dolly meant.

'Well darlin', you have to decide whether to do this or not,' Nellie said gently.

Drawing a breath Dolly answered quickly. 'If you're both that worried, then I won't do it. You're both very dear to me and I won't have you fretting.'

Nancy sighed with relief and Nellie nodded her admiration of the girl who was fast becoming a young woman. 'I'll let Ezra know straight away he needs to find another way to acquire that house. Dolly, do me a favour and whistle for one of his ragamuffins for me.'

Dolly grinned and hobbled away.

'Feel better now, Nance?' Nellie asked a moment later.

'I do, thanks, Nell.'

'Me an' all.'

The two old friends shared a warm smile as they awaited Dolly's return.

* * *

Ezra threw a tanner to the urchin who had delivered the message from Nellie, then he rubbed his chin as he contemplated what to do next.

He really should have known better than to approach Nellie Larkin for assistance, but he had done just that. Now he was in a pickle. A quick thought flitted through his mind of having Arthur disappear, but he dismissed it.

Taking the contract from the drawer he read it again. The deal was that Arthur would pay when Dolly was delivered to him and if he couldn't pay, then he would forfeit his property. There was nothing in the agreement about the necklace.

Ezra replaced the paper in the desk. It looked like he was going to miss out on the gems; would he lose the property too? As much as he didn't wish to, he thought he should meet up with Nellie again. Despite it sticking in his craw to have to go crawling to Nellie, maybe between them they could find a solution to his problem.

On his way out of the office he called to the two men he'd spoken to earlier. 'Hold off on that assignment...' Seeing their bemused expressions he sighed and clarified his statement. 'That job – until I tell you.'

'Righto, Mr Morton,' the more vocal of the two said.

Outside the works, Ezra whistled to a cabbie. 'Crown Saloon', he said as he climbed aboard. The cab crawled slowly through the snowy streets, the horse's hooves occasionally slipping on the icy cobblestones.

Delivered safely at last, Ezra asked the cabbie to wait before striding into the gin palace.

Nellie saw him coming; she had expected this and led him into the kitchen. Holding up a hand she said, 'Before you say anything, none of us were really comfortable with the arrangement.'

'Fair enough,' Ezra said with a little smile.

'Summat tells me you've had another idea, am I right?' Nellie asked warily.

Ezra nodded. 'Indeed, and this one doesn't involve Dolly!'

'Nance, best get the kettle on,' Nellie said with a laugh. Then turning to Ezra she asked, 'What's on yer mind then?'

Having outlined his plan, Ezra left Nellie to discuss it with the others; she promised to let him know the outcome the following day.

Pushing his way through the crowded bar, Ezra spied Mr Sharpe coming towards him. 'I didn't think to see you in a place like this, Mr Sharpe.'

'Likewise, Mr Morton,' the solicitor answered.

'On business, are we?' Ezra was fishing for information.

'Not yours,' Sharpe said with a raise of his eyebrows. Ezra wouldn't get a bite from this pool that was for sure.

With a huge belly laugh Ezra left the bar but his curiosity had been aroused. What was that solicitor doing in Nellie's place? Certainly not drinking gin. No matter, he felt sure he would find out sooner or later.

Back inside, Mr Sharpe was ushered into the kitchen where he laid the mortgage contract on the table. 'There you go, Nellie, your agreement with the bank to repay said amount each month,' Sharpe tapped the document lightly.

Nellie blew out her cheeks, feeling the enormity of what she was undertaking. 'What about the pub?'

'The landlord is packing to leave as we speak. He's off to live with his sister in Scarborough – she has a bungalow by the sea, apparently. This is your copy of the signed contract of sale.'

'So, when can we get in to start work?' Nellie asked eagerly.

'Tomorrow! Here are the spare keys, the landlord will drop the other set off at my office before he departs,' Sharpe said as he laid the ring of keys on the table.

'Blimey, that didn't take long! You'm as fast as shit off a shovel and no mistake, Mr Sharpe,' Nancy intervened.

'He's keen to be gone, so he said.' Mr Sharpe gave a little grin as he shrugged his shoulders.

'Well, I suggest we have a good look over the place before we decide what's to be done,' Nellie said with a smile.

'With your partner, Nellie, don't forget that Dolly's wishes as co-owner must also be taken into account ,' Sharpe reminded her.

'Naturally. I have no intention of pushing the girl aside, Mr Sharpe. She's saved my arse too many times and besides we love her like a daughter.' Nellie tilted her head towards Nancy who nodded her confirmation.

Standing just behind the door, Dolly covered her mouth with her hand to stifle the sob she felt rising in her throat. Then a couple of seconds later, and with a tap of her stick to herald her arrival, she walked into the kitchen.

37

Ezra's new plan was relayed to Dolly and this time she whole-heartedly agreed with it.

'Now, has Arthur seen that necklace before?' Nellie asked.

'He may have caught a glimpse of it when Mr Sharpe first gave it to me.'

'Right, you and I need to get off to the jewellers. We have to find something very similar for Ezra to present to Arthur.'

'But won't he be expecting to see me?' Dolly asked.

'Ezra is going to tell him he frightened you into giving up your mum's jewellery,' Nellie explained, 'so there's no need for you to be there.'

'Do you think Arthur will believe it?' Dolly was concerned everything could go wrong.

'Oh, he'll believe it, don't you worry about that. So, get your coat on – we've some shopping to do.' Nellie grinned as she fetched her own outdoor clothes.

The two walked steadily down the street with Nellie ensuring Dolly didn't slip on the frosty ground. Traversing the tramway, they passed warehouses whose brickwork was covered with grime. The Victoria Law Courts took up a massive expanse of land to the right and as the two walked on they saw the smaller building which was the County Court. Reaching the Old Square, they noticed small crowds of people standing around chatting, seemingly oblivious to the cold.

Nellie tilted her head and said, 'We'll go down Corporation Street.'

Dolly nodded and they continued on until they came to a staggered crossroads. Turning into Union Street they glanced into the windows of the small shops as they went. A milliner showed off beautiful hats of all colours; a butcher could be heard, slamming his cleaver into a sizeable chunk of meat, through an open door. Then came a shop selling boots and shoes as advertised by the massive wooden boot hanging from its eaves. There were solicitors' offices and insurance companies as well as a pianoforte manufacturer.

Turning right at the end they entered the High Street where smaller shops filled the thoroughfare on both sides. Wandering along, they scanned the articles for sale in each window.

Eventually they came to a shop displaying some old trinkets in its window. All the while, Dolly's eyes searched for something which could take the place of her mother's necklace. With a shake of her head she said, 'There's nothing like it, Nellie.'

'Let's look inside, cos we can't get anything that's new. Arthur would know then it was a trick.'

The shop was dark, lit only by a single gas lamp. Dolly explained what they were looking for and the owner rubbed his whiskers as he considered the challenge. Then he raised his index finger in a flash of inspiration. Rummaging in a drawer he drew out a white stone set in a gold surround.

Sliding it onto a chain taken from another piece he waited for the girl's reaction.

'Perfect!' Dolly said with a wide grin.

Nellie paid the asking price from money she had wheedled out of Ezra for that reason, and they left the shop, excited at having found just the right thing. Slowly they ambled back to the saloon in time to see Ezra arrive.

'Bloody hell, he's quick off the mark!' Nellie said.

'Avaricious – like Arthur,' Dolly replied.

Nellie nodded. 'Come on, let's get this to him then we can concentrate on sorting out the pub.'

After Ezra had left with the fake necklace, Dolly and Nellie went indoors, but as they entered, Nellie gasped. There stood a man with a duck under his arm.

'You can't bring that in here,' she said as she pushed her way through the crowd.

'I dain't. I came in and it followed me!' the crapulous man said with a look of surprise.

People around who had heard the exchange howled with laughter.

'Out! Now!' Nellie said, and pointed to the door just as Jim Jenkins appeared. The man and his duck quietly left the building.

Poppy and Noah were working the bar together and appeared to be getting on well. Nellie nudged Dolly saying, 'Look at that pair. That'll be the next wedding, you mark my words.'

Dolly smiled as she followed Nellie into the kitchen. Over hot tea Dolly told Nancy about the man and his duck; Nancy burst out laughing.

It was later that afternoon that the duck was mentioned again. Old Aggie came rushing in to say the bloke with the bird had been arrested.

'Apparently some bugger reported him for thieving the duck and the bobbies went to his house,' Aggie said so all could hear her.

Nellie passed over a Ladies Delight and Aggie took a gulp before resuming. 'He'd wrung its neck and was just plucking it when the coppers called. They found him with a handful of feathers and you know what he said?' Aggie paused in order to drain her glass, enjoying having everyone's ears tuned to her words. 'He said, 'I was holding its clothes while it went for a swim!'

The whole room erupted as folk fell about laughing. Nellie shook her head and poured Aggie another gin. Had she not seen the duck for herself, she wouldn't have believed it as Aggie was always quick with a joke.

Nellie retired to the kitchen as Matt Dempster took her place at the bar. He laughed loudly as Aggie repeated the tale yet again.

As darkness descended, Fred lit the gas lamps and the place sparkled in the yellow glow. He banked up the fire so the customers would stay warm while they drank themselves into oblivion.

Meanwhile, Dolly and Nellie were discussing their new venture, with constant interruptions from Nancy.

'Will you be having new gas lamps cos the ones on the outside wall are shite!'

'Yes, Nancy, we will most certainly have new lamps,' Dolly said with a grin.

'You'll need some new names for the gin an' all. What about... Nancy's Nerve Tonic, or Dolly's Surprise...' Nancy went on.

'Nance, for God's sake shut yer gizzard!' Nellie protested.

'I was only saying, anyway you still have to find summat to call the place,' Nancy said, feigning hurt.

'Nellie, Nancy's correct – we need to decide on a new name for that old pub,' Dolly said.

'You're right. You got any ideas, gel?' Nellie asked.

Dolly shook her head. 'No, The Castle was good enough for a public house – but for a gin palace? We need something catchy – something people will remember.'

'What about Daydream Palace?' Jack asked as he returned from his room where he'd been napping.

'Oh, Jack! That's perfect!' Dolly gasped.

'I think that's bloody lovely,' Nancy said.

'Me an' all,' Nellie concurred.

'It looks like it's decided then,' Jack said with a grin. 'So, Nancy, how's about a cuppa then? I'm spitting feathers here.'

'Cheeky young bugger!' Nancy muttered, but with a wide grin, for the mention of feathers reminded her to tell Jack about the man and his duck.

* * *

Meanwhile, over at the brewery the two men listened carefully to Ezra's instructions. 'Take this to Arthur Micklewhite and tell him I got it from Dolly. Ask him for my money and when he says he doesn't have it, tell him you have to report back to me. Understand so far?'

Nodding, the men said nothing.

'Then I want you to follow him. See where he goes and what he does. If he tries to flee, then you bring him to me.' Ezra dismissed them after one pocketed the glass jewel.

Now Ezra would wait. He guessed it would only be a couple of hours before Arthur was once again sitting in his office. He was expecting Arthur to try to sell the gem and once he discovered the diamond was a fake he'd be livid.

Knowing he'd been duped, he would try to abscond, but Ezra's men would be there to prevent that happening.

All was going to plan and Ezra shifted his thoughts to Poppy. He had spotted her working the bar with a young man he didn't know. He had seen the stolen glances between them and knew then and there he was out of the running for her affections. He had been convinced he was in love with her at one time, but now he knew it was merely an infatuation.

Mentally berating himself for being such a fool, Ezra wondered if it was his destiny never to marry. He sighed deeply; in his heart he knew that when the time came, he was set to die a lonely man.

Pulling out the contract made with Arthur, he asked himself why he was doing all this. What was it for? Yes, he was very wealthy, but was he any happier for it? Who would he leave his fortune to?

Shoving the paper back into the drawer he gave himself a mental shake. He determined to just live his life and not hanker after things he couldn't have. Besides, it wasn't too late, one day he just might have a wife and family.

The thought cheered him enough to resume working.

38

Arthur saw the two huge men in suits coming down the path and he grinned. Excitedly, he opened the door and let them inside.

'Ezra sent us,' one said.

'To give you this,' said the other.

Arthur frowned. 'Where's Dolly?'

'She was too scared to come,' the first man informed him.

'But our agreement was...'

'You got what you wanted so now we need Ezra's money!' the second snapped.

'I... I need to sell this first, then I'll bring the money to Ezra.' Arthur hooked his fingers through the chain and the stone swung in mid-air.

The two men exchanged a glance, playing their part to perfection.

'We'll have to report back to the gaffer then,' the first man said.

Arthur nodded and watched them leave the house. He

continued to stare out of the window until he was certain they had gone. He threw back his head and laughed loudly.

His eyes then moved to the necklace still hanging from his fingers. That went well, he thought, then, pocketing the gem, he grabbed his coat. He needed to get to the jewellers before it closed for the day.

Traversing the streets as fast as he could without slipping on the ice, Arthur rushed to the shop he had in mind. It was high class with lots of gold in the window, and Arthur felt sure he'd get a good price there. Rushing into the shop, he banged the door closed behind him and scuttled towards the salesman standing behind a counter.

'I need to sell this,' he said breathlessly as he pulled the necklace from his pocket and handed it to the jeweller.

The man placed his magnifying glass to his eye and turned the stone this way and that. 'Hmm.'

'How much?' Arthur asked impatiently.

'Five pounds,' the jeweller said as he removed the glass from his eye.

Arthur stared open-mouthed. 'Are you kidding me? Five quid! This diamond is worth thousands!'

The man shook his head. 'I'm sorry but it's not.'

'I don't understand,' Arthur mumbled as he rubbed his forehead.

'What's not to understand? This trinket is virtually worthless to me so I'm doing you a favour giving it a value of five pounds. May I suggest you take it to a pawnbroker; you may be offered more there.' The man wrinkled his nose in distaste.

'But...' Arthur began as he stared at the man.

'Sir, this piece of rubbish would not sell in our emporium." He waved an arm to encompass the whole room.

'It's a bloody diamond! Of course it would sell!' Arthur's

frustration was mounting. Was the man trying to dupe him by saying it was of no value.

'Sir, I say again, it's worthless – it is *not* a diamond! It is a piece of glass set in a cheap surround!'

'Glass!' Arthur's brain tried desperately to process what he'd been told.

'Yes, sir.'

'Glass...' he repeated. Then the penny dropped. 'Bloody Ezra!'

Snatching the gem back, Arthur turned and fled the shop, leaving the jeweller with a grin from ear to ear. Making his way home he fumed every step of the way. Ezra had fiddled him. Why? What was the point?

So incensed was he about being fooled, Arthur didn't see the two suited men following at a discreet distance.

Reaching home, he scuttled indoors and slammed the door behind him. Throwing the cheap jewel on the table, he paced the kitchen. Running a hand through his hair he tried to think. He slapped his forehead as the answer hit him like a thunderbolt. Ezra knew the gem was fake, he also knew Arthur wouldn't be able to pay the promised amount; therefore, he would be taking Arthur's house!

Pacing again, with his fingers tangled in his hair, he began to panic. What should he do now? He could try pleading with Ezra to give him more time to come up with the money, but he doubted that would work.

Finally, he had a flash of inspiration – the contract had been for Ezra to deliver Dolly – not the necklace. Clapping his hands together he grinned. Ezra had broken the agreement which surely meant he was home free.

Yes, he would remain poor but at least he was still breathing and it was Ezra who had reneged on the deal. Arthur began to relax, he had the upper hand over Ezra

Morton and it felt good. He would simply wait for another visit when he would politely point out that it was Ezra who was in the wrong. He would tell the man that if he didn't fulfil his part of the contract then the deal would be off.

Arthur would be no further forward but at least he could be free of Ezra and his underhand dealings. Picking up the fake stone again, Arthur smiled.

Nice try, Morton, but you'll have to get up earlier in the morning to get one over on me!

* * *

Ezra's men immediately reported back once they saw Arthur enter his property, after which they were sent back to keep watch and ensure Mr Micklewhite stayed where he was.

Ezra assumed Arthur was now aware the gem was made of glass and was holed up at home awaiting a visit from his people. The man was probably rigid with fear at being unable to pay his debt.

Of course, Ezra was aware of the agreement between them which he again pulled from the desk drawer. Reading it once more, he screwed it into a ball and threw it into the fire. Now there was no agreement concerning the young girl.

Reaching for another paper, Ezra grinned wickedly. This contract had been drawn up immediately after the first and was virtually the same but was for delivery of said necklace and not young Dolly. Ezra had completed his part of the bargain by sending Arthur the necklace given to him by Dolly and Nellie. He could always claim he didn't know it was fake. Now it was up to Micklewhite to pay what he owed. He smiled as he read the document again. The forged signature on the bottom was excellently done; even Arthur wouldn't be able to tell the difference.

Ezra always made sure he was well ahead of the game when dealing with clients and contracts.

Ezra folded the paper and tucked it into his inside pocket. It was time to visit Arthur Micklewhite in person.

* * *

Meanwhile, having been given the keys to The Castle public house, Nellie and Dolly threw open the doors and had a good look around. With pencil and paper in hand, Dolly made notes as the two began to formulate their plans for refurbishment.

'It will take a lot of work,' Dolly said as they moved from room to room.

'Yes, but if we renovate downstairs first, then the place can be open and making money while the upstairs is being done,' Nellie said.

'How long do you think it will take?' Dolly asked.

'If we get the blokes in who did The Crown – not too long at all. They're fast workers and will be eager for the job, I suspect,' Nellie replied. 'I was thinking – the Jenkins family would be glad of work here if you're in agreement.'

'John and Jim's family?' Dolly asked, and at Nellie's nod added. 'Yes, of course, but would you mind asking them, Nellie; they know you and might be more inclined to accept.'

'I will,' Nellie replied.

'Best get the builders and decorators in as soon as possible, don't you think?' Dolly ran her hand over the bar top and blew the dust from her fingers.

'Ain't no time like the present,' Nellie said with a smile.

Re-locking the doors, they crossed the road and entered The Crown where Jack was busy awkwardly changing the labels with his one good arm. Down came the Ladies Delight and up went Royal Poverty. White Satin was replaced by Cock my Cap.

It really didn't matter what the gin was called, it was all the same throat-searing stuff which would inevitably lead some folk to debtors' prison and drive others to madness.

'Jack, do me a favour and go down to the Hodges' and ask them to come and see me. Don't say what it's about cos I don't want Ezra to get wind of it all yet, and walls have ears.' Nellie said.

Dolly helped Jack with his coat before the lad set off.

'And you just watch out for the traffic!' Nellie yelled as Jack disappeared through the front door of The Crown.

The Hodges were a family of builders and decorators, and had transformed an old pub into the glittering gin palace that Nellie was so proud of. It transpired that the family were indeed glad of the work, for winter was their slowest time.

Later that day, Eli Hodges sat in the kitchen and pawed over Dolly's notes. 'This don't look too bad. O' course I'll have a better idea when I see it.'

'Well, young Dolly here will be running the place so it's up to her as to décor and the like,' Nellie said.

Eli's silver eyebrows shot up in surprise. 'You'm a bit young, ain't yer?'

'I know, Mr Hodges, but I know exactly what should be done and Nellie is giving me a free hand,' Dolly answered confidently.

'Fair enough. Right, let me at it!' Eli said, jumping to his feet.

Dolly took the older man to assess what she had planned so he could give them a price for the work to be undertaken.

An hour later he was back in Nellie's kitchen. 'It's an easy job, ladies.' Eli was careful to include Dolly in the negotiations. 'If my quote is acceptable to you both, me and my lads can start tomorrer.' He pushed a slip of paper to Nellie, who puffed out her cheeks before passing it to Dolly.

'That seems fair, Mr Hodges; and remember, once the bar is up and running, we will need the upstairs doing too.' Dolly gave the man a warm smile then turned to Nellie. 'Do you agree, Nellie?'

'Yes, gel, I do. After all, the bank will be paying, so I say – the sooner the better!'

'In the first instance, yes, but we will have to work hard to repay the mortgage,' Dolly countered wisely.

Eli Hodges went away a happy man having secured jobs for his family, and work in The Crown Saloon went on as usual.

39

Later that day, Ezra and his two thugs arrived on Arthur's doorstep and were invited into the kitchen. Ezra couldn't resist taking a quick look around the room, knowing it would belong to him before long. The floor was filthy and sticky beneath his boots. There was the distinct odour of rotting food and unwashed clothes at which he wrinkled his nose. Dirty dishes were piled in the sink and the window held months of grime.

Turning to the man he'd come to visit, Ezra said with a sickly smile, 'I've come for my money, Arthur.'

'Ah well, this necklace you sent, besides being worthless – was not a part of the deal we struck.' Arthur felt very confident as he spoke.

Ezra pulled out the contract and handed it to one of his men.

'I don't read so good, Mr Morton,' the man mumbled and passed it to his colleague.

The other read it, saying, 'It says you agree to pay Mr

Morton a fee for the jewellery inherited by Dolly Perkins.'
Then he returned it to his employer.

'That's not right!' Arthur said, snatching the contract from
Ezra's fingers. His eyes rolled over the words and he gasped.
'This is not what we agreed!'

'That is your signature, is it not?' Ezra asked.

'Yes, but...'

Ezra held out his hands in supplication.

'Ezra, for God's sake!' Arthur begged.

'Are you calling me a liar perchance, Arthur?'

'No, but... I don't have any money, Ez—'

'Mr Morton, to you!' Ezra snapped viciously. 'If you can't
pay, then your house is forfeit, Arthur.'

'Mr Micklewhite, to you!' Arthur suddenly stumbled back
into the table as a meaty fist shot out and landed on his jaw.
The man who had thrown the punch growled, 'Show some
respect! Mr Morton has tried to help you out and this is how
you repay him?'

Ezra waved a hand and his subordinate immediately
stepped back. 'The contract stands, Arthur!' Ezra's voice was
like a rasp on metal. 'Now, never let it be said that I'm not a
fair man,' Ezra said, ignoring the snort of derision from
Arthur, 'I will give you one week to come up with my money.
If, by that time we are still in the same predicament as we are
today, then this hovel will pass into my hands.'

Glancing at the bodyguards who frowned menacingly,
Arthur nodded and inwardly sighed with relief that he was
not to be pounded into the ground.

'One week,' Ezra repeated, before he turned and left, his
entourage close behind him.

Dropping into a chair, Arthur stared at the wall. It seemed
that in the blink of an eye he had lost everything. Ezra
Morton had fiddled him out of his house; Dolly had duped

him out of becoming rich, and Elizabeth Murray had ruined any chance he had with her mother or Ann Bradshaw.

Dragging his hands down his face Arthur groaned. Now what? Where would he go? How would he live? Yet again, he would be forced to steal simply to exist. Thievery was second nature to him but the thing that irked the most was that he was still so poor. He had thought to be living the high life by this time, but instead he found himself destitute.

After a while, Arthur got to his feet. Slowly he walked upstairs and once in his bedroom he glanced around. Other than his clothes, he had nothing. He packed a small bag and wearily trudged back downstairs.

Knowing he was beaten, he took one last look around him, before leaving his house, never to return.

Back in his office, Ezra was mightily pleased with his acquisition, a nice little property in Rea Terrace. Once it had been given a good clean, he could rent it out thereby swelling his coffers further.

Yelling, 'Come!' in response to a knock on his office door, Ezra then asked, 'Yes, what is it?'

His bodyguard tugged a forelock and said, 'Work going on at The Castle over in Aston Street, Mr Morton.'

'That old pub opposite Larkins?'

'Yes, boss.'

'Hmm. Find out who's doing it and on whose orders.' Ezra nodded and the man left quietly.

Standing by the window, Ezra watched the rain pattering down which was quickly melting away the last remnants of snow. He was intrigued about The Castle and the renovations he assumed were taking place. His spies had kept him abreast of the fact that the landlord was in no financial position to undertake any improvements, so he wondered what was afoot. No matter, he had sent out runners and would find out soon enough. Then his mind wandered back to Arthur; would he have any way of finding the money owed? Ezra doubted it.

Returning to his seat, he smiled. It had been so easy to acquire that house in Rea Terrace; the ruse had worked perfectly.

He was rubbing his hands together when a hand rapped the door and a head appeared. 'The work on The Castle is on Nellie Larkin's say-so, Mr Morton.' Then the head disappeared and the door closed with a quiet click.

Bloody hell that was quick, he thought. The ragamuffin crew of runners dispatched earlier had earned their coin and no mistake.

Ezra frowned and blew his cheeks out.

Larkin! What was going on? How was she involved? Unless –she had bought the place. If so, where had the money come from? Ezra was furious that his lackeys had been remiss regarding informing him about Larkin's nose being in another's business – namely that of the landlord of The Castle.

If Nellie had bought it, who was going to run it? Would it stay a public house or would she turn it into another gin palace? The more he thought on the matter, the more he was convinced Nellie couldn't possibly have purchased the pub. There was no way on God's green earth she could afford to.

Ezra needed to know and there was only one way to find out the full facts. Time to visit Nellie Larkin again and see for himself precisely what she was up to.

* * *

The two bully boys Ezra had left in Rea Terrace to keep

watch on Arthur were grumbling about the cold when they saw him leave the house, bag in hand.

'Where's he off to now?' one asked.

His friend shook his head as they followed where Arthur led.

Finally coming to the railway station, they watched as light fingered Arthur helped himself to a passenger's ticket which he expertly lifted from the pocket of a greatcoat.

Exchanging a glance of disbelief, the two quickly pounced before Arthur could make his getaway. The ticket was snatched from his fingers and returned to its rightful owner with an apology. Then Arthur was hauled away, begging for understanding and mercy with each step taken.

People stopped to stare at the unfortunate man being manhandled by two well-dressed men they knew to be in Morton's employ. They pitied the fellow, who was close to tears, as he was frogmarched down the street.

The men ignored his pleas and all but dragged him along the road towards the brewery.

'Please, you have to understand – I can't pay Ezra!' Arthur whined.

'You should have thought of that before you made a deal with him,' the bigger of the two replied.

'What's going to happen to me?' Arthur asked in a whinging tone.

'Ain't got a clue, mate, but you'd best believe – it won't be anything nice.'

Arthur's stomach rolled with fear and despite the cold wind he began to sweat. 'Come on, fellas, can't you just turn a blind eye?'

'Not a chance. If Ezra found out, we'd be turning a blind eye each for real!'

Arthur shuddered at the thought. Trying to flee had not

been one of his better ideas and if he'd taken more care, he might have noticed Ezra's men following him. As it was, he now found himself being presented to Ezra like a sacrificial lamb.

The three arrived just as Ezra was about to go to visit Nellie Larkin.

'Caught him thieving a ticket at the railway station, Mr Morton,' the shorter man said. He pushed a trembling Arthur towards Ezra's desk.

'Going somewhere, were we, Arthur?' Ezra asked sarcastically.

Arthur merely glanced at the two who had delivered him into the hands of Morton.

'May I enquire as to where you were headed?' Ezra's voice was menacingly calm. When no answer was forthcoming he asked, 'All right, can I ask again why you were leaving this delightful town?'

Ezra drew in a breath and swallowed before exhaling noisily.

Arthur glanced again at his captors, his eyes desperately pleading for help. They ignored him, their eyes on their employer.

Ezra began to drum his fingers on the desk as he waited.

'I was…' Arthur's mind was so full of fear that he could not find an explanation.

'Let me help you, Arthur. You see, I think, knowing you could not pay what's owed, you chose to abscond. Am I right so far?' Ezra's fingers stilled mid-air.

Arthur nodded then shook his head. Beads of sweat rolled down his face which had taken on a sickly grey colour.

Ezra's head imitated Arthur's gesture then he sighed loudly. 'What did you hope to achieve by running away, Arthur? That you wouldn't have to pay up? That I would write your debt off? Don't you realise there is nowhere you can hide from me?' Ezra stared at the man who was physically shaking. Pointing to a chair, he indicated that Arthur should sit before his legs gave way beneath him.

The two men stood on either side of Arthur and each placed a hand on his shoulder.

Arthur's head hung low on his chest and his heart hammered loudly.

'I don't understand, Arthur, I gave you a week in which to try and raise the money or you could have just given me your house.' Ezra's voice remained calm and even.

'I can't – I don't have the means,' Arthur croaked.

'I see. Then why not just hand over the keys to your property?' Ezra asked.

'Where would I live if I did that?' Arthur asked in a rush.

Ezra frowned. 'I'm confused, Arthur. You see, these two fine gentlemen caught you trying to board a train, which tells me you wouldn't be living in Rea Terrace any more anyway.'

'Why should I give you my house?' Arthur asked, suddenly finding courage through anger where before there was none.

'We had an agreement, don't you remember?'

'Yes, I recall, but not the document you hold now. We both know the truth of our original contract, which I suspect has been disposed of.' Arthur's confidence grew, fuelled by a fury building up inside him. He had nothing else to lose now so he would say his piece before the devil came for him.

'Mr Morton, I came to you to help me steal a necklace worth thousands of pounds, for which you were to be handsomely rewarded. You have reneged on your promise to deliver Dolly Perkins to me. You have lied and cheated regarding the written document we both signed. You gave me a glass stone in place of a diamond, which was another cheap trick.' Arthur's eyes held the frustration built up over many years and he watched Ezra's expression change from arrogance to pure hatred.

'I admit I was scared,' Arthur went on, 'but I'm not any longer. Oh, I've heard the rumours about your cruelty but I'm also aware of a certain lady who has bested you on more than one occasion. It's common knowledge around the markets.'

Arthur saw Ezra's nostrils flare as he tried to keep his temper in check and he plunged on, 'I wonder if it might be more prudent for you to watch your own back rather than go around scaring poor folk. You never know, one day you may well find yourself one of those needy people you are said to terrorise.'

Arthur could see his point hit home and although what he'd said so far was true, his next words were speculation only. Nevertheless, he said them anyway.

'From what I hear, that lady I spoke of is out to ruin you.' Arthur raised his eyebrows and drew his lips into a thin line.

'Enough!' Ezra slammed a fist on the desk. 'I'll hear no more!'

'Touched a nerve, have we?' Arthur said with a little laugh before he felt the hands on his shoulders tighten in warning.

'Nellie Larkin will never ruin me!' Ezra boomed.

'I never mentioned the lady's name, but she's evidently a thorn in your side,' Arthur gloated.

'Get him out of here! You know where to put him until I decide what's to be done with him!' Ezra barked.

Arthur was yanked to his feet and dragged towards the door. 'I think your days of running this town are numbered, *Ezra*!' he called loudly over his shoulder.

Ezra could still hear Arthur's mocking laughter long after he'd been removed from the building.

Leaning back in his chair he considered the facts before

him. Arthur seemed to know a lot about Ezra and he was a blabbermouth. Now, maybe it was gossip picked up from the townsfolk, but he had no intention of allowing Micklewhite to add to it by letting him go free. Although their contract stipulated the house would go to Ezra if Arthur didn't pay his debt, he thought things would be much easier if Arthur wasn't around when he came to collect. Maybe an accident could befall the unfortunate man.

40

Whilst Arthur was languishing in a cold dark cellar close to the brewery, work on The Castle was well underway.

Meanwhile Nancy, over at The Crown Saloon, was busy preparing for her wedding to Fred. Nellie had promised to close up for the day in order for everyone to attend and enjoy the celebrations.

In the bar, Nellie nodded as old Aggie sidled up to the counter.

'You heard the latest?' Aggie asked with a toothless grin.

'No, but I'm sure you'll enlighten me,' Nellie answered as she passed over a free gin in exchange for the information.

'Ta, Nell. That bloke – what's-his-name – young Dolly's step-father,' Aggie rubbed her forehead trying to recall the name.

'Arthur Micklewhite,' Nellie supplied the answer.

'Ar, him. Well, he tried to sell a jewel he thought was worth a king's ransom, only it was just a piece o'glass!' Aggie cackled before taking a slurp of her drink.

Nellie continued to serve impatient customers as she listened.

'I heard tell he's ticked off Ezra Morton good and proper an' all,' Aggie added.

'How so?' Nellie asked with mock surprise.

'Seems the neighbours heard he'd hocked his house to Ezra and now he won't give it up.'

'Big mistake,' Nellie said as she refilled Aggie's glass.

'He was spied being carted off by Ezra's goons and he ain't been seen since,' Aggie said, shaking her head.

'Good riddance is what I say,' Nellie answered.

'He was telling a bit about you as well apparently.' Aggie peeped from beneath hooded eyelids as she spoke.

'Me?' Nellie asked, her interest even more piqued now.

Aggie nodded. 'My source says he told Ezra you was out to ruin him.'

Nellie's laughter boomed out across the bar and everyone cheered in response. A happy landlady meant happy customers.

'There ain't much chance of that happening but I thank you for giving me a good laugh,' Nellie said at last.

Moving along the counter to serve another customer, Nellie stored the information away in her mind to be retrieved and chewed over later. Wherever Aggie got her information from, she had no idea, but it had given her a lot to think about and it might prove useful to share it with the others after closing time.

A while later, Nellie went to the kitchen for a well-earned rest, and she smiled at Poppy and Noah as they stood in the corner holding hands and whispering quietly together. There would be another wedding pretty soon if she was not mistaken. She was pleased the two had formed a relationship so quickly once Poppy had realised Ezra was not for her. She was a beautiful girl and deserved a good man like Noah Dempster.

Sipping her tea, Nellie thought about how easily Ezra had given up on the girl. In the beginning he had been intent on enticing her into his bed, but she had given him the cold shoulder. Then nothing – Ezra had appeared to have completely forgotten her. Then again, all he cared about was money and Poppy had none.

Nellie's mind came into focus at hearing Dolly praising Jack's efforts at reading. That young girl had come into the household by chance and had transformed all of their lives. Nellie felt the love swell in her breast for the two children she watched laughing together. She couldn't imagine life without them now. Her eyes moved to Nancy and Fred discussing wedding plans, and her peripheral vision registered Poppy and Noah going to the bar to help Matt with serving.

Nellie smiled inwardly, feeling very lucky to have such a close-knit family. Then she considered what Aggie had told her. Why would Arthur say she was out to ruin Ezra? How did he think she could accomplish such a thing? Was she seen as a threat by Ezra?

'Summat on yer mind, Nell?' Nancy asked.

Jack and Dolly's ears pricked up at the question.

Nellie nodded, then explained her thoughts.

'Why would Ezra be afraid of you?' Nancy asked incredulously.

However, it was Dolly who answered. 'He's probably concerned you're stealing all his staff.'

'I ain't, though!' Nellie replied hotly.

'I know, but I imagine he thinks you are coaxing them into your employ. He must see himself losing the power he once held over the town and that would frighten him,' Dolly said wisely. 'Look at it this way, you paid off your loan to him and he doesn't know how. You allowed Poppy to make up her own mind about him before she brushed him off and he has no idea why. You've invested in another property – which he's bound to know about by now – but he's at a loss as to how you've managed it. Oh, and you outsmarted him regarding the deliveries from another supplier – I almost forgot that.' Dolly grinned, seeing Nellie mentally ticking off her achievements.

'Yes, but all that was down to you really, sweetheart. You're the one who guided my hand and I'm grateful for it.' Nellie nodded with a beaming smile.

'Maybe I helped a little, but Ezra is in the dark about it all and that's what must irk him. He's not in control of you and your business any more. And another thing, his staff are like rats leaving a sinking ship, and where are they going? To you, Nellie.' Dolly glanced around to see Jack and Nancy nod in agreement.

'Nellie!' Poppy's voice echoed through to the kitchen.

'Now what? There's always a bloody crisis in this place!' Nellie grumbled as she got to her feet.

'Somebody to see you,' Poppy said as she led a couple of suited men into the kitchen.

'Gents. What can I do for you?' Nellie asked as she eyed the burly men standing meekly before her.

'No wonder Ezra's afraid,' Nancy muttered under her breath, 'two more defecating!'

Jack and Dolly giggled loudly at the malapropism. 'Defecting, Nancy,' Dolly corrected her gently.

'That an' all,' Nancy mumbled.

'We was wondering if you had any jobs going, Mrs Larkin,' one said.

Nellie sighed. Inviting the men to sit and take a sup, she listened to their reasons for wanting to leave Ezra. Much the same as the others, they were fed up of doing Ezra's dirty work and being shunned by the townsfolk.

'What's yer names?' Nellie asked.

'Billy and Bobby – we'm bruthers, ain't we?' the other said.

'Dolly, you'll need doormen over the road when it's up and running,' Nellie said.

The two men glanced at the young girl, unsure why Nellie was consulting her. Dolly nodded and their attention returned to Nellie.

'Right then. Here's the offer, gents. Dolly here is to manage The Castle once it's renovated – which should be in the next week or so. She'll need men on the door so you'd be working for her,' Nellie explained.

'Her? She's only a kid!' Bobby exclaimed.

'Offer is on the table this one time, fellas. Take it or leave it.' Nellie waited as the two exchanged a glance.

'What's the wages?' Billy asked eventually.

'Same as the Jenkins boys working my bar. I'm sure they will have told you already as I know you lot keep in touch whoever you work for.'

A sheepish look crossed their faces as they grinned. 'Nothing gets past you does it, Mrs Larkin?' Bobby said.

'Call me, Nellie, lads. So, you gonna look after my little wench and her gin palace then, or what?' Nods came quickly and Nellie spoke again. 'All right, but Dolly will be your boss – you remember that and treat her with respect.'

Billy turned to the young girl watching the proceedings and spoke quietly. 'Thank you, Miss Dolly.'

'You're welcome. I'll see you at the end of next week when hopefully we'll be open for business.'

When the men had gone, Nellie and Dolly burst out laughing when Nancy said, 'The animals came in two by two.'

Fred, who had gone outside for a smoke, suddenly rushed in saying, 'Dolly, your first delivery has arrived!'

Grabbing her cane, Dolly ambled outside, followed closely by Nellie and Fred.

'I'll get yer cellar sorted out with the barrels now that it's all clean and tidy,' Fred said.

Dolly smiled her thanks. A moment later Jack was at her side. 'Blimey, Dolly – it's really happening now!'

'Come over and have a look,' Dolly returned.

Jack, with his arm in a sling, and Dolly with her walking cane crossed the street and stood looking at the front of the building.

Shiny new glass had been fitted and gas lamps hung on the wall on either side of the door. The sign, Daydream Palace, written in gold on a black background, was in place and as they entered Jack gasped. The bar room was massive. There were gas wall lights and two great chandeliers hung from the ceiling. A huge mirror lined the back wall reflecting light back into the room. Small kegs displaying the names of the different gins stood like a line of soldiers in front of the mirror. A layer of clean sawdust on the floor gave off a woody fragrance as Jack and Dolly walked over it. The walls had been whitewashed, then painted with murals. Scenes from myths and legends adorned the room, bringing the whole place alive. The huge counter was polished mahogany and the big black till was placed between the central two kegs.

They heard Fred down in the cellar grunting with the effort of shifting barrels. The clinking of glass said the bottles and drinking glasses had also arrived.

'Dolly, you'll need a cellar man and bar staff,' Jack said at last.

'I know. Your mum is asking the Jenkins family, on my behalf, if some of them would like to work here,' she replied.

'Good. They're a nice bunch.'

'What is it, Jack? What's troubling you?'

'Everything is changing, Dolly. You'll be here and I'll be over there,' he tilted his head in the direction of The Crown, 'it won't be the same any more!' Jack said, stifling a tear.

'We have to move with the times, Jack. I know it's hard but that's life. Sometimes new doors open and we have to walk through them. Anyway, you can pop over any time you like,' Dolly assured him.

Having completed the grand tour of the whole building they returned to Nellie's kitchen.

'Ah, there you are, I've heard back from the Jenkins family. Juliet and Janice have accepted the offer to work the bar with you, Dolly. They'll be popping in later to have a word. Now, if you'll take my advice you'd do well to have them move in first so you ain't on yer own at night when you go over,' Nellie said.

'Good idea. I wonder, Nancy, if you have a few moments – would you help me get a couple of rooms ready. One for the Jenkins girls and one for myself. Then tomorrow I think it will be time to move in.' Dolly spoke gently knowing what a wrench it would be for the woman who was like a second mum to her.

Nancy simply nodded, unable to trust herself to speak for fear of bursting into tears.

The following day would see Dolly Perkins embark on a great new adventure and she could hardly contain her excitement.

41

Elizabeth Murray picked up the newspaper and frowned. The Birmingham Post had become the Birmingham Daily Post. Just another way to entice new readers and make more money, she thought with disgust.

Every day she had scoured the newsprint in the hope of seeing that Gabriel Short had been arrested, and each day she had been disappointed.

Laying the paper in her lap, Elizabeth thought back to the day she had visited the police station to report Short for thieving. She had heard nothing since. However, one good thing had come out of the whole debacle – her mother and Ann Bradshaw had become firm friends sharing afternoon tea and gossip as well as trips out to the theatre. Two lonely women drawn together by an inept charlatan.

Elizabeth stared into space as she wondered what had become of Mr Short. Was he still living in Rea Terrace? Had he in fact been apprehended and she had somehow missed the reporting of it? Maybe he had absconded with the intention of trying his luck in another town. He could, at this very moment, be duping some other poor woman out of her money and possessions.

With a small shake of her head, Elizabeth knew it would serve no purpose to revisit the police station; they would tell her nothing. She could take a little jaunt to Rea Terrace though, if only to satisfy her curiosity.

Tossing the newspaper aside she got to her feet. Dressing warmly, she set out and walked briskly to beat off the cold. *One way or another I'll see you behind bars, Gabriel Short,* she thought as she stepped swiftly but carefully along the frosty streets.

Eventually coming to number twenty seven, she rapped the knocker with gusto. After a moment she banged the door with her gloved fist.

'Can I 'elp yer?' came a gruff voice.

Elizabeth turned to see a well-built woman leaning on the fence that separated the properties. Her straggly hair looked like it had not been brushed in an age and her teeth were turning black.

'I hope so. I'm look for Mr Gabriel Short,' Elizabeth answered.

'Ain't nobody of that name living there, me duck,' the woman said in a friendly manner.

'Oh, has he moved away then do you know?'

The woman shook her head. 'Like I said, there's no Mr Short there.'

'But I visited him here a while ago with my mother and a friend,' Elizabeth said, confused.

'Ar, I remember seeing you.' The woman nodded as she spoke.

'Then you will surely know we met Mr Short,' Elizabeth said, the frustration building inside her.

'Look, missus, I can see you'm a lady which tells me you

ain't dim witted, so what part of this ain't you understanding?' The woman ran a sleeve beneath her nose and sniffed.

With a wince, Elizabeth said, 'Maybe we should begin again. Can you tell me who lives here?'

'I can that,' the woman answered.

Waiting for more, Elizabeth pushed her head forward. 'Well?'

'Well, what?'

'Well, who does live here?'

'Mr Arthur Micklewhite. Lived there for years. After his wife passed, it was just him and the little wench,' the neighbour said finally.

'Little wen... girl?'

'Ar, Arthur's step-daughter. About twelve years old I would say, but she run off shortly after her mum died.'

'Why?' Elizabeth asked.

'What am I – the Birmingham Daily bleedin' Post?!' the woman huffed.

'Sorry,' Elizabeth said, suitably chastised. 'Is Mr Micklewhite working then?'

The woman shook her head with a laugh. 'That lazy bugger ain't never worked a day in his life. Lived off his wife he did. Swaggering around lording it over everybody, but that soon changed when he was on his own. Living in muck now he is.' The woman wrinkled her nose and sniffed again.

'I see. Well, thank you very much for your help,' Elizabeth said and turned to walk away.

'Hey, missus,' called the woman and when Elizabeth faced her once more, she added, 'He was hauled away by two big blokes t'other day, and I ain't seen hair nor hide of him since.' Then she held out her hand saying, 'Nothing's for free in this world.'

Digging in her drawstring bag, Elizabeth produced a

florin and placed it in the outstretched hand. The woman nodded her thanks before biting down on the coin.

Walking away, Elizabeth's mind whirled around the information she had gleaned from the neighbour. So, Gabriel Short was not his real name after all. It could be that Arthur Micklewhite was not genuine either. If that was the case then who was this man? Where did he hail from and where was he now?

Reaching home, Elizabeth knew she had reached a dead end. She could go no further in her quest to see that dreadful man get his just deserts. The thought was like bitter aloes to her after all she'd done to try and get him off the streets.

The only thing left to her now was to continue to read the newspapers and hope to read that Arthur, aka Gabriel Short, had been detained at Her Majesty's pleasure in Stafford Gaol.

* * *

Whilst Elizabeth was endeavouring to track down the person she hated with a vengeance, Ezra Morton was trying to decide what should be done with the same man. Arthur Micklewhite had made a serious attempt to flee whilst owing Ezra money, and that simply couldn't be allowed to happen. Now he was being held in a cellar not far away. The question was – how to deal with him.

Ezra knew he would never get his money; Arthur was as poor as a church mouse. The house in Rea Terrace could not be his either while Arthur still lived. However, if the man was to pass into the next life, then Ezra could take possession of the property. Should he be challenged regarding ownership, then he had the contract to prove his legal right to the building.

Taking the document from the desk drawer, Ezra read it

through once more and smiled, then he gave a whistle. A moment later the door opened to admit one of his minions. Waving the paper in the air, Ezra said, 'I have a job for you.'

* * *

Meanwhile, over at Daydream Palace, the Hodges family were working like Trojans. The bar room and kitchen were all finished and now they were whitewashing the bedrooms. In the next couple of days Dolly and her new staff would move in and the place would be open to the public.

Word of the renovations had spread rapidly around the town and folk had taken a few minutes out of their daily lives to stop and watch. Some were eager to pass on the knowledge that a new gin palace was opening up; others were disgusted and grumbled that more lives would be ruined by mother's ruin.

Excitement in the kitchen of The Crown Saloon was building with everything they had to look forward to, from the grand opening of the new premises to Nancy and Fred's wedding.

There was a sadness too. Dolly was moving out and it seemed like the family was splitting up, for all she would only be across the road.

Nellie voiced this thought, and Dolly responded with, 'It's progress, Nellie. Nothing stays the same for long except our love for each other. That will remain strong for the rest of our lives.'

That night, when all were asleep and the saloon was dark and quiet, Nellie's thoughts roamed over all that had happened since Dolly had come into their lives. An old head on young shoulders, Dolly had sorted out each problem wisely. She had taught Jack to read well and eased his discovery of Nellie not being his real mother. She'd been like a daughter to Nancy and a good friend to Poppy.

Even though Dolly would only be a few steps away she would leave a space in the saloon kitchen that could never be filled.

Nellie's tears fell in the darkness of her bedroom. Silent and hot they trickled down her face as she prayed.

Dear Lord, take care of that young girl who I love like my own. Let her be successful in her endeavours and one day have a husband and children of her own.

Nellie buried her nose beneath the covers and the warmth helped dry her tears. She thought about all of those who had joined her *family,* and she thanked God for every single one of them. Closing her eyes, a smile lifted the corners of her mouth and before long she felt herself drifting into sleep.

42

The day for Fred and Nancy's wedding arrived and there was great excitement in the kitchen at The Crown.

Fred was having enormous difficulty in tying his cravat so Noah lent a hand. Matthew helped him on with his jacket and Jim passed him his top hat. Once ready, the men led a very nervous Fred out to the waiting cab.

'I want to wait for Nancy,' he protested.

'You can't, mate. You ain't allowed to see her on the wedding day until she gets to the church,' John said.

'Why not?' Fred asked innocently as he was bundled into the carriage.

'Cos it's bad luck, now come on!' Noah explained.

'Oh, right.' Fred settled on the seat and then began tapping his foot.

Laying a hand on the bouncing knee to still it, Jim assured him. 'Nancy will be getting ready now and you'll be wed inside the hour.'

Back in the kitchen, Poppy was tying a ribbon around the waist of Dolly's pale blue organza dress.

'Keep still, girl!' Poppy said with a laugh.

'I'm sorry, but I've never had sky blue shoes before!' Dolly replied as she leaned forward, yet again, to take another look.

Sat at the table, Jack slapped on his cap then shook his head. *Women!*

He sipped his tea, being careful not to drip it onto his new suit. Propping his feet up on another kitchen chair he admired his own footwear. His first pair of black boots which made him feel very grown up. All his life he'd had brown ones, as did most boys, but now he was one of the men.

He glanced at Poppy, who was looking very glamorous in a midnight blue velvet suit. Her hat, which she was just now fitting into place with a pearl hatpin, was a percher style made popular by their beloved Queen Victoria. Her black side-button boots were polished to give a brilliant shine.

A noise on the stairs told them Nellie was on her way down and they all gasped as she stepped into the room. Her suit was burgundy velvet trimmed with black silk. She had decided not to wear a bustle, the skirt was left to drape in a short train. On her head was a cartwheel hat of matching feathers.

'Oh, Nellie! You look beautiful!' Dolly said.

Nellie smiled as she patted her hair at the sides beneath the wide brim of the hat. 'Ta, sweetheart. You all look smash-ing, Nancy will be really pleased.'

Jack stared, never having seen his mother dressed in such finery before. 'You look bostin', Mum,' he said, taking his feet off the chair.

'And so do you, son,' Nellie grinned.

Checking the clock, she shouted up the stairs, 'Nance, get a bloody move on!'

'Keep yer bleedin' knickers on, Nell! I'm nearly ready,' Nancy yelled back.

Nellie tutted as she paced the kitchen. 'Whatever are you doing up there?'

'I'm putting my bloomers on if you must bloody know!'

Jack and Dolly burst out laughing and Poppy hushed them as they awaited the bride's appearance.

Eventually a stomping on the stairs heralded Nancy's arrival.

'Oh, Christ! This bloody skirt is getting on my nerves,' she blustered.

Once in the kitchen she smoothed the offending article, shoved her hat further back on her head and said, 'Right, I'm ready. I just hope this bloody net veil don't get in the way cos I'm fed up with it already.'

'Oh, Nance! You look bloody gorgeous! That cream silk suit really suits you,' Nellie said, willing her tears not to show.

'Ta muchly,' Nancy answered, 'you've all brushed up a treat an' all.'

'Right, Poppy and me in one carriage and you and Jack in t'other. Come on, let's get gone before Fred thinks you've done a runner!' Nellie said, ushering everyone outside so she could lock up.

The trip to St Bartholomew's church was short, Nellie and Poppy scrambled out of the cab and, picking up their skirts, they rushed inside. The driver moved forward and Nancy's carriage took its place.

Jack jumped down and helped Nancy alight. 'All set?' he asked.

'As I'll ever be, lad,' she replied, then blew on the short veil in an effort to move it out of her eyes. Prayer book in one hand she threaded her other through Jack's crooked arm.

With deep breaths, the pair walked forward into the church. Music sounded and Jack and Nancy walked steadily to where Fred was standing with his best man, John Jenkins.

Dolly moved from her place in the pew and followed along behind, a little posy in one hand, her stick in the other; she glowed in her role of bridesmaid.

The ceremony began in the quiet church as everyone hung on to every word.

The vicar turned to a beaming Fred. 'Do you, Frederick Dell...'

'Yeah.'

'Take Nancy Ann Sampson...'

'Yeah.'

'To be your lawful wedded wife...'

'YES!'

The vicar took a step back as titters sounded from the congregation. Then the rest of the words came out in a rush before he faced Nancy.

'Do you, Nancy Ann Sampson, take Frederick Dell to be your...'

'I do. Now bloody get on with it cos we'm wastin' valuable drinking time!'

Laughter and applause echoed around the church.

'I now pronounce you husband and wife!' The vicar heaved a sigh of relief as the ceremony came to an end. He watched with a smile as Fred lifted Nancy's veil and gave her a kiss.

After the couple had signed the register, Nancy called over her shoulder as they walked back down the aisle. 'Pick up yer cassock, vicar, and follow us.'

The newlyweds were pelted with rice as they climbed into the waiting cab, which led the way back to The Crown. Then the party began.

* * *

It was two days later when the grand opening of Daydream Palace took place. A red ribbon was stretched across the double doors which was cut by Dolly and Nellie simultaneously. The press were in attendance and crowds of people gathered along Gin Barrel Lane clapping and cheering.

Dolly took a breath and called out, 'The first drink is on the house!'

The new doormen, Bobby and Billy, threw open the doors, then stood back as the eager throng swarmed in. The bar staff were standing ready and in position before immediately beginning to pass out the first free drink. Before long the till was working to capacity as folk happily handed over their money.

Nellie and Dolly watched from the side-lines as the noise increased. There were people shouting for more gin; some bursting into song while others began to dance little jigs.

'Well, sweetheart, we did it!' Nellie said as she placed an arm around Dolly's shoulder.

'Yes, we did.' Then both threw back their heads and laughed loudly.

Their fears of not being able to attract enough customers melted away as more and more people pushed in through the open doors. Nodding to each other they knew they were set to become very wealthy women.

EPILOGUE

The end of the week saw a number of things happen.

Elizabeth Murray at last found what she had looked for for so long in the newspaper. She read out loud, '*The body of a man named Arthur Micklewhite was found by the railway track near New Street Station early this morning. It is believed he was hit by the steam engine whilst in a state of severe inebriation. Mr Micklewhite died of the injuries sustained. The train driver was not held responsible for the unfortunate accident.*'

Folding the newspaper, Elizabeth threw back her head and laughed until her sides ached. Composing herself once more, she realised her mother would not be upset by this news as Sylvia had only known the man as Gabriel Short, so Elizabeth opted not to enlighten her mother of the facts she had discovered, knowing now she could relax and get on with her life.

Number twenty seven, Rea Terrace passed into the hands of Ezra Morton unchallenged. It could never be proved whether he had had a hand in the death of the previous owner or not. Of course, speculation was rife that it was he who had disposed of Arthur Micklewhite, but without irrefutable evidence that he was to blame, Ezra was untouchable.

Fred and Nancy settled down quietly to married life, Fred having moved into Nancy's room as it was the largest of the two.

The post-wedding festivities had lasted long into the night and revellers had to be thrown out bodily to allow the wedding party to finally get some sleep. The celebrations would be remembered for years by the locals who had been invited to join in the revelry. Sore heads the following day did not deter hardened drinkers from frequenting The Crown for their much needed tot of throat-searing gin.

After being advertised in all the local papers, Daydream Palace had opened its doors for the first time and had been packed to the gunnels. The Temperance Movement members had stood outside desperately trying to convince people not to enter. Their efforts were wasted; folk crowded in, eager to spend their hard-earned cash on the liquid that could eventually see them driven to suicide, insanity or turn them blind.

'I really can't believe how well the Palace has taken off,' Dolly said on a quick visit to her friends in The Crown a few days later.

'Nor me,' Nellie said.

'I always knew it would be a good idea,' Nancy chipped in, ignoring the incredulous looks passed between those sat around the table.

'You're doing a grand job over there, Dolly,' Nellie said.

'Thank you, Nellie, I couldn't have managed it without all of you. Just think if Jack hadn't found me in your yard that night.' Dolly said with a smile.

'I dread to think what might have become of you,' Nancy

said, 'you could have been took off and sold to the bloody gypsies!'

Dolly laughed, then said, 'Right, no rest for the wicked. I'll see you all later.' She left them to their discussions about how lucky they all were.

Poppy and Noah were indeed planning their own wedding for the following year; their courtship having taken no-one by surprise, and Matt Dempster took a serious fancy to Janice Jenkins who now worked for Dolly. Within days of the Palace opening, they had been seen stepping out together, and bets were being taken on which of the brothers would be married first.

Jack spent his days between The Crown Saloon and Daydream Palace, helping out where he could. His arm was now out of its sling but still heavily bandaged and would remain so for some weeks to come to enable the bones to knit together properly.

One frosty morning just before Christmas, Jack and Dolly, who had become very close friends, took a short break from their work to take a stroll to the cemetery to visit Dolly's mother's grave. Placing a seasonal wreath on the plot, Dolly laid a hand on the iron-hard ground.

'Thank you, Mum, for all you've done for me. I think you would agree with the steps I have taken to get me to where I am now.' A lone tear slipped from her eye and a sob caught in her throat. 'I miss you so much, Mum. Goodnight and God bless.'

Jack held her hand and whispered, 'You would be as proud of your girl as we all are.'

Suddenly the dark clouds parted and a weak ray of sunlight shone down to rest on the headstone. Then in an instant it was gone again.

'Come on, Dolly Daydream, that was your mum giving her approval – now it's time for work.'

As the two walked from the churchyard, Dolly enjoyed what she thought were the last moments of her childhood. A new chapter in her life was just beginning and she looked forward to it with every ounce of her being. The tale of these two youngsters had spread all over Birmingham and beyond and people came from far and wide to see the children from Gin Barrel Lane.

MORE FROM LINDSEY HUTCHINSON

We hope you enjoyed reading *The Children From Gin Barrel Lane*. If you did, please leave a review.

If you'd like to gift a copy, this book is also available as a ebook, digital audio download and audiobook CD.

Sign up to Lindsey Hutchinson's mailing list for news, competitions and updates on future books.

http://bit.ly/LindseyHutchinsonMailingList

ABOUT THE AUTHOR

Lindsey Hutchinson is a bestselling saga author whose novels include *The Workhouse Children*. She was born and raised in Wednesbury, and was always destined to follow in the footsteps of her mother, the multi-million selling Meg Hutchinson.

Follow Lindsey on social media:

- facebook.com/Lindsey-Hutchinson-1781901985422852
- twitter.com/LHutchAuthor
- bookbub.com/authors/lindsey-hutchinson

ABOUT BOLDWOOD BOOKS

Boldwood Books is a fiction publishing company seeking out the best stories from around the world.

Find out more at www.boldwoodbooks.com

Sign up to the Book and Tonic newsletter for news, offers and competitions from Boldwood Books!

http://www.bit.ly/bookandtonic

We'd love to hear from you, follow us on social media:

 facebook.com/BookandTonic

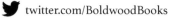 twitter.com/BoldwoodBooks

 instagram.com/BookandTonic

Manufactured by Amazon.ca
Bolton, ON